A DIFFICULT CHOICE

Anger burned in Jonathan's eyes as he grasped Elizabeth's arm with one hand. "Look at me, Elizabeth! I'm useless." He gave her a slight shake. "Take a good, hard look. Don't you see how my left arm hangs? It's no use for anything."

"You haven't given it time!" Elizabeth insisted. "Your arm will heal."

"Didn't you hear the doctor, Elizabeth? My arm is useless. You need a whole man, not half. You should have a man who can hold you with both arms." He'd felt her tense when he'd first put his arm around her. He expelled a frustrated breath, weary of the argument, then shoved her away from him. "Walk away, Elizabeth. Find what you need."

"You are saying that if you're not perfect, I won't love you. It doesn't work like ____ ____ Eliza-beth clenched her ____ ____ ____ 't hit him. "As far a_ ____ ____ n this house and rou____ ____ ____ s room and join the ____

She stormed towa____ ____ ____ around when she reached i____ There is a party tomorrow in honor of General Jackson. I expect you to escort me. If you won't, I'll get someone else! The choice is yours."

She slammed the door and ran to her room where she could cry in peace. She wanted her old Jonathan back. Not the cold stranger she'd just been with.

However, she had meant every word she'd just said. If Jonathan wasn't dressed and ready tomorrow night, she would leave him.

Even if it killed her. . . .

<u>BOOK YOUR PLACE ON OUR WEBSITE</u>
<u>AND MAKE THE</u>
<u>READING CONNECTION!</u>

We've created a customized website just for our very special readers, where you can get the inside scoop on everything that's going on with Zebra, Pinnacle and Kensington books.

When you come online, you'll have the exciting opportunity to:

- View covers of upcoming books
- Read sample chapters
- Learn about our future publishing schedule (listed by publication month *and author*)
- Find out when your favorite authors will be visiting a city near you
- Search for and order backlist books from our online catalog
- Check out author bios and background information
- Send e-mail to your favorite authors
- Meet the Kensington staff online
- Join us in weekly chats with authors, readers and other guests
- Get writing guidelines
- AND MUCH MORE!

Visit our website at
http://www.zebrabooks.com

LOVE ONLY ONCE

Brenda K. Jernigan

ZEBRA BOOKS
KENSINGTON PUBLISHING CORP.

http://www.zebrabooks.com

ZEBRA BOOKS are published by

Kensington Publishing Corp.
850 Third Avenue
New York, NY 10022

All Kensington titles, imprints and distributed lines are available at special quantity discounts for bulk purchases for sales promotion, premiums, fund-raising, educational or institutional use.

Special book excerpts or customized printings can also be created to fit specific needs. For details, write or phone the office of the Kensington Special Sales Manager: Kensington Publishing Corp., 850 Third Avenue, New York, NY 10022. Attn. Special Sales Department. Phone: 1-800-221-2647.

First Printing: August 2001
10 9 8 7 6 5 4 3 2 1

Printed in the United States of America

In Memory of
My mother, Bonnie Dittman, who died much
too young of breast cancer. A portion of the
proceeds from this book will be donated to
HOSPICE, so they can help those who can't
help themselves.

This Book is Dedicated to . . .
Ann La Farge, who told me to sit down and do
it when I didn't think I could,
and
My husband, Scott, and my son, Scott Alex, who
have helped me through a difficult year. I love
you.

Special Thanks

To my critique partners: Bonnie Gardner, Sue-Ellen Welfonder, Kathy Williams, Cindy Procter-King, Starla Crisler, and Diana Tobin, who helped me think this book through when I got stuck, and who put up with an awful lot of whining. Thanks for being there with all the cards and e-mails.

Chapter One

New Orleans
January, 1815

How the bloody hell had he gotten here?

Jonathan Hird sat astride his horse and glanced around. He wasn't sure he had the answer, but he knew he needed to find it quickly.

A dismal morning surrounded him with its fog-drenched air, obscuring his vision in every direction.

He listened.

Voices muted by the heavy mist a good hundred yards in front of him reminded Jonathan that he wasn't alone. He slowed his breathing, remained motionless while he waited, and listened, and wondered. All grew quiet. Much too quiet.

A flicker of a light breeze ruffled his hair and

began to strip the fog away, leaving in its wake a view of a battlefield waiting for the combatants to emerge. Jonathan, unfortunately, seemed to be in the center of the battle to come.

It was the wrong time and the wrong place.

He shivered.

The battle for New Orleans would be bloody.

Nudging his horse, he took a deep breath and raced across the muddy, rock-strewn field where the British, his countrymen, waited on one side and his best friend on the other.

Jonathan hadn't planned to put his hide in the middle of the skirmish, but it was the only way he could get to Adam Trent. And he must get to Adam, for he had vowed to support his friend and their cause.

The Highlanders swung onto the battlefront, their bagpipes skirling the blood-stirring music of Scotland. Thinking how strange it was to hear that heart-wrenching sound on American soil, Jonathan glanced to his left. Suddenly everything seemed to move in slow motion. He crouched down on his horse and prayed that this battle would not be his last.

Familiar voices caught his ear. "What's that god-awful sound?" one of Jean Lafitte's pirates shouted from behind their barricade.

"Look!" Dominic You chuckled as he pointed toward the field. "Just how tough can they be?" He laughed. "Look at them . . . they're wearing skirts!"

A bullet screamed past Jonathan's head. If he didn't make it to the American barricade in the next few minutes, he might end up in British hands.

His countrymen would never understand why he'd chosen to fight with the Americans.

Jonathan turned his horse and headed for the American side. He raised his head to search for Adam through smoke-filled air, and to let the men see who he was so he wouldn't be shot. Those bloody pirates would shoot anyone first and ask questions later.

There he was. Adam had seen him.

Just a few more yards and Jonathan would be safe behind the barricade.

That was when his luck ran out.

Suddenly, a pain hotter than any fire seared through him.

Wait a minute, he protested inwardly. This couldn't be happening. Elizabeth would be waiting for him. His sweet Elizabeth. The woman who'd finally made him see that he could settle down and give up the other women ... the gambling ... the drinking ... all the things he'd thought were making him happy.

"No!" He groaned as he grabbed his arm where the pain was concentrated. His hand was sticky and slippery with warm, red blood. He was losing his grip. He had to hold on.

He had to make it to Adam.

Blood seeped faster down his sleeve. He tried to grasp the horse's reins, but his fingers wouldn't obey. The ground rose to meet him as he lost his balance and slipped from the saddle.

He wasn't sure how long he lay there. The damp, cold earth chilled him.

The guns and battle cries seemed at a distance

now. Only the beating of his own heart sounded in Jonathan's ears.

Just for a brief moment, he saw her face ... Elizabeth Trent ... the woman he loved. Her raven-black hair flowed around her shoulders, and her slate-colored eyes glistened like black diamonds as she held her hand out to him. Yes, he could give up all his old ways for her. Her creamy skin and sweet smile would make any man think he was seeing an angel.

But beneath that angelic appearance was a feisty, headstrong woman who needed a strong man to tame her. A small smile tugged at the corner of his mouth, but it was quickly extinguished by the pain in his arm. He had intended to be that man. He couldn't die now.

Blackness closed in on him too rapidly.

Jonathan! He pushed himself up to listen. *Jonathan!*

Was someone calling his name? With a great effort he tried to rise to meet her, but he didn't have the strength.

Who was that fool running across the field?

He couldn't hold on much longer.

Again he reached out to touch Elizabeth, but his fingers wouldn't close over her hand and everything faded to black.

Now Jonathan Hird, the Earl of Longdale, had lost everything.

Chapter Two

What was that god-awful smell?

And just how long had he been lying here? Surely, a week had gone by, and they had yet to take care of his wound. Perhaps they were hoping he'd die. Then they wouldn't have to bother operating on an Englishman. That is, if he was in a hospital. He wasn't too sure about that part.

Some friend Adam was, to leave him in a place like this.

There was that smell again.

Jonathan twisted his head from side to side, trying to escape the odor. No matter which way he turned, the smell assaulted him.

Something cold brushed his face. He jerked at

the unexpected sensation. His eyes flew open, but several moments passed before he was able to focus on the white cloth someone was trying to put over his nose and mouth.

Chloroform!

Looking around him with blurry vision, he noticed he was on a table and there was a smaller table beside him where medical instruments had been laid out. He couldn't seem to clear his mind, but he did faintly remember being in another room with rows of beds and men near him, babbling with delirium.

Again, a white cloth covered his mouth. He tried to shove it away.

Good! At least he hadn't died. The unbearable pain shooting up his arm told him he was very much alive. A lesser man would be screaming.

"You must hold still, sir!" a stern voice sounded above him. "I don't have enough orderlies to hold you."

"Bloody hell! Get that stuff away from me," Jonathan shouted, struggling to raise his good arm. He tried to shove the man away from him. That's when he realized just how weak he really was. He had barely lifted his arm, only to have it fall limply back down.

"He's British!" the doctor shouted. "Get him off my table and bring me a good American soldier."

"No!" A strange yet familiar voice came from a distance as Elizabeth swept past the orderly who attempted to grab her arm.

"Jonathan fought for New Orleans, not against us, Dr. Blackman. This is my brother's friend," Elizabeth Trent said as she drew alongside the bed, placing her hand on Jonathan's shoulder. She looked at the haggard doctor who had been working many hours. His bushy eyebrows were arched together and beads of sweat dotted his brow.

"Who let her in here?" Blackman snapped at the nervous orderly.

"She insisted," the man replied.

"Get out, Elizabeth," Blackman ordered as he pointed to the door. "I'll not have a female fainting when I cut off this man's arm."

"No!" She reached out and grabbed the surgeon's arm.

"You will not take my arm off, sir!" Jonathan managed, despite a dry mouth. Damn, he needed water. And he needed to get out of this hospital, and fast. He attempted to sit up.

The doctor shoved Jonathan back down. "If I don't take your arm off, you'll die."

A commotion sounded in the other room just before the door swung open. Adam Trent marched through the door, his dark hair in disarray, his gray eyes sparkling with anger. His expression dared anyone to stop him. "I've just arrived to find my sister and my friend shouting. What's the meaning of this outrage, Blackman? You told me you'd take care of the man."

Blackman looked over his wire-rimmed glasses at Adam. "I just found out this man was your friend, sir. Taking care of him is what I'm trying to do. As a matter of fact, I was getting ready to operate before your sister burst in here."

"It's about bloody time, old boy," Jonathan said as he twisted his head to see Adam. Jonathan managed a small smile. "Please inform this gentleman, and I use that term loosely, that I'd prefer to keep my arm."

The surgeon grimaced with disgust before he picked up the end of his apron and wiped his face. "If I don't amputate, you'll die of gangrene. Even if I do save it, you'll never have the use of that arm again."

Elizabeth stood out of the way in the shadowy corner. Surely, she thought, the man couldn't be correct. Jonathan would be fine—he had to be. She glanced at her brother. Certainly, Adam wouldn't let this atrocity happen.

Adam stared at Jonathan. "If you hadn't tried that fool stunt and ended up on the battlefield, we wouldn't be in this situation."

"I took a wrong turn."

"You never did have a sense of direction." Adam shook his head. "Jonathan, it's your decision. What do you want to do?"

"There is no debating the issue. I'll keep my arm!"

The doctor grumbled about the odds, but Jonathan stopped him.

"I will take my chances," he said with quiet emphasis, signaling the end of any further discussion.

"You heard him. Clean up his arm and stitch it the best you can," Adam instructed. He motioned to his sister. "Elizabeth and I will wait outside."

"Where is she?" Jonathan asked, twisting his head to find her.

Elizabeth eased back over to the bed. "Here I am."

Jonathan looked up at the vision of loveliness

standing before him. Her long, black hair hung
loosely around her shoulders, reaching almost to
her waist. It glistened under the light like the sun
shining down on a raven's wing. How he longed
to run his fingers through the silky strands. Even
that small effort proved too much at the moment.
He couldn't lift his arm, much less hold her.

Gazing into slate-gray eyes so much like her twin
brother's, he saw the tears that threatened to spill
over Elizabeth's thick lashes and slide down her
cheeks.

"I'll be all right, my love." He took her hand in
his, rubbing his thumb back and forth across the
top of her knuckles. It was all he had the strength
to do.

"It will take much more than a bullet to stop
this scoundrel," Adam stated as he placed an arm
around his sister's shoulders and gently squeezed.
"Come. Let the man do his work, and then we can
take Jonathan home."

The surgeon, who had been working the whole
time they were talking, finished tying the last bandage in place. He looked at Jonathan, his grim
expression making his words chillingly clear. "As
far as I'm concerned, you can take him home now.
I can do nothing further for him." Blackman
looked at Jonathan for a long moment.

Finally, Dr. Blackman shook his head while he
wiped his blood-stained hands, then placed the
grimy towel on a white stand beside the bed and
tossed his instruments into his bag. "That arm will
be useless to you." He turned away. "If you live at
all," he muttered.

Jonathan's clear blue eyes darkened like angry thunderclouds. "Then I'll die in one piece."

"It's your choice." Blackman shrugged and hurried on to his next patient.

"He's one friendly soul," Jonathan remarked as he glanced up at Adam, noting his friend's bandaged shoulder for the first time. "What happened to you?"

Adam chuckled. "It seems a friend of mine thought he was invincible and could race across a battlefield with bullets flying all around him without being harmed."

"Seemed like a good idea at the time."

"Bloody stupid is what it was. And once you went down, I had no choice but to cut a zigzag across the field to rescue you."

"And I do appreciate it, old boy. Evidently the Scottish haven't lost their aim."

"Evidently." Adam frowned. With his good arm and Elizabeth on the other side, they managed to get Jonathan to his feet. "Let's get you home."

Carefully, they moved down the front steps of the old brick hospital. Adam nodded and his coach pulled up to meet them. The footman jumped down and opened the carriage door.

Soon they were safely settled in the carriage. Jonathan stretched out on the lush velvet seats, his head resting in Elizabeth's lap. Adam eased into the seat across from them so he wouldn't jar Jonathan.

"I'm so sorry I didn't ask sooner, but with Jonathan and all," Elizabeth rambled and finally got to her question. "How is Jewel? Did you rescue her? Is she all right?"

"You have been around Jewel too long," Adam teased. "She has a bad habit of asking several questions at a time."

"Don't criticize. Just answer me," Elizabeth's voice rose slightly with irritation. "Did you rescue Jewel?"

"Rescue Jewel?" Jonathan managed to ask, his voice slurred by pain. "From what?"

"Answer me!" Elizabeth shrieked as fear and anger knotted inside her. "Tell me she's not dead!" She reached over and grabbed Adam's knee.

"Jewel's dead? Can't be," Jonathan mumbled. He attempted to sit up, but finally gave up the effort. "I'm so sorry, Adam. I loved her, too."

Adam chuckled.

Elizabeth noticed the twinkle in his eyes as he looked at her and then Jonathan.

"Perhaps if the two of you would be quiet, I could answer your questions." He paused. "Jewel is not dead. You asked if I rescued her," he said to Elizabeth before addressing Jonathan. "And I seem to recall how you kept an eye on my wife for me."

Elizabeth glared at her brother. "You know bloody well what I meant, Adam! Don't frighten me like that. Is she safe?"

"Is Jewel safe?" Jonathan asked, too.

"You're both beginning to sound like parrots," Adam said, then folded his arms across his chest as he tried to relax. "Perhaps I should start at the beginning."

"Please be so kind," Jonathan quipped from his

reclined position. "It might be refreshing instead of frightening the wits out of us."

"Adam!" Elizabeth insisted, her tone warning.

"Jewel is as well as can be expected," Adam said patiently. There was a cold edge of irony in his voice. "After the fighting ended, I made sure you got to the hospital." He smiled at Jonathan. "I probably should have waited to make sure they didn't place you in the corner, which they apparently did. Anyway, I hurried home to see my wife. When I arrived at Four Oaks, all I found was a note telling me goodbye." Adam rubbed the back of his neck and Elizabeth could tell how upset he was. "I thought I'd lost her forever," he said.

"And?" Elizabeth prodded.

"It seemed our *friend*, Captain Lee," Adam snarled as he continued, "had kidnapped Elizabeth."

"He *what!*" Jonathan shouted, and this time he did come to a sitting position though he winced in the process at the pain that shot through him.

"Calm down," Elizabeth said as she patted his hand and braced her body next to his so he wouldn't fall over. She knew Jonathan couldn't handle the whole story.

"I hope you shot that bloody bastard. We should have done so in England. When he threatened to take Jewel. I remember how he claimed to be her uncle, but all that bloody bastard wanted was the treasure map that Jewel possessed." Jonathan took a deep breath, and looked at Elizabeth. "Sorry, love."

"I would love to have killed Lee, but I'm afraid

I was too late, which I'll explain in a moment,"
Adam said.

The carriage hit a rock and Jonathan moaned.
"I hope there are not many of those bumps," Adam
said, before continuing. "Anyway, Captain Lee
wanted Jewel all along. Elizabeth was merely bait.
He exchanged Elizabeth for Jewel."

Jonathan looked at Elizabeth with concern deep
in his eyes. "He didn't hurt you, love? Did he?"
he asked, taking her hand in his.

Elizabeth felt her face grow cold as the blood
rapidly drained, leaving her chilled. She couldn't
tell Jonathan what had happened. It had been hard
enough telling Adam.

Maybe later, when Jonathan was well. Then she
could explain everything, and hope he'd understand. With a great deal of effort, she calmly said,
"No."

Adam quickly cut in and Elizabeth knew it was
to save her from answering any more questions. "I
had to find Lafitte to see where Lee had taken
Jewel. All I knew is that they had sailed in search
of the treasure that only Jewel and Jean knew about.
What I didn't take into account was the raging
fever I had developed from this bloody wound."
He motioned to his arm. "I was so dazed by the
fever when I arrived at Grand Terre that Pierre
put me out of my misery with a good right fist to
the jaw." Adam rubbed the bruise on his jaw.

Elizabeth looked at him with sympathy, but her
concerns turned back to her sister-in-law. "What
about Jewel?"

"Jean and his crew arrived at the Bay of Pirates,

but not soon enough to save Jewel from being shot."

"Shot!" Elizabeth frowned. "How badly?"

"She was shot in the back of her shoulder. But she'll be fine," Adam said. "The doctor said she'd need plenty of rest."

Elizabeth breathed a sigh of relief. "Where is she?"

"At Four Oaks."

"What about Captain Lee?" Jonathan asked.

"Though Jean didn't personally see the black-guard die, Jewel told him that Lee had drowned in the inlet trying to save his precious treasure chest."

"Good riddance," Jonathan said, trying to ignore the rocking of the carriage.

"Yes, you could say that," Adam said with a nod as he shifted, trying to find a more comfortable position. "There was a long line of people who wanted to kill that bloody bastard!" Adam propped his arm on the window and looked out. "I beg your pardon, Elizabeth."

"You could probably put me on that list, too," Elizabeth murmured, more to herself than to anyone.

Jonathan managed to put his arm around her. "That's my tigress." He chuckled. "Do you realize, my love, that out of the four of us, you are the only one who hasn't been shot? I guess I can be thankful that you were not hurt."

Elizabeth forced a smile, but when she glanced at Adam she saw the compassion in the eyes that were so much like her own. Seeing the sympathy brought moisture to her eyes. She didn't want Jonathan to see, so she turned to gaze out the carriage window. The past would be something she'd have to live with for the rest of her life.

She glanced at Jonathan. "Yes, I was the lucky one," she whispered. "Now put your head on my shoulder." She gave him a small smile. "You need to rest."

Turning back to the window, she stared out at the trees stripped bare by chilly winter winds. Gray puddles dotted the road. At least it had stopped raining, but it was cold—just like she felt inside. Yes, she was the lucky one. She'd not been shot, but she had been wounded.

Deeply.

Elizabeth sighed. She wasn't a meek little lamb who would run and hide. She was a fighter like her brother.

She would lick her wounds. And she would survive.

But she could not bring herself to tell Jonathan . . . at least not yet.

Finally, the carriage swung into the lane that led up to Four Oaks. A row of live oaks lined both sides of the road, lacing their branches together in an overhead canopy. The carriage topped the rise and the white mansion, surrounded by four huge oak trees draped in Spanish moss, appeared before them.

Elizabeth had come to think of Four Oaks as home. It wasn't as large as their childhood home, Briercliff, in Cornwall, but it was warm and inviting with its stately beauty.

Eight Corinthian pillars graced the front of the house, and wisteria vines draped the two at the ends. On a warm, sunny day you could hear the constant hum of bees darting from flower to flower. But the cold winter days of the present season left the vines bare and the bees quiet.

Elizabeth missed Briercliff, where she and Adam had grown up playing in those castle halls. Briercliff sat on the gray cliffs of Cornwall, and Elizabeth had always thought of the magnificent estate fondly, because that was where she remembered her parents. If she shut her eyes, she could picture her mother's beautiful face and her breathtaking, laughing blue eyes. Elizabeth and Adam had taken after both their parents and ended up with unusual slate-gray eyes. She supposed it was a mixture of their father's black eyes and their mother's blue ones. She wished her parents had lived long enough to see how she and Adam had grown up. She hoped they would have been proud of their children, and she wished she could have asked her mother's advice about how to handle her present situation.

The carriage lumbered to a stop, halting Elizabeth's daydreaming. She noticed Jonathan had fallen asleep on her shoulder.

"Sit still, Elizabeth. I'll get someone to help me get Jonathan to a room," Adam said. "He's going to need plenty of rest before he's back to his old self." Her brother swung down out of the carriage.

Elizabeth watched her brother march up the front steps of Four Oaks. She glanced down at the face of the man she loved.

She and Jonathan had grown up together in England. But back then she was nothing more than an annoyance to him. He'd always called her Adam's little sister even though she and Adam were the same age.

However, over the years her place in his life had changed to something else . . . something more. She smiled. She had noticed how Jonathan had stared at her when she'd left England to come to America. It was a peculiar stare . . . as if he'd wanted to say something, but couldn't. That in itself was unusual for Jonathan. He was devilish in every way and never at a loss for words.

She'd heard the stories about him in England— the ocean wasn't that big! Jonathan Scott Winston Hird, Earl of Longdale, had become a rake. She wondered just how many hearts he had broken. Of course, Jonathan would let them down easy, but their hearts would be broken all the same.

She hadn't known what to expect when Jonathan had come home this last time. Did he remember her? Would he care?

Lifting her hand, she gently brushed a stray lock of sandy brown hair from his forehead. The warmth of his soft flesh was intoxicating, and she longed to have him hold her.

Elizabeth had loved Jonathan all her life. At first, the love she felt had been the love of a child, but it had endured over the years and had grown stronger. When Jonathan followed Adam across the ocean, and she'd finally seen him again as a man, from the perspective of a woman, she knew. For just a brief moment before Jonathan had hidden it, she had seen his love. He had looked at her with such a yearning, it had made her heart ache with longing, and she'd made up her mind then and there that Jonathan's bachelor days were numbered.

Adam leaned in the carriage door and grabbed Jonathan's good arm. "You've had enough time with my sister. Let's get you upstairs."

Groggily, Jonathan pushed to a sitting position and blinked several times. "Bloody hell, old boy. I'm not a sack of potatoes. Do be careful."

"No, a sack of potatoes would be easier to handle," Adam said matter-of-factly. "Here. Put your feet on the ground and Marvin will grab your other side so you don't end up flat on your face."

"I'm perfectly capable of walki—" Jonathan's voice trailed off as he stumbled. The servant and Adam grabbed him. "On second thought, old boy, some assistance would be most appreciated," Jonathan joked as he draped his good arm around Adam's neck.

Elizabeth was glad to hear Jonathan's easy sense of humor return. "Do be careful, Adam," Elizabeth pleaded, following them up the front steps. "He's been wounded, after all."

Adam turned his head a fraction to give his twin an incredulous look. "And I haven't?"

Elizabeth felt the heat of a blush as she trailed behind them up the stairway to a room directly across from hers. By the time they got Jonathan into bed, he'd passed out.

Annie, Elizabeth and Adam's old nanny and housekeeper, swept into the room. "Adam, ye need tae be in bed. Have ye forgotten yer wounded?"

Annie was a plump little Scotswoman, small in size but with the feisty determination of a much bigger woman. Her brown hair was streaked with gray and pulled back into a loose bun; her apple cheeks always glowed with good cheer.

"No, I haven't," Adam said curtly. "But I think Elizabeth has."

"Jonathan's hurt, too." Elizabeth touched Annie's arm, ignoring her brother completely.

"Saints above! Have ye all lost yer ever-lovin' minds? I should have locked all o' ye in yer rooms. Then ye wouldn't have these gapin' holes in ye." Annie clapped her hands and looked toward heaven, then back at them. "Now all o' ye out! The lad needs his rest."

"But Annie," Elizabeth protested.

"Ye not be doin' him any good if ye keel over from exhaustion. Now, shoo, all o' ye."

Reluctantly, Elizabeth left. She knew Annie was taking care of her, too, and Elizabeth had to admit she was exhausted.

When she entered her room, the bed looked very inviting with its fluffy pink goose down comforter and the eight white pillows piled up against the headboard. But she resisted the pull of the finely dressed four poster bed and tugged instead on the silken bell cord.

In a few minutes, Sally, her maid, appeared in the doorway. "Yes, ma'am."

Sally was an older black woman who'd run the kitchen until she'd hurt her back. Then Elizabeth had suggested Sally might like to have the easier job of lady's maid.

Sally had been so grateful that she took to caring for Elizabeth like a mother hen. Now Elizabeth had two mothers—Annie and Sally.

"Sally, can you help me with these hooks? I want to take a nap."

"Yes'um. You've not been takin' care of yourself, Miz Elizabeth. Just look at those dark circles under your eyes. Master Jonathan will be lookin' elsewhere ifen you keep it up."

Elizabeth swung around. "Do you really think so?"

Sally laughed. "Only if he's a fool. Ain't none to compare with you, Miz Elizabeth.

Elizabeth smiled and then climbed under the fluffy pink comforters. "I'll just sleep a little while," she murmured. She heard the click of the door then Sally slid from the room and Elizabeth drifted to sleep.

The afternoon turned into night.

She slept peacefully until the wee hours of morning.

That's when the demons slipped in. . . .

Chapter Three

No matter how much Elizabeth tried to forget, the nightmare would find her. Not every night—not when she first slept—but in the wee hours of morning, when she was very tired, the horrors would slither in like a slimy snake and encompass her until she could no longer breathe, or think, or remember it was only a dream.

And so the dream began . . .

She didn't want to be here!

Who were these men?

Why had they kidnapped her?

She glimpsed her attackers just before they threw a sack over her head. They tied her hands, and then one of the men pitched her over his shoulder. She tried to kick but the man just tightened his hold on her legs.

Dressed in dark navy, they had looked like seamen, but they could have been anyone. Their voices were British, yet *she* was British, so why did they want her? Did they think her a spy?

The next thing Elizabeth knew she had been placed face down on something hard and rocking. She smelled the salt air and knew it had to be a small boat because her feet could touch both sides. She rocked against the rough wood planking as the men shoved away from the dock. Droplets of water hit her arms as the oars lashed through the water. And the faint sounds of men bustling around the dock grew faint as they rowed away from shore.

"Wh—where are you taking me?" she demanded from her awkward position. They didn't bother to answer her.

Soon the little boat bumped the hull of a larger ship. Once again she was being hefted over someone's shoulder, and they were moving again, this time up and over.

After they boarded, she was taken to a small cabin where they set her on her feet and removed the blindfold. She tried to see who they were, but they deliberately kept out of sight. Her gaze darted around the ship's cabin, searching for a clue as to her whereabouts, but all she saw were the backs of the men as they left.

She knew the ship wasn't one of Adam's because she didn't recognize anything. The room contained a bed, a small desk with a chair, and an unlit kerosene lamp suspended from the ceiling. The room smelled damp and musty. It was dark and unclean.

Her first thoughts were of escape, and she began to struggle with the ropes that bound her hands.

The bindings seemed to grow tighter as she struggled to twist her hands loose. Unfortunately, they hadn't tied her hands in front or she could have used her teeth.

Elizabeth tried to see by the flickering light coming through the single porthole. She had no earthly idea how or why they had brought her here. The panic she'd tried so desperately to keep in check began to engulf her. Her heart raced. Chills crept up and down her spine. What was she going to do?

A squeaking sound caught her attention and she jerked her head toward the cabin door just as it swung open. A lone man strode through, kicking the door shut behind him.

She stared at the British officer before her, but had no memory of ever seeing him before. He stood tall and broad-shouldered and would have been considered handsome if not for an ugly, jagged scar that ran from his ear to the corner of his mouth.

He did not speak, but peered at her from hooded eyes. All the while, his finger absently traced the purplish mark on his face. What little of his eyes she could see in the dim light shone cold. And hard. Something about him made her think of death.

She shuddered with revulsion.

"What do you want from me?" she asked, dismayed at the quaking fear in her voice.

"I can think of a few things," the man said. His stern voice held no vestige of sympathy. "Sit down."

She didn't like the coldness in his voice and she dared not disobey. She backed up to the chair, thankful to put some distance between them, making sure she didn't take her eyes off him. "I am not a spy! I'm British."

He grinned, but it was not a comforting sight. "Just like myself."

"Then why have you kidnapped me? I don't understand. I don't know you."

The man's scowl was hot enough to burn leather, then he sneered, "But your brother and sister-in-law do. I am Captain Lee."

Elizabeth became more uncomfortable by the minute. "Jewel knows you?"

"That's right," he acknowledged with a nod. He jerked his hand to his face and pointed a slender finger. "She's responsible for this! Ugly, isn't it?"

"Sh—she did that?"

Instead of answering, he pulled out a knife and ran his finger over the edge, testing it for sharpness, then lifted his gaze back to hers.

He smirked at her discomfort, then slowly moved behind her. Elizabeth felt his warm breath on her neck, chilling her to the bone. She gasped. But instead of cutting her as she had anticipated, he sliced the ropes, freeing her hands.

"Yes, Jewel did this. And with this very knife," he said from behind her as she rubbed her wrists with numb fingers. She had no desire to turn and look at him.

Without warning, Lee jerked her head back and rubbed the blade up and down her throat. "You can rest assured that your precious sister-in-law will pay for her deeds, one way or the other. Then we'll see how much your brother thinks his Jewel is worth."

Elizabeth tried to contain the whimper that escaped her lips. She trembled with horror. She had no doubt Lee would cut her throat. She hated knives. She always had. Would this be the end?

Just as she felt the knife prick her skin, he moved away. After what seemed like an eternity, she could breathe again. Taking several deep breaths, she touched the spot where the knife had pricked her and drew fingers red with blood. Her blood.

She tried to calm herself while she rubbed her wrists again to get the blood flowing. She knew she should probably keep her mouth shut, but she didn't always heed smart advice. She couldn't allow this arrogant bastard to think she feared him. "Adam will never let you near Jewel," Elizabeth finally managed to blurt out.

"You are as spirited as your brother, I see." Lee grinned and closed the distance between them. "I won't have to get close to Jewel." He bent over, inches from Elizabeth's face, and whispered, "Jewel will come to me." He pulled Elizabeth up to him, wrapping his arms around her, his eyes gleaming with hatred.

Elizabeth struggled against his iron grip, but Lee merely laughed. "Your brother owes me. And you're just the person to pay his debt. Jewel will be the other half." Lee sneered before his mouth closed on hers.

The cold, revolting kiss made Elizabeth's skin crawl. She pushed hard against Lee's chest, but couldn't break his hold. His hand moved to her breast as he groped her, tearing at her clothing. The bile rose in her throat and she began to push harder. "No. Not this—please—" she protested.

But he was too strong. . . .

Then the dream was over.

The snake slithered away just as it had come in the middle of the night . . . quick and deadly.

Elizabeth jerked straight up in bed, laboring for air. Her gown, soaked with perspiration, clung to her damp body.

A dream.

Only a dream.

Or more a nightmare, one she'd relived over and over again.

If only she could forget.

She wiped the tears from her face. Would the past ever release her? If she was ever going to have a life with Jonathan, she had to forget.

Thank goodness, she hadn't been a virgin when Lee attacked her. That much she could be thankful for. Jonathan had been her first, and because of that she knew what physical love between a man and a woman could be like.

It definitely wasn't what she'd experienced with Lee.

Somehow, she was going to have to find the words to tell Jonathan what had happened, but for now he was much too ill. She didn't want to think of the possibility that he might walk away from her. She couldn't lose him! She'd loved him all her life, and she didn't want to think about a life without him.

Shoving the covers away, she was thankful for the burst of frosty air. She straightened her gown and slid from the high four-poster bed. The smooth wooden floor felt cool on her bare feet as she hurried to the window, nudged the curtains back, and peered out at the brightening sky.

Good. At least it was morning and she didn't have to worry about sleeping again. Perhaps a good hot bath and some food would help ease her fears and leave her dreams behind.

She went to the bellpull and rang for the claw-footed tub to be filled. Several servants arrived with buckets of steaming water and emptied them into the hip tub. As soon as they had finished, Sally came in with bedsheets draped across her arm and a saucer full of dried rose petals.

As Elizabeth relaxed in the rose-scented water while Sally fussed around her, the warm water began to ease her tense muscles. She closed her eyes and rested her head on the back of the porcelain tub and whispered a prayer that Jonathan would soon be his old self again.

"You goin' look like a prune ifen you stay in that tub much longer, Miss Elizabeth," Sally said as she wandered over to the wardrobe.

"But it feels heavenly," Elizabeth said with a sigh as she sat up in the tub and began to lather, feeling much more like herself than she had before her bath. "What do you think I should wear today?"

"It's still awful chilly outside, but I think you need somethin' bright. Somethin' cheerful. Folks been mopin' 'round here way too much," Sally said as she peered into the wardrobe.

All Elizabeth could see was Sally's big rear end sticking out of the doors. "How 'bout this one?"

Sally held up a pelisse of apple green *gros de Naples* material that fastened in front with circular slide buttons of the same color.

"I shall wear whatever you choose, Sally. You never fail to pick out the dress that suits me best." Elizabeth stepped out of the tub and rubbed herself off in a soft bath sheet. She slipped into her chemise, then Sally helped her into the lovely dress.

The long sleeves felt good today, Elizabeth thought as she adjusted the slit at her wrist. She was tired of winter already.

While Sally brushed her hair, Elizabeth sipped the hot chocolate Annie had sent up. "Just pull my hair up on the sides. I don't have the patience for you to fuss with it this morning. I want to see Jonathan."

"You sure have pretty hair, Miss Elizabeth. There are times I swear it's so black, it's blue."

"One of these days I'm going to cut it all off," Elizabeth teased as she pulled her long hair above her head and motioned with her fingers.

"You do, and I'll be tannin' your hide for sure."

"Now, Sally," Elizabeth said. She rose and started for the door. "I'm going to see to Jonathan."

Elizabeth hurried across the hall to Jonathan's room. The door stood ajar, so she slipped into the room unannounced. She'd expected to see Jonathan awake and sitting up, but what she found was Jonathan sound asleep and Annie holding a cloth over his forehead.

Annie turned at the sound of the door creaking

open. "Ye look much better this morning," Annie
greeted. "Did ye sleep well?"

"For part of the night," Elizabeth answered as
she placed her hand on Jonathan's forehead.
"What's the matter?" Her eyes darted from Jonathan to Annie. "Is he worse?"

"Dinna ye be a-frettin'. The lad's had a bad injury
and this fever is his body's way of fightin'. 'Twill
take time." Annie patted Elizabeth's hand. "I'll
pull him through this just like I always have with
ye and Adam, and then ye'll be havin' plenty of
time to be nursin' him back to health."

Two weeks passed slowly. Jonathan refused company, preferring to be alone. Elizabeth wasn't sure
what to do. She wanted to help, to do something.
Anything. A few days later when she tried to see
him, Annie met her at the door.

"I must see Jonathan," Elizabeth insisted.

"I'm sorry, lass, but he doesn't want to see anyone," Annie said gently. She took Elizabeth by the
elbow and steered her away from the door. She
leaned over and whispered, "Just give him some
time."

"Are you sure I shouldn't stay with him?" Elizabeth asked. "I feel so helpless."

"What ye can do is help Jewel. This will be her
first day out of bed, and she mustn't overdo. Ye
know how bullheaded she can be. That's one young
lady that doesn't know the meaning of the word
no."

"Where is Adam?"

"He and Derek have gone to the docks. Something about the sails being replaced on the *Wind-jammer*."

Elizabeth sighed, hating to leave Jonathan, but realizing that Annie had everything under control. "Promise me you'll call if he changes his mind."

"Ye know I will. Now shoo," Annie said, motioning with her hand as if she were waving away flies.

Reluctantly, Elizabeth left, then proceeded down the hall to Adam's room. She'd been so wrapped up in Jonathan, she'd ignored her sister-in-law. But on the other hand, she knew Jewel needed the time to rest and recover. Elizabeth knocked softly on the door.

"Come in," Jewel called.

Elizabeth saw her sister-in-law across the room as Jewel turned away from the window. Jewel's long black hair swung freely about her shoulders, and her rose-colored gown brought a soft glow to her face. The gown completely covered the bandage, and she didn't look hurt at all.

"Jewel." Elizabeth moved swiftly and embraced her, but drew back when Jewel winced. "I'm so sorry, but you look so well it's easy to forget about your wound." She held Jewel at arm's length. "Are you in much pain?"

"Yes." Jewel took a deep breath and adjusted her smile. "But I will live."

They looked at each other for a moment before they both laughed. "It's so good to see you. I had my doubts the last time we parted that I'd ever see you again." Elizabeth admitted.

Amusement flickered in Jewel's eyes. "That thought ran through my mind as well." She looped her arm through Elizabeth's. "I don't want to talk about those dreadful times. Let's walk outside. I've been cooped up here much too long. I need fresh air even if it is cool. How do *café au lait* and *beignets* in the gazebo sound?"

"Excellent."

"Good. I've made arrangements to have them sent out for us."

The day was crisp, so they had to bundle up in their long cloaks. The sun had risen high in a bright blue sky, but did nothing to warm them. They were quiet for a while, each lost in thought as they walked along. They walked through the garden, which looked bare now, but in the spring there would be lilacs, purple Japanese maples, magnolia, and jonquils and the air would be filled with the fragrance of honeysuckle. The birds even seemed silent today as if they sensed the two women needed some time alone.

Jewel thought back, remembering how scared she had been when she found out Captain Lee had kidnapped Elizabeth. . . .

Elizabeth had promised Jewel that she wouldn't ride far. When the sky had grown dark and Elizabeth hadn't returned, Jewel had paced the floor, reprimanding herself for not accompanying her sister-in-law.

That's when a noise in the distance had stopped her. She listened. The sound of a horse galloping out front got her attention. Thank goodness, Elizabeth had returned.

Jewel had run to the front door and pulled it

open. Her smile faded instantly. It wasn't Elizabeth, but a young boy with a package in his hand.

"I have a package for Mrs. Trent."

"I am Mrs. Trent." Something was wrong. She felt it. Her hands shook as she took the package. Looking up, she found the boy was still waiting. "Is there something else?" she asked before reading the attached note.

"I was instructed to wait for a reply, ma'am."

"A reply?" Jewel gave him a blank look. "A reply?" she questioned again. Who in the world was the message from? She wasted little time reading the note. Instead she tore open the package. "No!" She shook her head. This just couldn't be possible. It was a nightmare. The color drained from her face.

The innocent boy reached out and touched her arm. "You all right, ma'am?"

"Y—yes," Jewel stammered, trying to gather her thoughts. "If you'll come in and wait I will pen my reply."

Captain Lee had Elizabeth in his possession. So that Jewel would not think he was making idle threats, he had sent a small token—Elizabeth's chemise. The pink "E" embroidered on the front let Jewel know that it was indeed Elizabeth's.

Captain Lee had come back to haunt Jewel.

Jewel prayed Lee wouldn't harm Elizabeth, even though he had threatened to in the letter. Then it dawned on Jewel: Lee wouldn't hurt Elizabeth; she was the one Lee wanted . . . because only she could take him to the treasure.

So Jewel had traded places to free Elizabeth.

* * *

Jewel felt someone squeeze her arm and she turned, trying to focus on the present. "Did you say something?"

"You must have been deep in thought," Elizabeth commented with a half-smile. "I said, was it bad?" She repeated the question as they strolled toward the gazebo. She couldn't help feeling responsible for Jewel's injury. If she hadn't wandered away from Four Oaks and gotten herself kidnapped, things might have been different.

"It was a nightmare, but at least Captain Lee is dead. He'll not bother either of us again!" Jewel's curt voice lashed out before she caught herself and turned to her friend, placing her hand on Elizabeth's arm. "How are you doing?"

Elizabeth blushed. "You know, don't you?"

Jewel nodded. "It was the first thing Lee boasted about. I would have killed him myself if I'd had a weapon." Her lips thinned with anger. "I'm so sorry you suffered because of me," she said in a low voice taut with anger.

"It was my own stupid fault for riding too far from Four Oaks. You warned me, but I wouldn't listen. However, I didn't deserve that kind of punishment," Elizabeth said as they walked along. "I'm not sorry Lee's dead."

"I agree. But you still haven't answered me," Jewel reminded Elizabeth in a quiet voice. "Are you all right?"

Elizabeth stared at her feet. A tumble of confused thoughts and feelings assailed her, but her pride concealed her inner turmoil. "I'll be fine. If only I could make the nightmares go away, then I'd be free."

"This, too, will pass in time," Jewel said softly. "Trust me." She drew a long breath and changed the subject. "I'm worried about Jonathan—he's refusing to see anyone."

"How well I know." Elizabeth frowned. "It hurt at first, but then I decided he needed time. The question is, how much time?"

Jewel poured the cream-rich coffee into fine china cups. "I don't know that I'm the one who can give you that advice, but don't let Jonathan withdraw into himself. He has such inner strength and has helped me so much with Adam. I owe him a lot."

Elizabeth took a *beignet* and placed it on her plate. "What should I do?" she asked, brushing powdered sugar off her fingers.

"Adam said the people of New Orleans were giving a victory celebration for General Jackson and we are all invited. It would be the perfect time to get Jonathan out of the house."

"First we have to get him out of his bedroom." Elizabeth laughed bitterly.

"You can do it," Jewel encouraged and patted her friend on the hand.

"But how?"

"Demand that he talk to you now," Jewel said as she leaned back against the blue cushions.

Elizabeth thought about Jewel's suggestion as she sipped her coffee. "You're absolutely right. Jonathan has felt sorry for himself much too long.

He's going to get out of that bed if I have to drag him!''

Elizabeth smiled and took a bite of the sugary treat.

She was through being nice.

Chapter Four

Three weeks had passed, or so Jonathan had been told.

Lying in bed, he had never felt so helpless in all his life. He was used to being independent, doing as he pleased, and now he needed help to do such a simple task as stepping into his breeches. He didn't like it one bit. With each day of his slow recovery, his mood darkened.

He paced sluggishly about the room like a lame tiger trying to build his strength, trying to find the man he once was. He'd spent the last three days doing the same thing over and over again, refusing to see anyone until he felt stronger. No one could see him like this. Not even Elizabeth.

He chuckled, remembering how Annie had told him Elizabeth was none too happy about his refusal to see her.

A soft knock sounded at the door.

He ignored it.

The next time, the knock was a little louder. Again he ignored it. He stopped his pacing and stood in a dark corner where he could lean against the wall, look out the window, and not be seen. Whoever it was would soon give up and leave him alone. If it had been Annie she'd have already barged in.

Suddenly, the door flew open and Elizabeth swept into the darkened room, her green taffeta skirts rustling as she rushed over to the bed. She stepped back when she found the bed empty. She looked around the room. When she spotted him, her eyes narrowed. "You're up," she said.

"You could say that."

"Jonathan Hird!" She took a deep breath before continuing. "How could you refuse to see me?"

He moved away from the wall as she marched toward him. She hadn't changed a bit. She was still headstrong, determined, and beautiful. Her black hair hung loosely around her face and the vivid green of her gown made her face a warm, inviting color.

Before he could stop her, she threw her arms around him. He stumbled, but kept his balance as his good arm came around her.

"If you were any more enthusiastic," Jonathan chuckled, "we would both be on the floor."

"I'm sorry, darling," she said as she looked up at him with loving eyes. "But it's been so long. Haven't you missed me?" She cocked her head to the side and said with a sly grin, "Just a little?"

"Miss you?" Jonathan almost choked on the

words. Did she have any idea just how much he'd missed her? He tried to resist the desire that ran through his battered body, but it wasn't working. Hot lava poured through him at her mere touch. She pushed him to do things he hadn't intended to do or wasn't sure he had the strength for.

His hand inched up Elizabeth's back until it cupped the back of her head. She tensed beneath his fingertips. Lowering his face, he placed feather-like kisses down the side of her cheek. Miss her? Hell, yes, he'd missed her. It had been so long since he'd held her. It had been much too long since he'd tasted her sweetness.

Elizabeth felt his warm breath as it mingled with hers. She willed herself to relax. This wasn't Lee, but Jonathan.

Jonathan stared at her, capturing her with his eyes. A liquid warmth crept up her arms, and her heart raced as she waited for him to kiss her . . . to really kiss her as he'd done so many times before. He was the only one who could shut out the rest of the world . . . make her forget the hurt. He was the one who could make her yearn for something more.

He brought his lips down on hers, sending a jolt slamming through her. She froze. Panic seized her. She would have cried out if his lips hadn't smothered the sound. Determined to put the past behind her, she finally relaxed and let the pleasure flood over her.

His mouth moved on hers, possessively exploring each part of her mouth. Her arms slid up and around his neck. She wondered if he could feel the wild pounding of her heart.

When she pressed her body into his, Jonathan's mouth became more demanding, his tongue sliding into her mouth to seek all her sweetness. She trembled as she clung to him. This time from desire.

He needed her closer, Jonathan thought wildly. Her sweetness tormented him and reminded him of another time, a sweeter time, when they had made love. It was the only time they had both lost control, and Jonathan had eagerly made Elizabeth his.

And for a brief moment he was back in that bed. . . .

"Jonathan," Elizabeth had whispered.

He had to have her. He had to make her his.

Rolling Elizabeth onto her back, he'd deepened his kisses as his hands roamed over her body. He told himself to stop. He knew better, but this time he hadn't listened and couldn't stop. All he knew was that the woman he loved had moaned his name in a feather-like whisper. And his body had hardened quicker than it ever had before.

His kisses grew more demanding; his tongue stroked her tongue sensually as his agile fingers began to unfasten her gown. He needed to feel her bare skin next to his. One by one the buttons were undone, and he shoved her chemise aside and began to fondle her breasts.

"Perfection," he'd breathed.

Her breasts were full and firm and felt wonderful beneath his strong fingers. Teasing one nipple between his fingertips, he felt her squirm beneath

him, at first trying to get away and then giving in
to the pleasure. She deepened the kiss, taking his
tongue into her mouth as her hands explored his
back, pulling him closer.

Did she have any idea what she was doing to
him? The more she responded, the hotter his need
grew, and the thin thread that had been holding
him together began to grow brittle until finally it
broke.

"I want you, Elizabeth."

She moved back and looked at him from under
sooty black lashes, then she gave him that famous
wicked smile. "What are you waiting for?"

Jonathan moaned and looked to heaven for
strength, but it didn't come. He crushed her to
him, kissing her over and over again. He took all
that she offered until his searing passion engulfed
him. He wanted more, needed more. Sensual chills
ran up his spine.

He drew his mouth from hers and kissed a trail
to her breasts. His tongue circled her taut nipple,
then his lips closed, and he began to suck, tasting
the small bud until it tightened and she began to
gasp and arch her back.

Her needy moans intensified his pleasure. With
his free hand, he forged a path down her smooth
skin and over her stomach until he found the soft
nest of curls between her legs. He slid his fingers
into her warmth.

At first she was startled and tried to push him
away, but soon she begged him not to stop.

"Jonathan, please."

And then Jonathan found heaven as they made

love over and over again. Each time it was better than before.

He'd truly found paradise.

Jonathan took a deep breath, bringing him back to the woman in his arms, the woman who heated his blood now as she had then.

But, that had been before.

He realized he wanted her just as much as he had that night. He tried to raise his left hand to bring her closer, forgetting for a moment that he couldn't. The pain shot through his arm, reminding him he wasn't the man he used to be. He jerked away, and turned his back.

"Wh—what's wrong?" Elizabeth asked, placing her hand on his arm.

He shrugged away. "For a moment, I forgot."

"Turn around and face me!" She waited until he'd done so. "Forgot what?"

"That I'm only half a man. You deserve better, Elizabeth." Jonathan ran his right hand through his hair, hating how he felt.

She grabbed his shoulder and turned him to face her. "That is the stupidest thing I've ever heard!" She poked him in the chest with her index finger. "You're every bit the man you once were!"

Anger burned in his eyes as he grasped her arm with one hand. "Look at me, Elizabeth! I'm useless." He gave her a slight shake. "Take a good, hard look. Don't you see how my left arm hangs? It's no use for anything," he muttered. His expression grew hard and resentful.

"You haven't given it time!" Elizabeth insisted. "Your arm will heal."

"Didn't you hear the doctor, Elizabeth? My arm is useless. You need a whole man, not half. You should have a man who can hold you with both arms." He'd felt her tense when he'd first put his arm around her. He expelled a frustrated breath, weary of the argument, then shoved her away from him. "Walk away, Elizabeth. Find what you need."

Enraged, she drew back her hand and slapped him hard across the face. As the sound echoed around the room, Jonathan merely glared back at her. The red handprint was vivid on his cheek, but that didn't stop her or make her feel guilty . . . not one bit.

"I'll not have you speak to me that way again. You are saying that if you're not perfect, I can't love you. It doesn't work like that, Jonathan." Elizabeth clenched her trembling hands so she wouldn't hit him again.

"As far as I'm concerned, you can sit in this house and rot, *or* you can come out of this room and join the living," Elizabeth challenged him in a frosty tone.

She stormed toward the door, but swung around when she reached it. She lifted her chin and gave him an icy stare. "There is a party tomorrow in honor of General Jackson. I expect you to escort me. If you won't, I'll get someone else! The choice is yours."

She slammed the door and ran to her room where she could cry in peace. She wanted her old Jonathan back, not the cold stranger she'd just been with.

However, she had meant every word she'd just said. If Jonathan wasn't dressed and ready tomorrow night, she would leave him.

It had been a long time since she or Jonathan had laughed and had fun. But tomorrow she intended to do just that. . . .

Even if it killed her.

Chapter Five

Elizabeth sat on the velvet stool in front of her dressing table, browsing in her jewelry box while Sally brushed her hair.

Elizabeth picked up a pair of pear-shaped earrings and held them up to her ears. "Has Jewel dressed?" she asked Sally.

"Yes'm, she's real purty. What you gonna wear?"

"I haven't made up my mind," Elizabeth admitted as she glanced up and met Sally's gaze in the mirror. "I'm tired of all the dark winter colors. What do you think of my pink gown?"

"That'll be right purty, Miz Elizabeth, what with your pink cheeks. And ifen you wear a shawl when in the cool air, you oughta be plenty warm."

"Then it's settled."

"Better put on your gown 'fore I fix your hair," Sally instructed as she went to the wardrobe. After several minutes, she produced the delicate pink dress. "Here 'tis. Sure is purty."

Elizabeth stood and held onto the bedpost while Sally laced the whalebone corset. "Now you take a deep breath, Miz Elizabeth, while I pull on dese here strings." When the corset had been tightened and tied, Sally said, "It's chilly outside. You need to wear your flesh-colored pantaloons."

"I think you're right." Elizabeth smiled and stepped into the undergarment.

Sally dropped the fifteen yards of pink muslin, then hooked the dress up the back. The dress was perfect, Elizabeth thought. A lightly folded drapery in the form of a stomacher adorned the bust. The sleeves were short and extremely full. Long, white *crêpe lisse* sleeves inserted at the shoulder were confined at the wrist with broad bead bracelets and ornamental *mancherons*.

Elizabeth took her place back in front of her dressing table. "Have you seen Jonathan?"

"Ain't seen nobody since I come upstairs," Sally said as she started to twist Elizabeth's hair and pull it up so it was full on the top with side ringlets. She'd barely gotten it secured with pins when Elizabeth shot to her feet.

"Wait!" Elizabeth shouted and looked desperately around the room, then darted over to the washstand.

Elizabeth leaned over the porcelain bowl and emptied her stomach before letting out a pitiful groan. "Sally!"

Sally hurried over with a damp cloth. "What's the matter, honey?" She held the cloth to Elizabeth's cheek. "You goin' to be all right?"

"I think so," Elizabeth said weakly even though she wasn't too sure at the moment. "Maybe we got my corset too tight."

"I don't think so. You probably just gotten excited over the party." Sally shook her head, then took Elizabeth's hand and led her back to the dressing table. "Here." Sally reached in her pocket and pulled out some green leaves. "Bite on these peppermint leaves and you'll feel better. Now let Sally make you real purty."

"Don't forget the final touch," Elizabeth said and pointed to her waist.

"We don't want to forget that purty thing." Sally went over to the nightstand and brought back a piece of jewelry.

Elizabeth waited a few moments until her stomach eased, and then she stood so Sally could pin a gold watch set with rubies and a gold chain on her *ceinture*. The watch dangled just above her waist.

Elizabeth turned and looked at herself in the mirror. The watch had been her mother's, and she was proud of the small gift. Her eyes traveled up until her gaze rested on her face. She was beginning to look like an old maid. Women her age usually had been married for years and had several children. Why was she so different? Had she waited all these years for Jonathan only to have him turn away? She tugged at her bottom lip with her teeth. Maybe she wasn't pretty enough.

After she left her room, she hurried straight to Jewel's room, only to find it empty. Evidently everyone was waiting downstairs. She took a deep breath and started down the wide staircase, but to her disappointment, she found the hallway and foyer empty.

Was Jonathan going to leave her waiting? Had he slipped that far away from her? She hadn't bothered to check his room. Perhaps she should go back and see if he was upstairs. She heard the soft murmur of voices coming from the parlor, so she headed toward the sounds. Her heart pounded so hard her chest hurt.

Shoving open the door, she found the room bathed in the soft glow from a crystal chandelier; the three occupants who'd been in a lively conversation stopped and turned toward her. All except Jonathan, who stood at the fireplace already facing her way.

Jewel was seated on a rose-colored settee. Adam stood behind her, his hip resting on the back of the settee as he talked to Jonathan. However, as soon as the door opened, the conversation ceased.

"Elizabeth," Adam said after an awkward moment. He rose and came to her, placing a soft kiss on her forehead. "You look quite lovely tonight."

She let out the breath she'd been holding when she'd feared Jonathan would not be in the room. "Thank you." She smiled at Adam, but then immediately looked at Jonathan. Standing beside the Italian marble mantel, he looked like royalty. A fire blazed in the hearth behind him, seeming to surround him with a warm halo.

"I've not seen that dress, Elizabeth," Jewel commented, apparently wanting to break the silence that had settled upon the room. "It's definitely your color."

"Thank you," Elizabeth acknowledged and

moved further into the room. "I see you are dressed in my brother's colors as always."

"Of course," Adam commented with a grin, placing his hand possessively on his wife's shoulders. "She likes this color best." He ran a hand over her royal blue sleeve, then gave Jewel a wink.

Jewel's brow raised a fraction. "He's lucky it's my favorite color," she said to Elizabeth, completely ignoring her husband.

Elizabeth smiled at the easy way Adam and her sister-in-law got along, and she wondered if she'd ever have that kind of a relationship. With Jonathan.

Elizabeth started toward Jonathan. "I'm glad you are going tonight," she said when she stood in front of him. How handsome he looked, she thought. He'd lost a little weight, but it only made him more attractive. He wore a fine white satin waistcoat, and his breeches, right down to his stockings, were a deep slate gray, relieved only by the brilliance of his white shirt.

Jonathan straightened, then took her hand. "I believe I was threatened earlier," he reminded her as he drew her hand to his lips.

Elizabeth blushed. "Who? Me?" She pointed to herself. "Why, I'd never stoop so low."

Jonathan's sky-blue eyes twinkled with warmth as he stared at her. His face, dark and swarthy like a pirate's, made him stand out in a crowd. She longed to reach up and place a kiss on his lips, but she knew her brother would reprimand her for such unlady-like manners.

Jonathan couldn't believe the vision before him. He'd never seen a woman so full of life and surprises. Elizabeth never showed any outward concern for possessions. She liked having fun and enjoying life. As his gaze traveled up to her face, he couldn't help but notice that those expressive eyes held a sensual promise. He longed to have her next to him in bed with that glorious hair spread about the pillows and across his bare chest. And he wanted her, he realized, very badly. He'd just have to keep reminding himself he wasn't the same. But he wasn't going to remind himself at the moment. He leaned over, his lips very close to her ear, and whispered, "I could be talked into staying home with you."

Elizabeth felt her ears burn, and she blushed at the same time her brother said, "We'll not have any fraternizing until after you two have married."

"Adam, old boy, you're just too cynical in your old age," Jonathan said with his famous lopsided grin. He put his hand on the small of Elizabeth's back to head her toward the doorway, then he evidently thought of another jab. "Should I remind you of all the . . . fraternizing you did with Jewel before she became your wife? As a matter of fact, I remember one morning back at Briercliff. . . ."

"That's enough, Jonathan," Adam bit out, stopping him. "Besides, that was different," he added as he and Jewel followed the other couple from the room.

The huge, black traveling chaise waited for them and soon they were on their way to New Orleans. Elizabeth said a small prayer, thankful that a touch of her old Jonathan had returned.

She couldn't help but notice how his left arm hung limply beside him. But his spirits seemed

high, so maybe she could keep his mind off his
damaged arm.

Jonathan cleared his throat and turned to Adam.
"Have you spoken to General Jackson in the last
several weeks?"

"Not since the battle. I heard they crowned Jackson with laurel when he rode into New Orleans."
Adam smiled.

"Wait a minute." Jonathan chuckled. "Our
staunch general, our destroyer of Indians, rode
around the city with a leafy crown on his head?" He
leaned forward. "I'd like to have seen that."

Adam laughed. "I would, too. At least we'll get
to see him at his victory ball since it's being held
in his honor."

"I hope Uncle Jean and Uncle Pierre are there,"
Jewel chimed in.

Adam glanced at his wife and smiled. "I'm sure
they will be, my love. They have, after all, been
forgiven for their past sins, so they should be in
attendance. I believe Jackson has a soft spot for
those pirates, even if he won't admit the fact."

"Will you introduce me to your uncles, Jewel?"
Elizabeth asked. She'd heard many stories about
the pirates. Like the time it was rumored that Jean
had killed a man in a duel in Charleston . . . an
affair of honor in which a mysterious woman had
played a part.

"Of course. We are family."

Elizabeth could feel Jonathan's warmth. Without
thinking, she reached over and took his hand. A
little too late she realized it was his bad arm, but
she didn't let go when he tried to pull away with

his other hand. He'd have to learn how to use his arm sooner or later.

She rubbed her fingers back and fourth across his hand until he seemed to relax, and to her amazement he didn't move his fingers. She'd never let him give up. Maybe there was a chance that Jonathan would recover, and the past would be behind them.

The carriage halted in front of the French Exchange. Gaslights sputtered all around the building, casting a warm glow into the chilly night and showing off the elaborate decorations, Elizabeth noted as she embarked from the vehicle.

When they entered, they were informed that the upper part of the Exchange was for dancing. Dinner would be on the lower portion in precisely two hours.

Climbing the staircase, the murmur of voices grew louder. Flowers and colored lamps were everywhere. A huge banner, JACKSON AND VICTORY: THEY ARE BUT ONE!, was draped across the banister.

Elizabeth noted that all of society had turned out for the occasion, dressed in bright colors much like her own dress. Maybe the New Orleans culture had rubbed off on her.

She was escorted over to the receiving line where she was again introduced to the general. She was surprised at how haggard he looked. Evidently the battle had taken its toll.

"General, you remember my wife?" Adam said with a nod. "And my sister, Elizabeth."

Elizabeth took Jackson's extended hand. His long, thin fingers felt cold. "It is nice to see you again," Elizabeth said. "Congratulations on your victory. Our city will be safe once again."

Jackson smiled broadly. "We have the two gentlemen with you to thank for our safety." He patted Adam on the shoulder. "Without their help, the triumph could have gone the other way." Jackson regarded Jonathan. "I heard that you decided to take a ride across my battlefield, Son. How is your wound?"

"I'm left with a mangled limb, General, so I'm of little use to anyone."

"Nonsense! You are as good as you were. No, I take that back. You are better because now you have experience under your belt."

"I'm not too sure. They wanted to take off my arm. Said it would be useless."

"A good thing you didn't let them. Never did trust those old sawbones." Jackson waved his hand to clear the air. "Enough about war. Let me introduce my wife." He took her elbow in his hand. "This is Rachel."

"My pleasure," Elizabeth murmured to a short, plump lady who didn't look like she belonged to the general. He was just the opposite—tall and very thin.

The four of them walked over to a corner where they could talk and watch the dancing. Elizabeth didn't want to embarrass Jonathan. She knew he could still dance, but of course he would think otherwise.

Just one look at him told her he'd grown tense. She could almost feel him changing, and she didn't want him to. He was drawing away from her again.

Peter Thornbird approached across the floor, a

man Elizabeth had seen several times while Jonathan was in England.

"You look much too serious, Miss Elizabeth. Perhaps a dance would help," he said with a smile and a slight bow. He never took his gaze off her, and that made her feel quite uneasy. "That is, with your permission, sir," he added, addressing Jonathan.

Jonathan simply nodded, his expression more distant than before.

Did he even care if she danced with Peter? Blast Jonathan for feeling sorry for himself. She needed to do something to shake him up and bring some life back into him. So, she took Peter's hand and he led her to the dance floor.

After several whirls, she felt herself relax. Soon, she was laughing, and before she knew it, she had danced three straight dances with Peter.

Jonathan felt his collar tighten as he watched Elizabeth swirl across the floor. He hadn't been able to take his eyes off her. She looked like an angel dressed in that beautiful pink gown. Just as the music ended, another man approached her and asked for the pleasure of the next dance. It seemed every man in the place was smitten by her beauty. He looked around and counted dozens of eyes on her.

Jonathan forced a blank look, but he was feeling increased frustration. He didn't care for those men holding her so close. However, they did have two good arms and could offer her much more than he could, he thought, deeply lamenting his loss.

Elizabeth was tired. Just as the music started, Peter asked, "Would you care to go again?"

"I'd better get back to Jonathan," she answered breathlessly.

Peter offered the crook of his arm to escort Elizabeth off the dance floor. "I heard that you've been keeping company with the gentleman. Are you engaged?"

"No," Elizabeth murmured. She frowned as the question began to run through her mind over and over again. The way things were going, she might never marry. She was doomed to be an old maid, but it was worse since she'd finally found love. Perhaps it was time she took the matter into her own hands. She looked at Jonathan as they came closer.

He stood leaning casually against a post watching her approach, and he didn't look very happy. A warning cloud settled on his features and a muscle quivered at his jaw.

"Thank you for the dance, Miss Elizabeth," Peter said, and bowed graciously.

"Try *dances.*" Jonathan's dry voice cut through the air like a sharp knife.

Peter's face reddened. He glanced at Elizabeth, then made a hasty retreat, not bothering to say more.

Elizabeth's blood pounded, causing her face to grow hot with humiliation. "That was rude, Jonathan Hird!"

"Monopolizing your time is rude," he informed her sarcastically.

She lifted her chin. "You could have asked me to dance."

"You know damn well—" Jonathan never finished his sentence because of a commotion at the staircase. Murmurs rippled through the crowd.

Elizabeth swung around to see what had drawn Jonathan's attention and that of everyone else. Two very tall gentlemen had just emerged. Every woman in the room started turning one by one to stare at them, including Elizabeth. "Who are they?"

"Those two gentlemen, my dear, are Jean and Pierre Lafitte."

Elizabeth took a quick breath in utter astonishment. "They're nothing like I expected." The taller one, who, she assumed, was Jean from the stories she'd heard, stood at least six feet tall and was extremely handsome.

"Did you expect eye patches and bandannas tied around their heads?"

"I—I'm not sure. There have been so many stories circulated about them. And here they are, dressed like the rest of the gentlemen."

Jewel and Adam greeted Jean and Pierre first, and before Elizabeth could move, the four of them were coming their way. Jean's hair was sleek and black and his profile classic. He was dark and slender. Pierre was tall, too, but not as impressive as his brother.

"Jean and Pierre, I would like you to meet Adam's sister, Elizabeth," Jewel began.

"Mademoiselle," Jean said in his delightful French accent as he brought her hand to his lips. "What a rare flower in our midst."

Jean's sparkling dark eyes would be hard for any woman to resist, and Elizabeth could tell he was accustomed to using those charms with women.

His mischievous smile proved that. "I have heard about you," Elizabeth said before she thought.

"I assure you none of it is true," Jean said with a grin. "I wish I could say the same of you, but your brother has done a good job of keeping you secret."

"Look elsewhere, Lafitte," Jonathan said with a silken thread of warning in his voice.

Jean looked at Jonathan with an arched brow. "It's good to see you, too, Jonathan. I suppose the wound has made your disposition . . . what shall we say? Sour?"

"A bit," Jonathan admitted.

"Pierre and I will be sailing soon. We could take you with us and have you back in shape before we return to port. The sun and the sea have never failed to cure anything."

"I wish it were that simple," Jonathan said, his tone a trifle wistful.

"There you are!" General Jackson called as he approached the group. He shook Pierre's hand and then Jean's.

"If you will excuse us," Pierre spoke his first words as he took Jewel's hand and led her onto the dance floor, "I would like to dance with my niece."

At the same time Adam took the general's wife for a whirl around the floor.

"Anytime you want to fight with my men, you are more than welcome. Your men are almost as good as my coon hunters," Jackson joked to Jean.

"Almost?" Jean stared at the general. "I will give you that point on land, my friend. But on the sea, my men would be fighting while your coon hunters would be hanging over the side of my ship heaving."

Jackson laughed. "You are probably right. But in all seriousness, it was an honor to have your men fighting with my own."

"Ladies, gentlemen. Dinner is being served downstairs," Governor Claiborne announced as he laid his hand on Jackson's shoulder. He bowed toward Elizabeth. "I'm afraid I must steal our guest of honor."

Jean turned to Jonathan as the general and Claiborne strolled away. "Claiborne is one man I have no use for."

"Nor I," Jonathan agreed, shrugging. "But, he is our host. And we should be cordial for at least one night," he added, then looked at Jean. "Shall we dine?"

Chapter Six

The dining room glittered with hundreds of candles set in gold candelabras up and down two long, white tables.

Elizabeth entered the room on the arms of both Jonathan and Jean. The envious looks of the other women made her smile as she and Jonathan neared the table where some dinner guests already sat. A servant dressed in white greeted them and directed each to their respective seats.

Elizabeth was seated on the opposite end of the table from Jonathan. It was probably just as well, she thought as she looked far down the table at him. She felt a pang of longing so strong she wanted to cry. They needed time together, not apart. She dared glance at him again, but he wasn't looking her way. He'd turned to speak to Jackson.

As the servants poured champagne, Elizabeth

half listened to the conversations around her, shrugging her shoulders in halfhearted answers. Meanwhile, Jonathan seemed to be entertaining the two ladies on either side of him, and Elizabeth couldn't stop the twinge of jealousy that skittered through her.

One of the ladies smiled at everything Jonathan said; now and then her eyelids dropped a little in a flirtatious manner. Jonathan's mouth twitched with amusement.

Elizabeth ground her teeth, but managed to keep her temper in check. During all the excitement of actually getting Jonathan out of the house, she'd almost forgotten that she wanted to speak with him. She needed answers. She was tired of this state of limbo.

And she would talk to him tonight.

The servants entered with the food, drawing her attention. Soon the spicy aroma of the Creole dishes filled the room. She had learned to love the special Louisiana food that was so different from that of her English homeland. The first course was gumbo, followed by spicy shrimp in tomato sauce served over fluffy white rice. Some of her favorites.

Elizabeth looked at Jonathan again just in time to see one of the women grab his arm possessively. She stiffened, her eyes flashing with anger. It took all her control not to jump up in the middle of dinner and have a word with Mr. Hird.

She took a deep breath and managed to finish the gumbo, but when the main course was served she found her appetite had left her. She barely touched her food, pushing the rice around her plate, eating only a few bites.

As soon as the meal ended, Elizabeth made her way over to Jonathan. She figured if she had to wait for him to escort her out, she might never leave the table, since the other women were keeping him company.

"Excuse me," she said quietly, then waited until he looked at her. When she had his full attention, minus the giggling young lady next to him, she finished her request. "I would like to see you on the terrace," she stated firmly, daring him to argue. His dinner companions would have to do without his company.

She didn't bother to wait to see if Jonathan followed. Elizabeth made her way to the foyer where a servant retrieved her cloak. She wrapped the gray-brown silk taffeta garment around her, pulling up the hood to protect her hair from the wind.

Perhaps he could tear himself away from his dinner companions for a little while. In her present mood, she wouldn't hesitate to make a scene.

Once she was outside, the crisp night air quickly cooled her body, if not her temper. The starry heavens peeped through the bare branches. A breeze blew a loose strand of hair across her nose that tickled and made her want to sneeze. She tucked it behind her ear as she nervously went over what she wanted to say.

It was now or never!

She wouldn't let anything stop her now that her mind was made up. Lost in thought, she jumped when Jonathan touched her shoulder.

"I believe you summoned me, my dear."

Elizabeth whirled, her hood falling about her shoulders. "Summoning you," she spat out contemptuously. "It seems to be the only way to get your attention these days."

Jonathan's face showed no trace of emotion. He looked at her, waiting to see what she wanted. She realized then that he didn't intend to make any of this easy.

Damn man!

"Before your injury, I was hopeful that we'd have a future together . . ." Elizabeth said, then paused as Jonathan tensed. His eyes grew hard and his jaw tightened.

Good, at least she had his attention even if he was thinking the wrong thing.

"I thought you loved me." Her voice cracked as unwanted tears sprang to her eyes; she fought to hold them back, not wanting to cry. She needed to say what had to be said without her emotions getting in the way.

"I did," Jonathan stated flatly.

Elizabeth stiffened. She noticed he used the word "did" instead of "do." "Well, for me, nothing has changed."

"I am not the man I was then." His words sounded as cool and clear as ice water. "Why can't you see that?" he said angrily, his scowl hot. "The battle changed everything."

"Your injury changed nothing!" Elizabeth shook her head stubbornly. "You are the same man to me."

"You deserve better," he replied in a low voice. "Someone whole."

"I deserve to be happy."

"Precisely, my dear." Jonathan sighed. "And I

completely understand that you want to end our relationship."

"I never said anything about ending our relationship, which is exactly the point. There is nothing to end, Jonathan Hird. You have never made a commitment to me!" She grabbed both his arms and shook him hard. "I love you. Will you marry me?"

"I—I," Jonathan stammered, and gave her a look as incredulous as if she'd just slapped him.

She couldn't remember ever seeing such a shocked look on his face before.

"That is not an answer," Elizabeth pointed out. "It's simple . . . yes or no."

He regarded her quizzically for a moment, and then answered, "Yes."

"What do you mean, no?" Elizabeth shouted and stomped her foot in a childish gesture. She had known he would say no. Damned man. "Don't I mean anything to you? Don't you lo—" She hesitated, blinking with bafflement. "Did you say yes?"

He nodded with a sly grin. "Just remember, I warned you."

Elizabeth threw her arms around him and planted kisses all over his face. "I'm so happy, Jonathan." Joy bubbled up and shone in her eyes. "I don't want to wait because I've been waiting for you forever. I want to be married three weeks from today before Annie and Derek sail back to England. Annie would never forgive me if I got married without her. As a matter of fact, she's probably given up hope."

"Whoa. Slow down, my love." Jonathan pulled back a little. A smile tugged at his mouth. "We'll have the wedding of your dreams. I promise." His breath stirred her hair.

She felt a flood of uncontrollable joy.

"You shall spare no expense. But don't you think we should seal the bargain with a kiss?" he asked with a gentle whisper.

Imprisoned between the porch rail and Jonathan, she looked at him and grinned. As though his words had released her, she flung herself against him. He held her close with his good arm and lowered his head to hers. She wanted to yield to the burning sweetness. His warm lips pressed gently on her own, sending the pit of her stomach into a wild swirl. Passion rose in her like the hottest fire, clouding her brain. To save her soul, she couldn't stop with a chaste kiss and pull away like a lady should. Instead, her arms slid up and around his neck as she pressed her body into his and savored the feel of his hard muscles against hers. Nothing mattered but the taste of him. The brandy he'd had earlier made his lips sweet and produced a delicious sensation.

Suddenly, he deepened the kiss and persuaded her to open her mouth. His tongue explored the recesses of her mouth, teaching her how exquisite a kiss could be. She kissed him with a hunger that matched his own.

However, a little sanity returned and she pulled back slightly. "W—we shouldn't be doing this."

"I know," Jonathan agreed, his mouth grazing her earlobe. She quivered at the sweet tenderness of his kiss. The warm breath on her ear made her go limp. Jonathan had to tighten his grip to keep her from falling.

To hell with what is proper, Elizabeth thought.

She was so happy, she could burst. After all these years, she was finally getting married. And, best of all, to the man of her dreams. Perhaps it would be enough to wipe out all of the bad memories. She looked up at Jonathan and whispered, "Are you happy?"

"So much has happened in such a short time, I think I'm numb," he answered slowly. Too slowly.

Elizabeth frowned. "That isn't exactly the response I expected."

"Of course I'm happy." He gave her a smile that warmed her to her toes. "How could I not be?"

"I guess you're going to make me ask this, too." She frowned and drew in a deep breath. "Do you love me?"

Jonathan's hand rested casually on Elizabeth's shoulder for the longest time. The look in his blue eyes held a warmth that left her breathless. "I have known you since you were in pigtails and I wore knickers. Over the years, you grew up and attempted to follow Adam and me around. I admit back then, I thought you were a royal pain. Then the strangest thing happened. I started asking Adam where you were and what you had been doing. I had to know everything about you.

"Unfortunately, Adam got a wild idea and decided that both of you should go to America. I almost asked you then. . . ."

She saw heart-rending tenderness in his gaze. "I remember the strange look in your eye that day," Elizabeth exclaimed. "It was as if you wanted to say something to me."

"I did," he said, lifting his hand to her soft cheek.

"I wanted to ask you to stay with me, but I thought you were too young. You had yet to experience life, so I waited and hoped."

She frowned in exasperation. "Until I was a ripe old age and no one wanted me."

Jonathan chuckled and tapped her under the chin. "Remember, wine is not at its best until it is aged."

Her brow rose a fraction, and she felt her cheek twitch. "Are you avoiding the question?"

"Only leading up to it. When I arrived at Four Oaks this last time and saw you, I knew then that I had loved you for a very long time. Perhaps, forever."

She watched the play of emotions on his face and felt a few of her own. "So, why didn't you tell me?"

"Because I didn't know how you felt. It had been such a long time. But do know, Elizabeth, that I love you as no other."

Her heart melted at the words she'd longed to hear. She had loved only one man in her life, and he stood before her.

Her arms went around his neck at the same moment his lips found hers. The kiss was so tender and poignant that she never wanted this moment to end. Suddenly, everything was so right in her life.

Before she knew what was happening, she was parting her lips to let Jonathan deepen his kiss, and she felt his automatic response. She began to tremble. Her conscience again reminded her that it was very unacceptable behavior to be out on the terrace unchaperoned, much less having her body pressed against a man and her arms wrapped around his neck. If any of the society matrons were to walk through the door and discover them, they would swoon immediately.

However, it wasn't a mother who came through the French doors. . . .

"Unhand my sister, Jonathan Hird," Adam's deep voice growled behind them.

"*Mon Dieu,* I shall run him through with my sword for taking such liberties with your sister," Jean shouted.

Adam's head snapped around to look at Jean. "Haven't you learned that I can fight my own battles?"

"*Oui,* but we are kin, are we not?" Jean winked at Adam. "So, my friend, your battles become my battles."

Jonathan had jerked up at the intrusion, but he didn't bother to let Elizabeth go. Slowly, he turned so they both could see the two gentlemen arguing with each other and ignoring them.

"That may be true," Adam said and folded his arms across his chest. "But I'll ask for your help when I need it."

Jean folded his arms in a stubborn stance also. "There are times, my friend, when you'll not know that you need help," he said with a grin. "Or should I remind you of Pierre's right to the jaw?"

"Remember it!" Adam's voice rose as he flung his hand in the air. "I still have the bloody bruise as a reminder."

Jonathan had had enough. "Do you mind taking your conversation elsewhere, old boy? Your sister and I were having a very serious conversation before we were so rudely intruded upon."

Adam turned back to Jonathan. "I could see which way the so-called conversation was headed," Adam said dryly. "You should know better than to compromise my sister."

"I could still run him through for you," Jean suggested amiably.

"Some friend you are," Jonathan said as he glared at Jean.

Jean merely shrugged. "Blood is thicker than water, my friend."

Elizabeth thought the whole thing quite comical. She was surprised at Jean's easy wit. "Perhaps I was compromising Jonathan," she suggested. "It was my idea to come out here, after all."

"No one could compromise a rake," Adam stated firmly.

"I take offense to that, old boy."

"Well?" Adam stared hard. "Is it not true?"

Jonathan shrugged. "In the past, perhaps. But I still take offense, especially since I'll be marrying your sister in a fortnight."

"Bloody hell," Adam roared. But an easy smile played at the corners of his mouth, indicating that he was pleased.

"I'm truly offended that I was not invited," Jean protested.

Adam cut his eyes at Jean. "I can't invite you to something I know nothing about myself!"

"Are you not excited, Adam?" Elizabeth asked softly, gaining her brother's attention.

"Then it's true?"

She nodded.

Slowly, a grin spread across Adam's lips before he reached over and clasped Jonathan's arm. "It's about time you came to your senses." Then he turned and hugged his sister. "Of course I'm happy for you. See? I told you things would work out."

"See?" Jean said with a laugh. "You were getting excited over nothing, my friend," he said, slapping Jonathan on the back.

"Congratulations," Adam said.

"Thank you, Adam," she said, then kissed her brother's cheek. "Now, if you'll excuse me, I must tell Jewel. We have a wedding to plan, and there is much to do in the next two weeks."

"Two weeks?" Adam shouted, but Elizabeth ignored him as she hurried through the French doors.

At the moment, life was wonderful.

Chapter Seven

The week was a whirl of activity. Elizabeth wasn't sure who was happiest—Annie or Jewel. Every time Elizabeth saw Annie, she would grow misty-eyed and say, "My wee bairn is gettin' married. But look at ye. Ye positively glow."

As for Elizabeth, she'd never been happier in her life. She suddenly had the energy of three women, and it was a good thing, since there was so much to do.

Her carriage pulled to a stop at the dress boutique on St. Charles Avenue in the Vieux Carré. Elizabeth stepped out of the carriage and looked at the brick building. How lovely it was with its beautiful wrought-ironwork across the balustrades. New Orleans was much prettier than London, and rich in cultural diversity.

The bell above the door rang as she entered the little shop.

"Miss Trent," the young woman acknowledged as Elizabeth entered. "We heard that you were going to pay us a visit. Come this way. Mrs. Claremont has set everything up in the back."

"*Oui,* you'll make a lovely bride," Mrs. Claremont greeted Elizabeth taking both her hands. "Come sit down. We have much to do."

Elizabeth looked at yards of silk and lace and pored over the latest fashion plates from Europe. Mrs. Claremont gave her suggestions and finally they agreed on the perfect dress. It would be made out of white muslin and satin trimmed with the most delicate lace Elizabeth had ever seen.

"I would also like to plan for a breakfast after the ceremony, keeping the tradition of my homeland," Elizabeth said. "Do you have any suggestions? I want everything to be perfect."

"That sounds lovely. We can handle the food and we must have many flowers, which will be hard to find this time of year. However, I do have some friends with hothouses. I will pay them a visit tomorrow."

"When do you think I can be fitted?" Elizabeth asked as she stood to leave.

"I will be at Four Oaks in a week for our first and, I hope, final fitting. That is a promise I make to you, because you have been so good to me since you've arrived. I'll make sure your wedding is perfect."

Elizabeth hugged the dear little lady. "Thank you. I can't wait to see what you've created."

The invitations came next. Elizabeth bought very

fancy paper to take back home with her, where she'd address the invitations herself, and then have the servants deliver them to their friends.

Today was the final fitting for her wedding dress.

Elizabeth stood patiently while the seamstress pulled and pinned the soft material. Outside the large window in her bedroom, leafless trees were dark silhouettes against the winter sky. She wondered what Jonathan was doing at the moment. Was he thinking of her? Would he like to kiss her as much as she'd like to kiss him?

The chattering of the seamstresses faded into the background as Elizabeth's attention turned back to the window. This week had been milder than usual. The rain had let up and the sun had begun to dry out the soggy ground. She hoped the weather would be perfect for her wedding day.

"Please turn," Mary, the head seamstress, said.

"What?" Elizabeth had been so interested in the view outside that she hadn't been paying attention.

"Please turn, Lady Elizabeth," Mrs. Claremont repeated.

"Oh, sorry," Elizabeth said as she complied with their request. She caught a glimpse of herself and smiled. The gown's design was new, and to keep the surprise, Elizabeth wouldn't let Jewel and Annie come to any of the fittings. They had protested strongly about being left out, but in the end, Elizabeth had won the argument.

The design Elizabeth chose was very feminine. The bodice had an off-the-shoulder top made with delicate Brussels lace. The long satin skirt fell to the floor. Around the hemline, the seamstresses had embroidered pink roses connected by snowy pearls. She would wear a simple wreath of roses around her head to hold her veil, and carry a single pink rose in honor of her mother.

Elizabeth looked down to see that they were finally pinning the hem of the dress, and she sighed as she tried to stand perfectly still. She'd never had the patience for things like this, and today it was taking a lot of concentration to put up with the seamstresses.

Looking back out the window, she wondered about the prickling sense of foreboding that kept nagging at her that something was about to happen. It gave her an uneasy feeling that she wanted desperately to dismiss. Maybe it was just anticipation of her upcoming wedding.

"There. We have finished, Miss Elizabeth," Mrs. Claremont said as she offered her hand to help Elizabeth down. "Your gown will be ready in two days. I'm not sure I've ever created a gown so lovely," Mary said with a proud smile. "It will be long remembered."

"I don't know how to thank you. You have accomplished an almost impossible task, finishing this lovely gown in such a short time," Elizabeth said, squeezing Mary's hand. "You have truly outdone yourself. I cannot believe you took my idea and turned it into something so enchanting." Elizabeth stepped out of the garment and handed it to the seamstress.

Mrs. Claremont beamed. "You will be a beautiful bride." She gathered her pins and tape measures, placing them in her sewing basket. "I must say, you're the most excited bride I've seen in a long time. There seems to be a special glow about you that I don't often see. I am very happy for you."

"If you knew Jonathan, you would be excited, too."

"I have seen him," Mrs. Claremont said with a sly grin. *"Oui,* he is a fine one."

Elizabeth blushed. "I think so."

During the next week several parties were held in the honor of the future bride and groom. It was about the only time she got to see Jonathan, because Adam kept him so busy.

However, before the last party, Jonathan made a surprise visit to her room. Elizabeth shut her eyes, remembering.

"May I come in, love?" Jonathan asked, but didn't wait for her to answer as he closed the door behind him.

"May I help you, sir?"

Jonathan's brow had risen a fraction at her comment. "You can help me in many ways," he said seductively. "However, I came to give you a present."

Elizabeth rose from her dressing table. "A present? I thought maybe you had come to kiss me."

"Well, now that you've made the suggestion," he said, pulling her into his arms.

Their hot, passionate kiss made her warm all over, a small promise of things to come. When she parted her lips, she heard him moan with pleasure. She slid her arms up his chest and pressed her body into his.

After a few moments, Jonathan pulled back and

looked at her. "It won't be long before we're crawling into that bed if you keep kissing me like that."

Elizabeth laughed and stepped back. "How is this? Is it a safe distance?"

"The only safe distance would be at another plantation," he admitted with a grin.

"You said something about a present."

He slipped his hand under his jacket and pulled out a long box. "Indeed I did."

Elizabeth wasted little time opening the box. There before her was a necklace of blazing red rubies and diamonds. "It's beautiful!"

"Just like the lady who will wear it," he said, and pulled the necklace out of the box. "May I?"

Elizabeth smiled and turned so he could fasten the precious stones around her neck. Then he turned her back toward him. "The rubies remind me of your temper—"

"I'm not so sure that's a compliment," Elizabeth pouted.

"If you'll let me finish. The diamonds remind me of your beauty. The rubies remind me of your fire."

Elizabeth leaned up and kissed him on the lips. "That's better."

"Good." Jonathan traced the stones of the necklace along her neck. "I'm so glad you will soon be mine. If any other man ever touched you, I don't know what I would do. I can't bear to think of you with any man but me," he added in a whisper.

"I don't want anyone but you."

* * *

The *Windjammer* floated peacefully at anchor, softly nudging against the dock as the deckhands pushed loads of supplies up the gangplank, stocking the ship for the return trip to England.

Adam and Jonathan were at the New Orleans dock, trying to help out where they could.

"When do you set sail?" Jonathan asked Derek, who was repairing some riggings.

"The day after your wedding," Derek replied with a smile. "Are you ready for the big day, Son?"

"Is anyone ever prepared?" Jonathan laughed.

Adam walked up. "I most certainly wasn't."

"And he isn't joking," Derek quickly added. "Almost had to hit the boy over the head to make him realize he was in love with Jewel."

"I remember," Jonathan admitted. "He was pretty stubborn about the situation in England, also."

"Let's not talk about past history," Adam said to put a stop to the teasing. "You look natural onboard my ship. Now that you're going to be family, maybe you would like to be part of my shipping business."

"You know I've always been a land lover." Jonathan leaned back against the mast. "Perhaps I'll buy a small plantation and raise cotton. Of course, I will have to return home and check on my holdings. I just didn't want to return so soon after the war. You can just imagine if someone had recognized me during the battle. The thought of my neck being stretched isn't very appealing."

"I know. I have the same problem," Adam admitted. "But with Derek and Annie returning and a good solicitor looking after my property, I believe I'll remain here for a while."

"I haven't heard from my father in some time," Jonathan said. "But he's getting on in years and will need some help in the future, I know."

"I can't believe the marquess will ever be old," Adam said. "He's always been feisty."

"He may never admit to being old, but his body is telling him a different story. I think his fourth wife robbed him of what was left of his energy."

Adam and Derek started laughing, then Derek said, "Takes a lot of stamina to have one wife, much less four."

"Amen," Adam added.

"That's my father, gentlemen. I could not hold a candle to him, nor would I try. Elizabeth will be enough for me," Jonathan admitted. "It has taken me a long time to finally take the step. Once will be plenty for me."

"Said by someone who already knows his place," Adam teased. "Now let's get some work done before my friend here goes back to daydreaming of his upcoming wedding."

Finally, the week of her wedding arrived . . . and Elizabeth's euphoria ended.

Her nausea had returned—sometimes in the morning and sometimes at night. At first, Elizabeth tried to pass her unsettled stomach off as nerves. She was just overly excited about the wedding, she tried to convince herself. She also realized she was using that excuse more and more.

The only person who knew about her sickness

was Sally. She had never commented, but she was always there to soothe Elizabeth and to assure her that everything would be fine.

A cloying uneasiness followed Elizabeth as she moved through the week. And again, she had the strange foreboding that something terrible was about to happen, something she wouldn't be able to control. She'd always been able to control most things in her life and she felt safe and secure, but what if something happened that she couldn't stop . . . something that might change her happiness. That scared her.

Then reality struck.

The night before her wedding, Elizabeth was very sick.

"I'm so tired of feeling like this. What's the matter with me?"

Sally held a cool cloth to Elizabeth's brow. "Now don't go gettin' excited. It's only natural. Some women don't ever get sick, but honey, yo ain't one of them."

"Are you saying everybody gets this sick before their wedding?"

"Ain't the wedding that's makin' you sick," Sally said softly and looked at her with knowing eyes. "I've done seen this many times." Sally nodded her head. "Let me go get you something cool to drink," she said before she left the bedroom.

This time Elizabeth knew that she wasn't sick due to nerves. It was something much more permanent.

She was pregnant.

Captain Lee had left her with more than nightmares.

She shut her eyes, hoping to stop the tears burning her eyes. What was she going to do? Standing up, she swiped at her tears and began to move about the room.

She hated Captain Lee and all the unpleasantness he'd caused her family. She wanted no part of his child.

Yet the child also belonged to her.

She had to tell Jonathan. But what would his reaction be? Could he accept another man's child? Would he feel sorry for her and marry her out of pity? Or would he simply walk away? She remembered his words the other night: *If another man ever touched you, I don't know what I would do.* Elizabeth sighed. She would have to tell him the whole ugly truth and hope for the best.

She couldn't bear the thought that she might never see him again. He'd been so loving these last two weeks, and she couldn't help thinking that she was responsible for easing his bitterness over his arm.

Elizabeth dropped down onto a green velvet chair. Just when she thought everything would be all right, this had to happen. She couldn't bear to throw everything away. She had loved only once in her life and that man was Jonathan. Somehow, she had to keep him.

Finally, she stood and moved over to the wardrobe and took out her nightgown. She threw the gown on the bed and then started unhooking her dress. When Sally returned, Elizabeth took the drink and Sally finished helping Elizabeth undress. Then she dismissed her, preferring to be alone.

As she climbed into bed that night, she knew what she had to do. She would go through the ceremony, then try to convince Jonathan that the baby was his. It might be deceitful, but at the moment she couldn't see any other way.

She couldn't lose Jonathan.

When she finally closed her eyes, sleep was not peaceful. It was filled with nightmares of Captain Lee taunting her.

Captain Lee had finally gotten his revenge.

After three hours donning petticoats, satin, and lace, Elizabeth was finally dressed. She stood in a small room near the front of the chapel where the service was to be performed. Sally spread out her skirts, smoothing the material with her hand.

"You sure is purty, Miz Elizabeth."

Elizabeth turned and looked at herself in the mirror. She saw a beautiful dress, but she didn't like the person who stared back. Her face was very pale and dark rings circled her eyes. The happiness that should be shining through was missing.

She couldn't do this!

"Sally, please get Annie and Jewel," Elizabeth said quickly before she changed her mind.

"Are you sure, Miz Elizabeth?" Sally asked as she stood. "It's about time for you to go into the church."

"Yes, I'm sure." Elizabeth took Sally by the arm and pushed her toward the door. "Now hurry!"

After several anxious minutes, Jewel and Annie appeared in the doorway at the same time. "You're beautiful!" Jewel exclaimed.

Elizabeth looked at the two people she loved as

much as Jonathan and only hoped that they would understand her decision. "I can't do this."

"Of course ye can," Annie said, moving over to pat Elizabeth on the hand. " 'Tis nerves."

"Annie is right," Jewel agreed. "I felt the same way."

"No! You don't understand," Elizabeth protested, pacing as she tried to find the words to explain. "I cannot go through with this!" she said a little more forcefully.

"What do you mean?" Jewel raised her brows in surprise. "Jonathan is out there waiting for you. He's very handsome, I must admit, and you've told me over and over again how much you love him. You have waited so long for this day. So what is the problem?"

Elizabeth suddenly stopped. "I—I'm pregnant." The words tore from her mouth with a rush as the tears gathered in her eyes.

"What?" Jewel and Annie both said together.

"All the more reason to get married," Annie said quickly. "Jonathan will make a fine father."

Elizabeth shook her head. "You don't understand. Jonathan doesn't know," Elizabeth hesitated, not wanting to tell the whole truth.

"But he'll understand," Annie insisted.

"I don't think so."

"Then you don't know Jonathan very well," Jewel argued. "He even offered to help me if Adam threw me out."

"The baby isn't Jonathan's," Elizabeth said with quiet but desperate firmness. "It's Captain Lee's."

"Oh, my God!" Jewel gasped at the same time

her hand flew to her mouth to keep her from saying more.

"I'm so sorry, lass." Annie took Elizabeth in her arms. "I'd never wanted anythin' like that to happen to my girl. And if the man wasn't dead already, I'd do it myself."

"I—I thought I could marry Jonathan," Elizabeth sobbed. "And make him think the baby was his. But I can't do that to him. It isn't fair. He'd probably hate me and the baby when he found out who the father was."

"My poor lass," Annie whispered, rubbing Elizabeth's back.

Elizabeth pulled back and clutched both of Annie's arms. "Don't you see . . . I've got to leave. It's the only answer. You told me Derek was ready to sail? I must go with you. I won't be able to look Jonathan in the face," Elizabeth said sadly.

"For heaven's sake!" Jewel cried. "This isn't right. You must speak with Jonathan."

"I—I can't. I just can't." Elizabeth shook her head firmly. She clutched Jewel's hand. "You have to promise not to say anything to him about this. He must never know."

"I won't," Jewel assured. "But you have to talk to Adam."

"Yes, you're right. Go get him," Elizabeth instructed as she reached down and picked up the train of her skirt, tossing it over her arm. "I'm going back to the house. Tell Adam to meet me at the carriage." She pulled off her veil and looked at Jewel for a final time. "Please take care of Jonathan for me. Tell him I'm sorry."

Jewel gave her a teary smile. "I really wish you would think about this and speak with him."

Elizabeth hung her head in shame. "I can't. I can't bear to see the look on his face when he finds out I'm having another man's child."

"But it wasn't your fault."

"Men don't think like we do," Elizabeth said.

"I guess you're right." Jewel whispered, then gathered Elizabeth into her arms. "I'll miss you, but at least you'll have Annie taking care of you."

"I'll miss you, too. You have really become my sister." Elizabeth turned around to flee, but paused and looked back over her shoulder. "Please ask Jonathan to forgive me."

Then, barely holding back her anguished tears, she hurried from the room.

Jewel entered the church on wobbly legs. She clutched a pew to steady herself. All eyes turned to look at the bride, but saw Jewel instead. She looked straight ahead as she slowly walked to Adam, then whispered into his ear that she needed to see him in the vestry.

"For God's sake, Jewel. A wedding is about to take place," Adam hissed.

"Keep your voice down," she whispered, not wanting to draw everyone's attention any more than she already had. "There is a problem that needs your immediate attention."

"Is something wrong?" Jonathan leaned over and asked.

"Yes. I need Adam for a moment. We'll be right back." She clutched Adam's arm and swiftly walked

him to the back of the church and out the side
door to the carriage where Elizabeth waited.

"Elizabeth!" Adam stuck his head in the carriage's door. "Why are you out here, with a church
full of people waiting for you?"

"I'm leaving, Adam."

"Leaving? What the hell is that supposed to
mean? There is a man inside that church," Adam
pointed, "waiting to become your husband." He
looked from Elizabeth to Jewel, who stood beside
him on the outside of the carriage, then back to
Elizabeth. "Someone had better explain and
quickly."

Elizabeth started in a shaky voice and didn't stop
until she'd blurted out the whole story. She
watched the anger build in Adam's eyes. A muscle
twitched in his cheek as he tried to hold his temper
in check.

"I should have killed the man before we ever
left England," he ground out through clenched
teeth.

"That's in the past, Adam. I can't undo what has
happened, but I can prevent another mistake. I
will not ruin Jonathan's life."

Adam's large hands took Elizabeth's face and
held it gently. "I love you, Elizabeth, but you're
making a terrible mistake. Jonathan loves you. He'll
understand."

"But he won't accept me when I'm carrying
another man's child. He won't understand that
I've been with another man even if it wasn't by
choice," Elizabeth told her brother. She clutched
Adam's hand tightly. "You must respect my wishes.
Do not tell Jonathan where I've gone. I must have

this baby," Elizabeth said, trying to hold the tears back. "I'll have Annie and Derek with me. And I will write to assure you that I'm all right." Her eyelids felt like lead weights and her lips quivered. "I've already sent someone for my things. We're going to the ship now."

Adam backed out of the carriage and straightened. "Is there nothing I can say that will make you change your mind?"

"N–no." Elizabeth shook her head. "I've made up my mind. Jonathan needs someone worthy of him. Someone who can be truly his. I won't ruin his future."

"I think you are making an enormous mistake. One that you'll regret for the rest of your life."

"It will not be my first," she said, her voice barely above a whisper. She watched Adam shut the carriage door and motion for the driver to leave. That's when she realized she would not be seeing her brother for a long, long time. As the carriage pulled away, the tears flowed freely down her cheeks.

Adam couldn't move. He watched the carriage rambling down the road until all he could see was the cloud of dust. Turning to his wife, he said, "I don't know how I'm going to tell Jonathan." Adam sighed and ran his fingers through his hair.

Jewel stood shoulder to shoulder with her husband. "Captain Lee has caused us all so much grief, and he still does, even after his death. What are you going to do?"

"I don't know. But first, I must tell Jonathan that there will be no wedding." Adam started for the doors of the chapel. "I wish to God I knew the right thing to say. This will be one of the worst things I've ever had to do. . . .

"God help me!"

Chapter Eight

Jonathan stood at the front of the church, anxiously awaiting the appearance of his bride. What could delay the woman who'd all but demanded he marry her?

He stared at the back of the church, hoping the sheer force of his will would make Elizabeth appear. He'd been waiting for a good ten minutes, even though it seemed much longer. The crowd grew restless, their murmurs becoming louder as they shifted in their seats.

And just what was the bloody delay? Jonathan wanted to know.

As the minutes ticked away, an uneasy, prickling sensation inched up his spine. He didn't like this one bit. Something had to be wrong.

Finally, Adam appeared in the doorway and motioned for Jonathan to come to him.

Immediately, Jonathan stiffened. *I don't like this,* he thought as he made his way to the back of the church, ripples of whispering following him. He felt as if a hand were closing around his throat.

"I need to talk to you," Adam said in a low voice as he pulled his friend over to the little side room where Elizabeth had been earlier.

As soon as Jonathan stepped inside, he saw Jewel standing in the corner, a stricken look on her face. The knot tightened in his stomach, and he immediately swung around to Adam. "Where is Elizabeth? Has something happened to her?"

Adam rubbed the back of his neck before he looked Jonathan in the eye. "That's what I need to speak with you about. Elizabeth is gone."

"Gone?"

Adam took a deep breath. "Elizabeth has left Four Oaks."

"Left?" Jonathan asked with deceptive calm. "And gone where, might I ask?"

"That I cannot tell you."

"What the bloody hell does that mean?" Jonathan exploded. "You cannot tell me? Or you won't?" He gritted his teeth. "The woman I'm waiting to marry has suddenly left, and you can't tell me where or why she has gone?"

"I'm afraid that is true, Jonathan." Adam sighed. "There will be no wedding."

"Did she not even bother to leave me a note?" Jonathan's voice was cold and exact.

Adam shook his head.

After a long pause, during which Jonathan fought for self-control, he asked again, "Nothing?"

"No. I'm sorry." Adam paused. Awkwardly, he

cleared his throat. "I wish I could tell you more, but Elizabeth has her reasons, and she will have to be the one to explain her rash decision."

"And, of course, I'd have to find Elizabeth to hear this so-called explanation," Jonathan stated sarcastically. "Well, that will not be necessary, because I already know. Your sister is a coward," he ground out between his teeth. "She can't face me and tell me the truth. She thinks I'm only half a man." He glowered at Adam. "She has lied to me all this time, professing how much she loved me only to run when the time grew near when she would actually have to marry me. She couldn't bear the thought that I might touch her with this damaged arm."

Jewel rushed over and grabbed his good arm. "That isn't it at all. I know Elizabeth loves you—"

"Then tell me the truth!" Jonathan cut her off.

Sadly, Jewel shook her head. "I can't. Only Elizabeth can give you the answers you need."

Jonathan shrugged away. "Please spare me." He turned and started for the door.

"Where are you going?" Adam asked.

"To end the most miserable day of my life. Don't you think the guests need to know there will be no wedding?"

Jonathan made his way to the church doors. Once he got out of this embarrassing situation, he'd make damn sure he never made the same mistake again. His father had always told him he didn't raise a fool. Well, apparently he had. But a fool didn't repeat his mistakes. He would never let another woman hurt him. He could feel a creepy coldness invade his body, sucking out the warmth and leaving him dead inside. He never wanted to see Elizabeth Trent again.

Standing in front of the altar, he cleared his throat. "Excuse me, ladies and gentlemen. I'd like to thank you all for coming today, but you've come for nothing," Jonathan said, his voice sounding like it came from a long way off. "There will be no wedding today." Everyone starting talking at once as they stood slowly and started for the door.

Adam clasped a hand on Jonathan's shoulder. Jonathan tensed. He didn't want anyone's pity, especially Adam's. Elizabeth had not only made him look like a fool to strangers but also to his friends.

Jonathan stepped to the side as the congregation filed out of the church. Most didn't bother to look his way. He nodded politely toward the few who did. His pride had taken a severe beating today, but no one would ever know. He felt like his heart had been ripped out and only a cold, hollow shell remained. As far as he was concerned, Elizabeth was dead. He never wanted to hear her name again.

Jean and Pierre Lafitte were the last to leave. They stopped as they came to Jonathan.

"Sometimes, women are very fickle, my friend." Jean clasped Jonathan's bad arm and, to his surprise, Jonathan actually felt the pressure. It was the first time his arm had responded to anything. He'd thought he'd felt a prickling sensation in his fingers yesterday, but he had shrugged it off when he couldn't move them.

"I'm through with women. You give them your heart, and they rip it to shreds," Jonathan said with the certainty of a man scorned. He had to fight not to show his sense of betrayal any more than he had so far, but bitterness was building in him at an alarming rate.

"Oui," Jean said. "Pierre and I have experienced such pain, I'm afraid." Jean folded his arms across his chest. "If you have nothing better to do, my offer still stands. My men grow restless with this peaceful occupation. They are more than ready to return to smuggling." Jean chuckled and held up his hand when Jonathan was about to speak. "Such a course is not possible at this time."

"I hear that your home was destroyed," Adam said.

"Not only my home, but my ships. *Mon Dieu,* I am not happy about this. The government is but a thief."

Jonathan leaned against the wall, relieved to talk about something other than Elizabeth and the wedding that didn't happen. "What have you done to rectify the situation?"

"My first thought was to lead a raiding party to take back what is mine," Jean said with a grin. "I have filed suit, of course. I'm truly learning to be civilized. My attorneys, Gryes and Livingston, have filed the necessary papers to recover damages from the United States. And Livingston has written to the President. I have confidence that he'll leave no stone unturned, my friend. And if all else fails," Jean paused with a sly grin, "then we take matters into our own hands."

"When do you set sail?" Jonathan asked.

Jean smiled a knowing smile. "In five days. The ships are being readied."

"Jonathan, are you sure you want to go to sea?" Adam asked his friend, then pointed out, "You've never been interested in my ships."

"Adam does have a point." Jonathan said tentatively, as if testing the idea. This just might be a damned good way to rid himself of Elizabeth. He couldn't be any more miserable than he was at this moment. "I am more of a land lover, and don't know the first thing about sailing."

"Ah, but you will learn very fast, I guarantee." Pierre chuckled. "Or Jean and his crew will toss you overboard."

Jonathan couldn't help his smile, and he felt some of his tension ease. "That's what I'm afraid of. But I'm game, if you think there is something I can do."

"I guarantee"—Jean winked at Jonathan—"that you will return a different man. There is something about Mother Nature and the sea that cures all wounds."

The group turned to leave the church. "Where are we sailing to?" Jonathan asked, even though he really didn't care. Anywhere but here would be a blessing at the moment.

Jean moved ahead of Adam and Jonathan. "Does it matter, my friend?"

Jonathan laughed sarcastically. "I don't suppose so. Just as long as I don't see any women."

Jean grinned and looked back over his shoulder at Jonathan. "There will be none at sea. But I'll wager you'll be glad to see a pretty mademoiselle upon our return."

"Or an ugly one," Pierre added.

"Would you like to make a wager?" Jonathan's

voice was heavy with sarcasm. A woman was the last thing he wanted to see. He'd be careful to keep his heart well protected.

Jean gave a parting sly grin. *"Oui,* I always bet on a sure thing."

Elizabeth had done two stupid things in her life: First, she'd left the only man she'd ever loved, and second, she'd climbed on this infernal rocking ship.

It had been two weeks since she'd left New Orleans ... two long, miserable weeks. Between the pregnancy and the ship's tossing, she'd thrown up constantly. And now she was so weak, Annie had confined her to bed.

"I've brought ye some bread, lass," Annie said as she entered Elizabeth's cabin. "Look at ye. Yer sittin' up."

"Yes, but for how long? That is the question," Elizabeth joked for the first time in days. "I even feel I might live."

"That's my lass." Annie patted Elizabeth on the hand. "I know exactly how ye feel. I was sick on the voyage over, ye know."

"Well, I wasn't on my trip over, so to be this sick surprised me," Elizabeth admitted.

"Ye weren't expecting a wee one before."

Elizabeth frowned. "I guess you're right. Surely, this can't go on for nine months?"

"I think maybe we've seen the worst. Now we have to build yer strength back so ye'll be strong for the baby."

"Baby," Elizabeth whispered "I've never thought about being a mother before."

Annie's mouth curved into an unconscious smile. "Ye'll make a fine one. Just like yer own dear mother. Do ye realize it will be the third generation o' Trents for me?"

Elizabeth smiled affectionately as she sipped the tea Annie had given her. "You've been with us a long time. And to tell you the truth, I remember you more than I can recall Mother." Elizabeth reached out and squeezed Annie's hand. "You were always there when I fell down and scraped my knees. You were the one who hugged me and wiped my tears away."

"Yer mother was a fine lady, lass."

"I'm not saying she wasn't, but in a way you are my mother, too."

Annie stood abruptly. "Dinna ye go getting me all sentimental," she said gruffly. She brushed away a stray tear with the back of her hand. "If ye feel like it tomorrow, I'll take ye up top and let ye get some sun."

"That sounds like heaven."

The morning dawned with a dull gray light as the clouds opened up and released a cold rain that pelted the *Shanna Lee* for the third day in a row.

Jonathan prowled the deck, holding onto the ropes and riggings so he wouldn't be washed into the choppy sea. Wrapping his coat tighter around him, he made his way to the helm to visit Jean's captain, Dominic You.

Dominic stood behind the big wheel, his feet

spread apart as he guided the ship. He was a small man, but broad-shouldered and strong. His hair was light even though it was wet and plastered to his darkly tanned face. When he was angry he resembled a ruffled eagle, but his outbursts were rare.

"I hope this damnable weather doesn't follow us the whole trip," Jonathan said when he drew up next to You.

"Aye," Dominic said. His response held a note of impatience. "Here, take the wheel. I have to find another hat. Mine blew away."

Jonathan grasped the wheel with his left hand, his injured right arm hanging as usual by his side.

"No, no. You must use both hands." Dominic grabbed Jonathan's right arm and placed it on the wheel.

"I have no strength in that arm." Jonathan said.

"Nor will you if you do not use it." Dominic reached down in a box beside the wheel and retrieved a fresh tricorn hat, which he pulled down tight so the water would run off away from his eyes.

"Look," he said as he pulled up his shirtsleeve and revealed a twelve-inch gash on his arm. "I was injured once, and I almost gave up until I started lifting those wooden pins that we use to play skittles." He pointed. "There are a few pins over by the ropes. It takes time, but I believe you'll regain the use of your arm just like I did. Remember, you're no longer a landlubber."

When Dominic retook the wheel, Jonathan went over and picked up a couple of pins that were about twelve inches long and rather heavy. What the hell, he thought as he returned to his cabin. What could it hurt?

After several weeks at sea, Jonathan wasn't sure he liked sailing, but he could tell he was changing. This environment was nothing like the ballrooms in England, but for now he was content here. He associated with men who flashed dirks and wore cutlasses hanging from their belts.

He was learning that they had their own community aboard ship. Jonathan had been assigned the job of Sailing Master. He read the maps and planned where to sail. The "where" was always where Jean said he wanted to go. Everyone always obeyed the captain.

Jonathan knew most of the crew by name. There was Bobby, the pegleg cook, Henry, the ship's surgeon, and Jamie, the carpenter, who took the surgeon's place when needed. God help him should he require a doctor. Jonathan would have to be half dead before he allowed Henry to touch him.

They all dressed in wild costumes to frighten their victims. A few wore tricorn hats, while the others had scarves tied around their heads or necks. They wore baggy canvas breeches that came to their knees, which Jonathan found very comfortable.

Pistols were worn in several places—in their breeches or in a string of leather across their chests, strapped to their ankles, and probably a few places he hadn't seen. They were a rough—yet likable— lot.

The food was vastly different than that found in the dining rooms of London or New Orleans. Beer was the common beverage. He was glad of that when we saw the food that was served. They had meat that was salted and stewed in a large iron pot, and then there was the crew's favorite: green turtles. All Jonathan could think was, "Thank God for the beer!"

He had wanted a change, Jonathan had to remind himself more than once, and that was what he was getting. Even though he was on a ship of cutthroats, Jonathan found he was losing the tension he'd felt for so long. And it felt damn good to shed the bitterness he'd bottled up for months.

They'd been a month out to sea when they came upon a Spanish craft.

"She sits heavy in the water, my friend," Jean said as he pointed toward the vessel. "I believe the Spanish can do without a ship or two." Jean laughed. "Are you ready for a little adventure?"

"I'm as ready as I'll ever be," Jonathan admitted.

"Good." Jean nodded. "They are Spanish. We show no mercy."

"You mean we take no prisoners?" Jonathan asked.

Jean barely nodded before he issued the command. "Fire broadside!"

The cannons fired and the ship shook. Jonathan grabbed a rail as a hole appeared in the hull of the Spanish ship. The second shot brought the sails down.

The Spanish ship managed to shoot one round, but it went long, landing way past the pirate's ship.

The *Shanna Lee* drew near, and the pirates threw grappling hooks onto the crippled boat. Quickly, ropes were tied off. The pirates swarmed onto the Spanish ship like a plague of seagoing locusts.

Jonathan drew his sword and defended himself. He hated to admit it, but exhilaration ran through him, energizing him, as he defeated one sailor after another. Most he spared and threw overboard. Civilization was now a blur in his memory.

Once all the spoils had been loaded aboard the *Shanna Lee,* the order was given. "Sink the ship!" Jean smiled with satisfaction as he watched. Then without a word, he went to his cabin, leaving Pierre and Jonathan on deck.

Jonathan placed his hand on Pierre's shoulder. "Tell me something, Pierre."

Pierre nodded.

"Why does Jean hate the Spanish?"

"For good reason." Pierre looked from beneath craggy brows. "You see, Jean was in the West Indies when he fell in love with a rich and beautiful woman by the name of Marie. I joined them and lived there for a time. She was a wonderful woman, and Jean was very happy.

"Jean made plans for a trip to France. We loaded everything aboard our ship and set sail. While sailing through the West Indies we were overtaken and captured by a Spanish Man-of-War. The no-good Spaniards took everything. And worse, put us ashore on a barren island." Pierre's eyes were hooded like those of a hawk.

"They left us with nothing," Pierre spat, his vexation evident. "Do you understand? Nothing! Jean and I were used to outdoor living, but Marie was not and soon she became ill.

"Finally, an American schooner noticed us and sent a boat to rescue us. Marie had developed a bad fever, but there was no one on the American ship that could help. By the time we landed in New Orleans, Jean rushed her to the hospital, but it was too late." Pierre's eyes darkened with pain. "Three weeks later, Marie died."

"I didn't know," Jonathan said solemnly, shaking his head.

"Jean doesn't speak about what I've just told you. But it has always been a festering sore, and he's reminded when he comes across a Spanish ship."

"Thanks, Pierre. I'll not mention what you've told me." Jonathan excused himself and went to his cabin. So Jean knew what it was like to love and lose. No wonder he'd understood that day at the church.

Once Jonathan was in his cabin, he lay down on his small, hard bunk and closed his eyes. Without warning, the black-headed Elizabeth materialized in his mind, her dark eyes flashing desire.

He could picture her running ahead of him, laughing with the carefree nature that he remembered much too well. Suddenly, she turned, holding her arms out to him . . . begging him to come to her. He moved toward Elizabeth, wanting to lose himself in her sweetness, but just before he reached her, she disappeared.

Slowly, Jonathan opened his eyes and reality set in.

Elizabeth would always be a painful part of his past.

Chapter Nine

Adam thumped the letter against his hand as he made his way to his study. His wife was already seated across from his desk in one of the green chintz chairs.

Jewel patiently waited for Adam to take his seat, then asked. "What's wrong?" She frowned at her husband.

He waved the letter in the air. "This is a letter from Annie," Adam informed her. He took the letter out of the envelope, taking his seat behind the large oak desk.

"Well, it's nice that she writes you."

"You don't understand." Adam glanced up from the letter. "Annie never writes me. And that's why

I'm afraid to read what she has written," he told her. He quickly skimmed the letter, then he began to read it out loud.

> *Dear Adam,*
>   *I fear that I've waited too long to send this letter.*
>   *It has been almost two years since we've returned to Briercliff, and during that time, I've seen many changes in your sister.*
>   *Elizabeth is a wonderful mother. And Dawson is growing up to be a fine lad. He's the spitting image of his mother, and you would fall in love with him the minute you laid eyes on him.*
>   *But my concern is Elizabeth. She refuses to leave Briercliff and go to London, and I fear she'll never marry. The few gentlemen callers she has had, she has sent away after the first day.*
>   *The lass is becoming very headstrong, and no man will be able to control her. She has even begun to ride unchaperoned.*
>   *Adam, you need to come and find the lass a husband. She won't listen to me. And Dawson needs a Da.*
>   *Elizabeth should be as happy as you and Jewel. So please hurry.*
>
> *Annie*

Adam folded the letter after reading it out loud to his very pregnant wife. "What do you think?" he asked, placing the letter down on the desk.

"I think Elizabeth is still in love with Jonathan, and doesn't want any men in her life. I know if I couldn't have you, I wouldn't want another," Jewel told him with a twinkle in her eye.

Adam gazed at his wife affectionately. She was so beautiful that she absolutely glowed, even in her eighth month of pregnancy. She could still stir his desires, which wasn't doing him much good at the moment. He needed to concentrate on his other problem. "I'm not sure what to do about Elizabeth."

"You must go to her," Jewel urged. "It sounds like she needs you."

"I'll not leave you and miss the birth of my son," Adam stated flatly.

"You mean your child," Jewel gently reminded him.

"Precisely."

Jewel shifted in the chair. "Well, I'm in no condition to travel."

"Point taken." Adam nodded. "So that means I must find someone else to go. The question is, who?"

Jewel thought for a moment. "It must be someone we can trust. Elizabeth needs guidance. Perhaps someone who lives close. Of course, you know she will not like the idea of someone picking out a husband for her."

"She's going to be very difficult." He smiled. He remembered very well how his sister could be a temperamental child. "It will have to be someone who is strong."

Just then a loud knock sounded on the study door.

Adam glanced up. "Come in," he said.

"You have company, sir," the butler informed him. "Shall I show him in?"

"Who is it?" Adam asked as he stood.

"A gentleman, sir, by the looks of his clothing. But he said I was not to give you a name."

Adam frowned at the so-called gentleman's audacity. "Then send him away."

The door opened wider and the butler was shoved to the side as the gentleman in question barged through. "You would send me away without finding out who the bloody hell came to pay you a visit? My, my. Your manners seem to have disappeared, old boy."

"Jonathan!" Jewel stood and went to him. "Look at you, you've changed," she said and hugged him.

Jonathan stepped back, then arched a brow at Jewel. "Me, changed? Apparently, Adam has been feeding you much too well."

"Oh, no, it shows?" Jewel teased him.

"Yes, my dear, it does." Jonathan laughed, the rich sound filling the room.

"She does earn her keep." Adam gave his wife a loving glance, then moved over to his old friend and grasped his hand to shake it. "Where the bloody hell have you been? I thought you were just going on a short sail with Jean and then coming back."

"Look!" Jewel pointed. "Your arm. You can move it."

"By God, she's correct," Adam said as he looked down at the hand he'd grasped. The handshake was firm. "I had forgotten about your injury."

"Lafitte was correct about the sea curing me. And thanks to his crew, I had to quickly learn to use my arm again. They have no time for anyone who cannot do his share of the work."

Jewel couldn't quit staring at Jonathan. He'd

changed a great deal. Where he had been boyishly good-looking before, he was dangerously good-looking now. His shoulders seemed broader and definitely more muscular. His skin was bronzed, and there was a recklessness about him that hadn't been there before. He had aged, and there was a hard glint in his eye much like the one she remembered in Adam's before she had tamed and softened him.

"Please, be seated." Adam pointed to a chair. "Tell us what you have been doing."

Jonathan chuckled before sitting in the chair opposite Jewel. "I've learned to be a pirate, of course. You would be proud of the way I've mastered the high seas. I'm now ready to enter the shipping business you've always nagged me about."

"So that's why you've returned?" Jewel asked.

"Not really." Jonathan stretched his legs out in front of him. "Jean and Pierre have decided to move their operations to Galveston. They have gone there now. However, I've received word that my father is very ill, so I must return home."

"I'm so sorry," Adam said. "Is his condition serious?"

"Sounds like it." Jonathan admitted. He pressed both hands over his eyes and rubbed before he continued. "He has been bedridden for the last month. Word was slow to find me, so I'm not sure how he is at the moment."

Jewel realized Jonathan's usually lively eyes were dulled with weariness. "You're going home?"

"That's right. I'm leaving tomorrow." He broke into a leisurely smile. "But I couldn't depart without seeing my friends first."

Jewel glanced at her husband in silent communication. When she saw a slow smile touch Adam's lips, she knew they were thinking the same thing. "If you'll excuse me," Jewel said, rising, wanting to give them some privacy to talk. "I have some things I need to take care of. I'll see you before you leave," she said to Jonathan.

After his wife left, Adam went to the liquor cabinet and selected a decanter of dark liquid. "Would you care for some brandy?" Adam offered, but didn't wait for an answer. He picked up the crystal decanter, removed the cork, and poured two drinks.

"Brandy? It's been a while since I've had fine brandy. What's up?"

"I beg your pardon." Adam turned to Jonathan and tried to look innocent. This was going to be a tough subject.

Jonathan stood up and rubbed his chin and warily watched Adam. "I've known you for a long time. I believe I can tell when you're up to something, and you have always saved that bloody brandy for serious discussions."

Adam couldn't contain his smile as he handed his friend a leaded crystal glass. "Ah, you know me too well."

Jonathan nodded. "That's what I thought."

Adam waved his hand. "Shall we sit again?"

Adam sat in the chair beside his friend, slowly sipping his brandy and savoring the burning liquid as he decided where to begin. He wondered just how Jonathan was going to handle his request. Could he refuse a friend in need?

Jonathan knew Adam was stalling. He'd seen the

keen, probing eyes and inscrutable expression before. "Well? Are you going to tell me?"

"I need your help."

"You know you can always count on me," Jonathan quickly said. "What's the problem?"

"Adam set his glass down. Jewel and I were discussing a very important issue when you came in. As you can see, she is expecting next month."

"Yes, I could very well see that," Jonathan admitted as he leaned back in the chair. "Congratulations—I do believe I forgot to say that earlier."

Adam leaned forward and propped his arms on his knees. "That's why I need your help."

Jonathan chuckled. "With Jewel?"

"No," Adam snapped, "of course not. It's Elizabeth."

Jonathan felt like he'd been doused in ice water. "Not bloody likely." Abruptly, he stood. "I've heard enough."

Adam jumped to his feet and reached for Jonathan's arm. "You could at least do me the courtesy of listening."

"I don't want to hear anything about your heartless sister," Jonathan replied with as reasonable a voice as he could manage.

"I understand how you must feel."

Jonathan stiffened. "Do you?"

"Well, maybe I don't," Adam admitted. "But, listen to me. I received a letter from Annie telling me that Elizabeth has grown wild, and she wants me to come over right away."

"Wait a minute. Annie?" Jonathan stared at Adam, baffled. "Then Elizabeth is at Briercliff?"

Adam nodded. "That is correct."

"So that's where she went." Jonathan's lips thinned with irritation. "Well, she can rot there as far as I'm concerned."

Adam was hoping that Jonathan had lost some of his bitterness. Apparently, that wasn't the case. But the fact remained that he still needed Jonathan's help. Adam would love to tell Jonathan about the child, but he'd promised his sister that he wouldn't, and Adam was bound by that promise. "I understand your bitterness, but Elizabeth needs a husband."

"I hope the bloody hell you don't think it will be me," Jonathan said curtly.

"Of course not," Adam quickly responded. But deep inside he believed if he got Jonathan and Elizabeth together again, they would work out their differences . . . or kill each other. "I know you don't love her," Adam lied. "However, you do know her very well."

Jonathan threw his head back and roared with laughter. "I know her too bloody well."

"See?" Adam let out a sigh of exasperation. "You'd be the perfect one to find her a husband."

"Adam, you are asking the impossible." Jonathan shifted in the chair. At the moment, he couldn't find any comfortable position and the conversation wasn't helping. "I want nothing to do with your sister."

"I wouldn't ask if I could go myself, but I need you to do this for me," Adam persisted. "Besides, you have no feelings for her, so it shouldn't bother you to seek out a perfect husband."

Damn, the man was being persistent, Jonathan thought. If Adam were not such a damned good friend, Jonathan would have stormed out at the mention of Elizabeth's name. "I cannot do this!'"

"Why?" Adam asked with a pensive stare, knowing he was pushing Jonathan, but in the long run perhaps doing the right thing by them both. "Maybe I was wrong, and you still care for my sister." Adam arched an eyebrow.

"Don't be absurd."

"Then who better than her childhood friend?"

"You'll owe me the world for this, old boy."

"Then you'll do it?"

"Yes, Adam." Jonathan gave in as he swallowed the lump in his throat. "But I warn you. I just might stick her with the oldest, ugliest bastard I can find."

Adam laughed. "I believe you'll find my sister has changed a good bit since you parted. She might not be the easiest person to find a match for."

"Then this shall be an interesting reunion since I, too, have changed." Jonathan offered a salute with his goblet. "May the best man win."

On the rocky shores of Cornwall, a lone rider raced along the beach, the ocean spray shooting from her horse's hooves.

Elizabeth felt alive and carefree when she rode, but all too soon the ride came to an end, and she remembered she was a lady with many responsibilities. She glanced up at Briercliff, her childhood home. It stood high on the granite cliffs, overlooking the sea below. Its massive gray rooftop gave the castle a grim appearance, but it wasn't as it appeared. One couldn't call it cozy, however, because it was cold and drafty.

The castle had thirty-four rooms; the rear of the building had the most beautiful leaded windows that stretched across the back of the house and overlooked Annie's lovely gardens.

Reaching down, Elizabeth patted Star, Adam's horse, on the side of his neck. "You miss Adam. Don't you, boy?"

Star pawed the sand as if he understood. "I miss him, too," Elizabeth breathed in a choked voice. And most of all, she missed Jonathan. No matter what she did, she could never put Jonathan completely out of her mind. A thousand times she had asked herself what would have happened if she'd just confronted Jonathan with her problem. She would never know. It was too late for them, she thought sadly. She wasn't even sure what he was doing. Adam was still angry with her and refused to discuss Jonathan.

She nudged Star to a group of gray-colored rocks and recalled the time when Adam had found Jewel washed up, half dead on this very shore. Elizabeth smiled, wondering if she looked under a rock maybe she would find the person she was meant to spend the rest of her life with. The rocks certainly had been a blessing for Adam and Jewel.

One thing Elizabeth did know was that Dawson, her baby boy, was a blessing. No matter the circumstances of his birth, he was her beautiful child, and he looked just like her with his dark hair and gray eyes. He did have a strange birthmark on his ankle in the shape of a heart, which only made her love him all the more. Other than that he was perfect, and very, very active.

A flock of seagulls flew overhead. It was time to

get back to the house before Annie started worrying about her. Carefully, she wound her way through the gray rocks until she made it to the top of the cliff. Then she nudged Star into a gallop, heading home.

She rode Star to the stables and handed him over to a groom. "Make sure he gets a carrot," Jewel told the groom. "He deserves a treat."

In no time, she'd strolled to the main house and was just coming to the last step when the front door opened and Giles said, "I saw you approaching, Lady Elizabeth. Did you have a nice ride, mum?"

Elizabeth smiled as she walked past the stiff butler. She'd wager that Giles hadn't smiled in twenty years. "It was lovely, Giles. Where is Dawson?"

"The nanny has him in the nursery, mum."

"Thank you," Elizabeth called over her shoulder. She made her way up the stairs and went straight to the nursery, where she nudged open the door and looked inside. Dawson sat in the middle of the floor, stacking blocks.

"Has he been good?" Elizabeth asked Mary, the nanny.

"Yes, mum. He's always a good little chap."

"Mummy," Dawson said as he placed his hands on the floor and shoved his plump bottom into the air before he stood. He remembered his blocks and reached for one, then toddled over to her. "Block."

"I see you've learned a new word today."

"Block," Dawson repeated.

"Yes, I see your pretty block. You can use it to build things."

He looked up at her and smiled. For a moment, he reminded her of Jonathan, with that small dimple in his left cheek. And she felt a lump form in her throat. What if Dawson was really Jonathan's child and not Lee's? Then all her running would have been for nothing.

"Story?" Dawson asked and pulled on her hand.

"All right," Elizabeth said and followed her child to the rocking chair. She sat down and lifted him to her lap. Opening the big book, she began to read him a story. It wasn't long before she felt his head resting gently on her chest, his breathing slowed, and he slept.

These were the times she enjoyed most. When she held him like this, all her problems seemed to melt away. She hoped Jewel would have her baby soon and then Dawson would have a playmate when they went to visit.

Eventually, Elizabeth would return to America, but not until she felt she could face Jonathan again.

The door swung open, and Annie stuck her head inside and smiled. "I'd love to have a picture of ye two. I just wanted to let ye know that one of the servants came over from Foxmore."

Elizabeth stood and took Dawson over to his crib where she placed him down, covering him up. She motioned for Annie to leave the room so they wouldn't wake the baby. Even the mention of Jonathan's estate, Foxmore, had sent chills up Elizabeth's arm.

"Is there something wrong?" Elizabeth asked finally.

"The Marquess of Middlesex has taken to his bed in London. One of the servants came over earlier to see if ye knew Jonathan's whereabouts. And, of course, I told then ye dinna know a thing. Sounds serious.''

"I'm sorry to hear of his illness. The marquess is such a dear man. I used to so much enjoy talking to him when I was younger." Elizabeth thought for a moment. She didn't like the idea that the dear old man was alone and not feeling well. "Perhaps I should go to London to see him. I can't bear the thought of him dying alone."

'' 'Tis very noble of ye, lass.''

"He is a good man," Elizabeth said as she tiptoed toward the door. "Annie, tell Mary to pack enough for a week. I'll take Dawson with me."

Annie followed her out of the room. "The lad will be needin' new clothes before long. 'Twill be a good time to have him fitted."

"You have a good point." Elizabeth stopped and smiled at Annie. "I can't remember the last time I've been to London. Perhaps I'll order some new clothing for myself."

Chapter Ten

The black brougham displaying the Duke of St. Ives's impressive coat of arms lumbered down the road on its way to London. The crest was sapphire blue on the outside edges and in the center a bold knight dressed in armor sat astride a mighty black stallion. The mantle draped above the helm was blood red. Underneath the knight was sprawled the Latin for the motto *One So Bold*. It was the only marking on the sleek black carriage, one of the most impressive in all of England. The Trents had two carriages, but this was the one Elizabeth always took on long journeys.

Elizabeth had brought two coachmen to take turns driving so they wouldn't have to stay overnight at an inn. She leaned back on the green velvet squabs which made the ride very comfortable. Adam had always hated long trips, so he made sure that he and his family had every convenience when traveling. Elizabeth smiled as she thought of her brother and how he had to have his way.

Jonathan was a different story. He loved to drive a sleek black phaeton, which only seated two people. But then Jonathan had never had to worry about a family. His taste ran more to racing than settling down. He used to brag that his phaeton was much grander than the one the Prince of Wales owned.

Strange that her thoughts had drifted to Jonathan. She presumed it was because she'd been thinking about his father.

Glancing out the window, she saw that morning had dawned and the sky was turning a beautiful azure blue. Small white clouds resembling puffs of smoke dotted the sky. They rode through a field of daisies, and Elizabeth decided it was a perfect day in May. They had been traveling for hours, having left before dawn, but so far the trip had been uneventful. She hoped it stayed that way. There hadn't been any reports of highwaymen in a long time, so she wasn't worried about being robbed.

She was pleased that Dawson was playing and not fussing about his confinement. She gazed at the chubby little pink-cheeked face and smiled. If she'd done nothing else right, Dawson was one thing she was proud of. He was perfect.

Excitement shimmered in the air; she realized she was happy to be traveling and doing something other than her normal activities. Her life had been simple and routine over the last year, and she was ready for a change. She'd learned to manage Briercliff. She also found she had a rare gift for caring for the sick, so she had taken many trips to St. Ives to visit the townspeople and help out where she was needed.

She couldn't remember the last time she'd been to Adam's town house on Park Lane. Trent House was a four-story building made of yellow brick, and looked like every other house on the street. London was so densely populated that the nobility and gentry had to be organized around vertical rather than horizontal space. That's why she'd always preferred Briercliff, where there was plenty of room and open sky.

It was time for the Season with its whirlwind of parties and balls. She couldn't remember the last time she'd seen any of the nobility and gentry that would soon be filling London for the Season. She'd kept away for good reason. She didn't want people asking questions about Dawson. Oh, she already had a story made up about how his father had died and how she was now a widow, but she hated lying, so she kept Dawson her secret.

Elizabeth heard a snap and looked down at Dawson, who held his small wooden horse in one hand and one of the horse's hooves in the other. Dawson's lip stuck out as he tried to decide whether he should cry.

Finally, he looked up at his mother and said, "Broke."

"I see that," Elizabeth said as she scooped Dawson up onto her lap. She examined the toy before saying, "We'll have to pretend your horse is hurt until we can get him fixed."

Dawson studied his toy a little longer before wrapping his arms around it. Laying his head on his mother's chest, he settled down to sleep. As her child slept, Elizabeth had plenty of time to think.

She was sure she would see many of her old friends, and her secret would come out. Probably most would be married, she thought with a sigh, but as long as she could make them believe her story she could hold her head high.

But that wasn't the reason she was going to London, she reminded herself. She was making the trip to see Jonathan's father. If his son couldn't find time to see his father, then the least she could do was take his place.

She stared out the window, watching the greenery fly by. Unfortunately, just the thought of Jonathan brought his face to her mind. She could almost see him, and her pulse automatically quickened as she pictured his sandy brown hair and blue eyes that used to sparkle so brightly when he was in one of his mischievous moods.

It was one of the things that she'd loved most about him. He had taught her how to laugh at things instead of taking everything so seriously. Then it all changed.

Her memories fell back to the night they'd first made love.

They had been at Four Oaks in her bedroom. It had all started out so innocently. Jewel and Adam had been in New Orleans, and the servants were busy elsewhere, so they were very much alone. Elizabeth had wanted to play a game of chess, but the game was in her room, so she'd told Jonathan to come and help her bring the game board downstairs.

They had just gathered all the playing pieces when Elizabeth accidentally bumped into Jonathan. The chess pieces scattered to the floor . . . neither of them had noticed.

She hadn't known that anything could be so wonderful. They had never intended to consummate their love before marriage, but that night . . . that wonderful night. . . .

Jonathan had placed his fingers beneath her chin and lifted her face. At first, he'd placed soft, feather-like kisses on her cheeks and lips. His mouth slanted over hers and his arms went around her with a fierce yet tender possession. She'd slid her hands around his neck, clinging to him and innocently molding her body to his. This was how she'd always imagined it would be.

His tongue touched her lips, and Elizabeth opened her mouth slightly as his tongue slid between them, seizing her with a passion that took her breath away. His tongue stroked and explored. It was wild and deliciously wanton and sensual. She had never imagined desire could be so strong.

His arms tightened about her, and Elizabeth knew then that he was experiencing some of the same pleasure she felt. He aroused yearnings in her that she hadn't known existed, and suddenly there was an urgency to let him touch her. She began to tremble as her clothing fell to the floor piece by piece. Liquid heat flowed through her body, and she trembled. And then ...

Elizabeth moaned out loud. Her eyes popped open.

"Is anything wrong, mum?" Mary asked with an alarmed expression.

"I—I. No. Nothing. Just having a dream," Elizabeth managed. How embarrassing. She was living in the past with no hope for the future. She was behaving like a love-struck schoolgirl, when in reality she had to face the fact that she was nothing but a spinster, even if the rest of the world thought she was a widow. She shuddered. Would she ever know real happiness again, or would she have only memories?

Would she ever be able to think of Jonathan and not hurt inside? And what had he been doing since the last time she'd seen him? Had he married? Did she want to know? The thought of Jonathan with another woman made her feel cold and dead inside, as if a part of her were missing. And it was: her heart.

Did love have to be so painful?

Shutting her eyes, Elizabeth pressed her forehead against the window. She laid Dawson on the seat beside her. The sun had eased behind the trees and the shadows had grown long. It wouldn't be long before dark. Mary had fallen asleep. Maybe a little sleep would do Elizabeth some good, too.

The rocking carriage and fatigue from her early-morning departure made it impossible for Elizabeth to keep her eyes open. Soon she fell into an exhausted, dreamless sleep ... sleep where she couldn't think or wonder about what-ifs.

They arrived at Trent House in the wee morning hours and were escorted to their rooms. Her room was on the second floor, the nursery on the third.

After sleeping late, Elizabeth went upstairs to make certain Dawson was settled in before she visited the marquess. She smiled as she walked past the paintings of her and Adam at various ages. She remembered how they'd hated sitting still for so long. No wonder they were not smiling in any of the portraits.

Peeking in the door, she saw Mary reading to Dawson as they rocked back and forth. Elizabeth decided not to interrupt, because Dawson would only cry when she started to leave. At least she knew they were fine.

Returning to her room, Elizabeth found that Miss Greenow, Adam's resident housekeeper, had laid out her clothes. She had chosen a gown of chartreuse *faille française* that was plush to the touch. The skirt had vertical pleats caught up on one side with the other side falling straight. The front of the dress was similar to a man's cravat of white crepe. It was a lovely dress, Elizabeth thought—plain yet elegant. She pinned on a dark green hat and started on her mission.

"I'll be back shortly," Elizabeth told Miss Greenow, who, more or less, ran Adam's house. They only employed a small staff since they didn't come to the city often. "Mary will take care of

Dawson, but if I'm needed I'll be visiting the Marquess of Middlesex.''

"Yes, mum." Mrs. Greenow bobbed. "They have said he's right poorly," she said as she followed Elizabeth downstairs.

"I've heard the same thing."

She couldn't picture Lord Middlesex in a feeble condition. He'd been married at least four times and had survived all four ladies. He was feisty, to put it mildly, and spoke his mind at the drop of a hat.

Elizabeth didn't have to take a carriage, since Jonathan's father lived directly across the street. She made her way over to the gray-colored town house and rapped on the front door.

Jeffrey, the butler, answered. He was an elderly gentleman who'd been with the Marquess of Middlesex since his early teens. Jeffrey's hair was snow white, his eyes a faded blue.

"May I help you?" Jeffrey said in his haughty tone.

"Where is your monocle, Jeffrey?" Elizabeth asked with a smile. She knew he didn't see well, but he was very stubborn about wearing his eyepiece.

He drew himself up straight. "I don't need a monocle. Now state your business, young woman, or be off with you." He waved his hand as if he was shooing away a pesky fly.

"Please inform the Marquess that Lady Elizabeth is here to see him," Elizabeth said.

"I–I don't believe you. L–Lady Elizabeth is on the continent," Jeffrey stuttered and fumbled in his pocket until he found his monocle. After placing it in his right eye, he peered at Elizabeth. "It is you," he said. A slow smile formed, and he reached out and tugged on her arm. "Come. Come in," he dithered as he ushered her through the door. "When did you grow up?"

"I'm not sure." Elizabeth laughed. "Time goes by so quickly."

"Yes, ma'am." Jeffrey nodded slowly. "That is the only thing that is moving quickly these days." He chuckled, then started for the stairs. "Follow me. The marquess will be glad to see you. We've not had much company."

Elizabeth followed the butler and helped him when he stumbled on one of the steps. "You should get one of the younger men to go up and down these stairs."

"Rubbish! My knees just give way once in a while."

He opened the door and stepped quietly inside, leaving Elizabeth in the doorway while she was announced. "I have a visitor for you, sir."

Elizabeth peered inside while she waited. The room was much too dark, she thought, and very depressing with its mahogany furniture and dark rosewood panels. Thick, dark-green carpet stretched across the room. There were two floor-length windows on each side of the bed, but the drapes were drawn. A single candle by the bedside provided the only light.

From a large bed in the middle of the room, an older gentleman with white hair leaned up on his elbows. "Who the bloody hell is it, Jeffrey? Can't they let an old man die in peace?"

"If this isn't a good time, Lord Middlesex, I can

return on a later day," Elizabeth said from the doorway.

He collapsed back upon his pillow. "I might be dead at a later time," he snapped. "Come closer, so I can see who this voice belongs to."

Instead of going to him as the marquess had directed, Elizabeth went to the windows and drew open the heavy, green-and-gold curtains. She tied them back with the matching cords and tassels so the sunlight could shine brightly into the room.

Then she stepped beside the bed and took the marquess's hand. "Don't tell me you have forgotten who I am?"

He stared at her a long time, but the gold in his eyes flickered with recognition. "How could I forget our lovely Elizabeth?" he murmured, his voice choked. "Child, you have grown even lovelier, if that is possible."

"Thank you, sir." Elizabeth hesitated. She'd never seen Lord Middlesex looking so ill. His skin had the wrinkled appearance of parchment paper, and his blue eyes had lost the sparkle she remembered so well. He'd always been so full of life, and now he seemed a withered shell. "How are you feeling?"

"Not worth a damn." His lips thinned with irritation. "That old sawbones said I'd be gone before the end of the month," Lord Middlesex said, and then smiled. "But that was two months ago. I do believe I showed him."

"Indeed, you did," Elizabeth agreed. "I don't think anyone except the Lord can predict when we die."

"Only if they have a gun in their hands." He

chuckled, and patted the bed beside him. "Tell me all about yourself and Adam. And what has happened to that sorry son of mine?" The marquess shifted so he could see her better, and Elizabeth helped by propping pillows behind his head so he'd be elevated just a bit.

"Is that better?"

"Much better." Lord Middlesex smiled, then said, "The last I heard from him, he was going sailing with pirates." He drew both his brows together and reached out and squeezed her hand. "Has he lost his bloody mind? He has responsibilities and estates to run." Lord Middlesex waved his hand in a dismissing gesture. "Well, that's another story. Now tell me about yourself."

Elizabeth felt hysterical laughter build within her, but she couldn't say anything. Jonathan had gone sailing with Lafitte? Why? That tidbit of news disturbed her. Had he wanted to be reckless, maybe losing his life, or had he done it for the fun and adventure, never thinking twice about her?

Adam had refused to mention Jonathan in his posts since she wouldn't tell Jonathan anything about herself, so Elizabeth had finally stopped inquiring. But pirates? She had assumed Jonathan was farming. Pirates?

"Elizabeth. Are you going to speak or just sit there and stare at me?"

Elizabeth smiled. She could see so much of Jonathan in his father. Of course, she wasn't sure what Jonathan would be like today. Pirates? She just couldn't let that news rest. Would he still be carefree?

She need not worry about things she couldn't

change, she reminded herself, so she got her mind off of Jonathan and began to tell Lord Middlesex about where they lived and what they had been doing. She skipped the part about Jonathan fighting with the Americans and his injury. That information and knowing his son was a traitor would definitely send the marquess to his deathbed. She also skipped the part about their wedding that didn't happen. No need to get a lot of questions she wasn't willing to answer.

Before she knew it, Elizabeth had spent the whole afternoon with Lord Middlesex, and she'd loved every minute of it. She couldn't help wondering if she enjoyed his company because he reminded her so much of Jonathan or just that it was so different to see someone new. It was like having a small part of Jonathan here with her.

She stood up to go. "I'm sorry if I've overtired you." She fluffed his pillows and smoothed the covers over him.

"Nonsense, my girl," he said in a voice that sounded much stronger than when she'd first entered the room. "I've enjoyed our visit, and you must promise to come see me again. And don't wait too long, or you may miss me." He chuckled and winked at her, showing there was still some spirit in the old body.

Elizabeth laughed, too. "I don't think you're going anywhere. I'll be back soon, I promise."

She felt lighthearted as she hurried down the stairs. It had truly been an enjoyable afternoon. She hoped Dawson had been a good boy, she thought as she made her way to the door.

"Come back soon, Lady Elizabeth," Jeffrey said

as he reached for the door handle. "And I'll have my eyepiece in next time." Jeffrey opened the door for her.

I will—" Elizabeth didn't finish her sentence.

"My, my. Fancy seeing you here," Jonathan Hird said to an astounded Elizabeth.

This wasn't possible! Elizabeth's mind screamed. Jonathan couldn't be standing in front of her. Hadn't his father just told her he'd gone to sail with Lafitte? Maybe she should turn and ask Jeffery if he saw Jonathan, too.

"Lord Jonathan," Jeffrey said. "It is good to have you home, sir. You remember Lady Elizabeth."

"Unfortunately," Jonathan clipped.

Elizabeth promptly shut her mouth. Jonathan stood before her and he looked magnificent. His skin was darkly tanned, swarthy, and his eyes were hard. He'd been good-looking before, but now he was so much more so. He seemed bigger and bolder. He fairly reeked of sensuality.

Keeping his gaze fixed on her, he asked, "What? Nothing to say for yourself?" His voice was cold and exact.

She clenched her jaw to kill the sob in her throat. "I—I was visiting your father," she finally managed to get out.

Jonathan leaned against the railing and stared at her, taking in her appearance. She looked well and beautiful. There was a glow of innocence and promise, but he knew better than to be suckered in by that. As his gaze traveled downward, he noticed she was breathing heavily. Then his gaze rose to her stubborn chin and those damnable eyes. She flinched and retreated a step.

He wasn't ready to deal with Elizabeth yet. He'd intended to see his father, get settled in, and get some much-needed sleep since he'd not done so in two days. He hadn't expected to see her so soon. The problem of Elizabeth would have to come later when he informed her of his mission.

Now he stood face-to-face with her and, of course, the guilt was plainly visible in her eyes. "I hope you didn't make my father any promises you don't intend to keep," Jonathan bit out as he ignored the mocking voice inside him that wondered why.

Elizabeth flinched again. She could sense the barely controlled power coiled in Jonathan's body. "No, I did not." She should have realized he'd still be angry, but she didn't want to face Jonathan at the moment. As she stared at him, she realized, much to her horror, that she still loved him. She had hoped that time would lessen her love, but that wasn't the case. The love and the hurt were still there.

If possible, he was much more commanding in appearance than he had been when she'd first fallen in love. His shoulders seemed broader, his hair a bit longer. The arrogant line of his jaw told her he wasn't happy to see her at all.

Elizabeth simply wasn't prepared, but she had to say something. She swallowed and moistened her lips, forcing herself to settle down. "Your father will be glad that you are home," she said as she struggled to maintain an even, conciliatory tone. "How long have you been back?"

"I just arrived," he stated curtly with absolutely no emotion.

This wasn't her Jonathan. His eyes were cold,

and the devilish personality that had always made her laugh was nowhere in sight.

It was gone.

Perhaps it was lost forever. Had she done this to him?

He shifted impatiently and crossed his arms over his chest. "Your coloring isn't good, my dear. One would think you'd seen a ghost."

Her eyes grew wide as her gaze shifted. "Your arm! You can move it."

"Your observation is correct. I'm not the cripple you left at the altar."

She felt a nauseating wave of despair. "I never thought of you that way." Elizabeth's throat tightened. "I—I must be going."

"Of course. Running away is your style."

He might as well have slapped her, but she deserved it. Tears stung her eyes, but she would never let him see them. She lifted her chin, picked up her skirt, and stepped quickly around him. She hurried out into the street, tears blurring her vision. She had to get away from Jonathan. Now!

She never saw it coming.

Chapter Eleven

"Watch out!" Jonathan shouted.

Everything happened in a split second. She didn't have a chance.

The black carriage came out of nowhere and bore down on Elizabeth.

The horse reared, his powerful hooves beating the air.

Elizabeth screamed and fell to the street as the driver fought to bring the carriage to a halt.

Jonathan's heart caught in his throat as he helplessly watched the whole thing. How many times had he wished she were dead? But he knew deep down he'd never meant any of those thoughts.

He sprang forward. Though he ran as fast as he could, it seemed like forever before he reached her. He grabbed the horse's bridle and backed the vehicle away from Elizabeth, then turned and looked at her.

She lay very still, her head thrown to the side, her black hair spilling across the cobblestones. Her gown was torn and dirt-smeared.

"I didn't see her," the heavyset coachman rasped while he scrambled down from the carriage. He grabbed the horse's bridle to make sure the animal didn't move forward and injure the lady further. "Is she dead?"

"You had better hope not," Jonathan muttered as he knelt beside her. Elizabeth looked so small and frail. Carefully, he lifted her head, and immediately felt something sticky and warm. He looked at his fingers to see that they were covered in blood. He felt for a pulse, and let out a deep breath when he found one.

"She's alive." Scooping her up into his arms, Jonathan looked toward the driver. "She darted out in front of you. It wasn't your fault," he said grimly. "You may leave."

"I hope the little lady will recover," the driver said, politely touching his cap.

"I do, too," Jonathan said as he carried her back to his house where Jeffrey stood in the doorway, his face as white as his hair, his eyes wide with terror, and his mouth dropped open. Jeffrey did manage to step aside as Jonathan entered with Elizabeth.

"Send someone for the physician posthaste!" Jonathan ordered as he went by the butler.

"R—right away, sir."

Jonathan climbed the stairs, taking Elizabeth straight to his room. Kicking open the door, he entered and, in four strides, laid Elizabeth on the bed.

Her face was as pale as the linen sheets and the blood stained the pillowcase a bright scarlet. "Elizabeth," Jonathan whispered, but didn't receive a response. He took her chin in his hand and gently moved her head back and forth. "Elizabeth." She still remained deathly quiet.

Her black lashes rested on her creamy skin. Though her skin was still soft as a child's, there was a maturity about her that only heightened her beauty.

Jonathan glanced at her hand and noticed it was without a ring. Had she not married? He could only wonder. Then he remembered that one of his duties was to find her a husband. He was to be matchmaker to someone he'd once loved. He must have been bloody stupid to agree to help Adam.

It was a good thing he didn't love her or it would make his job just that much harder. He traced the side of her face. Finding Elizabeth a husband would be easy.

"Jonathan," Dr. Toogood said as he crossed to the bed.

Jonathan jerked his hand away from Elizabeth as if he'd been caught with indecent thoughts. He felt the heat in his cheeks.

When he didn't answer, the doctor continued, "It is good you've made it home." Placing his bag on the Queen Anne table beside the bed, Dr. Toogood shook his head slightly as he glanced at Elizabeth. "I thought I was being summoned for your father." He put his hand on her forehead. "What happened? Who is she?"

"Lady Elizabeth," Jonathan supplied, then added, "the Duke of St. Ives's sister. She stepped into the path of a carriage not more than ten minutes ago. I found a gash on the back of her head, but I'm not sure about any other injuries."

"I see." Toogood lifted her wrist and felt for a pulse. "Has she regained consciousness?" he asked, his brows drawn together in a frown.

"No."

"Let's take a look." First, the doctor pulled up her eyelids and peered into her eyes. Then, carefully turning her head, he frowned. "This will take a bit of work and a couple of stitches. I need hot water and some bandages."

When Jonathan failed to move, Dr. Toogood turned and stared at him. "Quickly, man, I must stop the bleeding. I cannot do everything myself."

Jonathan straightened and glared at the doctor's impertinence. Then he realized there were no servants about, and someone had to do something. He strode across the room and out into the hallway, where a cluster of servants had gathered just outside the door. They all jumped when he approached.

"Mary," Jonathan addressed the upstairs maid, "go get bandages and water for doctor Toogood, and don't waste any time. Also, please send Mrs. Roby up here immediately."

Once his father's housekeeper came into the room, Jonathan told Mrs. Roby what the doctor needed. "I'm going to see my father. You can fetch me right away should I be needed."

Jonathan realized the marquess would have heard his voice by now and would wonder what the commotion was and why Jonathan hadn't come straight to his room.

Jonathan pressed his lips together as he made his way to his father's room, feeling much like he did when he was a child. He would sit on the big bed and talk to his father as he prepared to go to his club. My, how time changed things. He just couldn't picture his father as a helpless invalid.

"Father," Jonathan said, fighting to keep the worry from his voice as he entered and drew near to his father's bed.

"My boy! Is that you?" Lord Middlesex shoved himself up on his elbows. "This has truly been a day for happenings. Place some pillows behind me. I want to see you."

Jonathan complied, then stood back and gazed at his father. He had aged. His hair was thin and his eyes dull.

"I thought never to see you again." Lord Middlesex's voice came as a choked whisper.

"Rubbish," Jonathan said and leaned down to embrace him. "You knew I would be here sooner or later. I was at sea, and it took a while for the message to reach me."

"At sea?" The marquess quickly regained his composure and his brows shot up. "You, my boy? I didn't believe it the first time I heard the story—still don't."

Jonathan chuckled. "I know it sounds farfetched, but it was something I had to do. Believe it or not, I grew to enjoy the adventure." He propped his hip on the bed. "But I'm home now."

"I could hear that just a moment ago," his father

said. "I'm not deaf yet. What was the ruckus in the hallway?"

"Elizabeth Trent was struck by a carriage, and we've summoned the doctor."

"Elizabeth?" The marquess frowned. "She was just here visiting me. You go tell Toogood he better take damned good care of her. That girl is a ray of sunshine." He pushed on Jonathan's arm. "Now, go do as I say. We'll catch up later."

Jonathan smiled at the gusto in his father's voice. There was still some life left in him after all. It just had been hidden for too long. Perhaps his father had only needed a reason to come out of hiding.

He stood staring at his father as he drifted off to sleep; evidently the doctor had given him some medicine to make him sleep. When he was sure his father slept, Jonathan slipped from the room.

Returning to his room, he saw the doctor straighten and rub his back. Jonathan stepped inside. "How is she?"

"That was a nasty bump and took several stitches," the doctor said, straightening his equipment. "My concern now is that she hasn't awakened. I've done all I can. However, someone needs to stay with her in case she has a seizure. We never know what will happen with such injuries, but she's young and strong and, God willing, she'll be fine."

Jonathan felt cold inside. Had it been his fault that she'd darted into the horse's path? If she hadn't been so preoccupied, she'd have stopped and looked instead of trying to escape. He had to say something, but his throat was tight. He swallowed and finally managed to say, "Thank you for coming on such short notice."

Dr. Toogood chuckled. "I'm used to coming to this house on a moment's notice. Your father isn't a patient man." The doctor's eyes crinkled with amusement as he patted Jonathan on the arm.

Jonathan laughed at the truth. "That I well know."

"If you don't mind me saying so, you look like the devil, Son. When is the last time you slept?"

Jonathan massaged the back of his neck. "I believe it was two days back. I've been traveling and have only just arrived."

"Then I suggest you leave Mrs. Roby to sit with your young woman, and you get some rest before you collapse," Dr. Toogood suggested on his way out. "I don't want to have to come here again today. Mrs. Roby will be back in a moment."

When Mrs. Roby returned, Jonathan followed the doctor's advice. He instructed her to get him if anything should happen, then he proceeded to take a long-needed bath.

In no time he was relaxing in a tub of hot water. He sighed as he laid his head back against the rim. His weary bones seemed to melt into the water; after a while the tension in his shoulders eased, and he began to feel better.

Since he'd returned from sea, nothing had gone as he planned. At the moment, he felt as if he were caught in a whirlwind and unable to control anything, especially his destiny. Whatever that might be. Perhaps he was just tired and could think more clearly after he'd rested. But sleep would have to wait a bit longer, he decided. He climbed out of the tub and dried off.

After he'd dressed, he went into his father's study

where he quickly scanned the ledgers of their estates. He knew his father hadn't been up to snuff and probably hadn't looked at the books for a while. When Jonathan closed the last book, he realized he would have to spend a good bit of time straightening everything out. The books were a mess.

By the time he shoved the chair back and stood, it was late. He stretched, then rubbed the back of his neck as he climbed the steps to his room. His head felt like a lead ball—it was taking a lot of effort to hold his head upright.

He entered his room and nodded for Mrs. Roby to leave. He would stay for a few minutes and give her a break from caring for Elizabeth.

Glancing down at Elizabeth, Jonathan couldn't stop himself from touching her cheek and caressing her skin. It felt like satin beneath his fingertips. She didn't feel warm, so he doubted she had a fever, yet he would have thought that she would have awakened by now. Earlier, he'd sent a message across the street to Trent House that Elizabeth had been injured and probably wouldn't be home.

Evidently, Annie wasn't in residence or she would have come over posthaste. Jonathan gave Elizabeth a speculative glance. What was she doing in London? He knew how much she hated city life. Had she come just to see his father?

Jonathan did know she hadn't expected to see him. That had been evident from her shocked expression. Wait until he told her he was here to find her a husband. He would probably receive more than a look.

Suddenly her breathing changed. It seemed

labored, heavy. He became anxious. What if Elizabeth died?

He moved the chair closer to the bed and sat down. "Everything will be all right," he muttered fiercely.

Reaching over, he took Elizabeth's hand in his and held it. Ironically enough, her breathing returned to normal. Perhaps she was frightened, he thought.

He rubbed the back of her hand and gazed at her face. Her cheekbones were delicate and pink. Sooty black lashes rested on her cheeks. His gaze traveled past full lips to her small but stubborn chin, and he wondered where they had gone wrong. He would never forgive her for the hurt she had caused him. A man's pride and his word were all that he had.

Again, Elizabeth gasped for air, and he tightened his grip on her hand as terror built inside him. "Don't you die on me, Elizabeth!" he demanded as if she could hear him. "Don't leave me again. We have some unfinished business, and I won't let you die until we're done. Do you hear me, Elizabeth?"

When she'd settled again, he brushed his lips across her hand then breathed a sigh of relief. He would hate her tomorrow, but tonight he'd give her his support.

And then as an afterthought, he looked up. "Please don't let her die," he prayed.

Because if Jonathan knew Elizabeth, she would die just to spite him.

Unable to hold his head up any longer, Jonathan laid it on the soft blankets. Just for a moment until

Mrs. Roby returned, he told himself, but sleep soon claimed him.

Sometime in the early morning, he woke with a terrible catch in the side of his neck, and his back was killing him. He stood and stretched, trying to get some of the kinks out of his body.

He felt Elizabeth's forehead again, and found it still cool to the touch. Her breathing appeared normal. She twisted her head away from his touch and murmured, "Dawson?"

It was a good sign, Jonathan thought. It was the first time she'd moved. But why did she call out Dawson? His father's first name was Dawson, but Elizabeth wouldn't refer to his Christian name. So just who was this Dawson? Was he her husband? A lover? Jonathan frowned. He needed some rest, but all he really wanted to do was shake Elizabeth and ask some questions.

Jonathan looked down at Elizabeth's sleeping form. It was apparent that he wouldn't have his answers now. He'd have to be patient.

He summoned Mrs. Roby, then made his way to a spare bedroom where he didn't even bother to undress. He simply sprawled across the bed. Maybe tomorrow Elizabeth would be better and out of his house.

She had to be.

Elizabeth opened her eyes and blinked several times before the world came into focus. Her eyes hurt. Her head ached. As a matter of fact, her entire body felt as if she'd been beaten.

She turned her head. A stabbing pain shot

through her so suddenly that it brought tears to her eyes. She moaned. What had happened?

"Where am I?" she asked the empty room.

It took several minutes of concentrating before she remembered running from Jonathan. Had he caught her? No, Jonathan might be angry, but he wouldn't have harmed her. But what had really happened?

She thought some more.

Finally, she remembered a glimpse of black and a horse's hooves. She must have stepped in front of the carriage. No wonder she felt so sore. The whole carriage must have run over her. What a foolish thing to do! But it wasn't all her fault. If Jonathan hadn't gotten her so flustered she'd have been more careful.

Jonathan. Jonathan was here! In England.

It hadn't been a bad dream. He was back in her life. And he definitely hadn't forgiven her.

She had to be in Jonathan's house. She tried looking around again, and though her body screamed with pain when she moved, she recognized her surroundings. This was Jonathan's room. She remembered it from their childhood.

She also remembered how good Jonathan had looked when she saw him. Her longing for him hadn't diminished over time. If anything, it made her want him more.

Biting her lip, Elizabeth turned slowly toward the door and let out a deep breath as the pain eased. There wasn't anyone in the room with her. Had Jonathan just thrown her in a room to let her live or die?

She knew he hated her. The thing she didn't know was how much.

Well, she'd just leave, and then he wouldn't have to worry. She attempted to sit by pushing herself up on her elbows; however, the pain was so intense that she gave up that notion right away.

"Good morning, mum," an upstairs maid said as she came through the door. "I'll go and tell His Lordship that you are awake."

"No, wait," Elizabeth called, but her voice was so weak that the woman didn't hear her.

"Dawson," Elizabeth murmured. She wanted to see her baby, but she couldn't have him brought over because then she would have to answer Jonathan's questions. Damn. How was she going to get out of here?

"I see you're awake," Jonathan said as he strode through the door, dressed in a rich brown frock coat and a cream-colored shirt. He regarded her with a speculative gaze.

Elizabeth didn't know which hurt worse, her head or her heart. No matter what had happened, she loved Jonathan just as much as she ever had, and seeing him only made her want him more. She had to put some distance between them so she could think straight.

"I need to go home," she said, and then added, "May I have some water?"

Jonathan poured her a glass and held it to her lips. He supported her back with his arm, something anyone would do, but to Elizabeth it seemed more personal. God, Jonathan smelled good. He'd evidently been smoking his pipe because he smelled of cherries and tobacco.

"Thank you," she murmured.

"You're welcome. Now tell me—how do you feel today?" he asked pleasantly enough, though his eyes were still hard.

"My head hurts."

"Let me show you why." He took her hand and gently placed it behind her head where a huge knot had formed.

"What exactly happened?"

"You ran in front of a carriage that couldn't stop. Luckily the horse hit you first and threw you to the side or the whole vehicle would have run over you," Jonathan explained.

"My goodness," Elizabeth said. "That was a crazy thing to do."

"I agree."

Elizabeth's cheeks heated. He didn't have to agree with her so readily when it had been just as much his fault. "If you hadn't gotten me so—"

Jonathan placed his hands on either side of her and leaned down. "So *what?*" he said in a seductive voice.

"I heard our patient is conscious," Dr. Toogood said, entering the room.

Jonathan immediately straightened and stood away from the bed as the doctor placed his bag on the table.

Dr. Toogood sat on the side of the bed and took Elizabeth's hand between his. "You are a very lucky young lady."

"I want to go home."

The doctor chuckled. "I'm sure you do. But not yet. It will take several days before your head stops hurting, and then you'll be able to leave. Would you like someone to send for your maid?"

"Yes, please."

Dr. Toogood examined the back of Elizabeth's head. "That is a nasty cut but looks to be healing quite well. How is that brother of yours? It's been a long time since I've seen His Grace in London."

"I haven't seen Adam in a while myself," Elizabeth said.

"I saw Adam and Jewel before I departed for England," Jonathan said from the end of the bed. "Adam is in high spirits, waiting for the arrival of his first child."

"Jewel wrote that she was expecting and I was so excited for her. How did she look?" Elizabeth asked. She was surprised that Jonathan had gone to Four Oaks. She'd assumed that he'd just sailed directly to England.

"She is growing larger every day, but other than that she is fine."

"I hadn't heard His Grace had gotten married. But it is good to hear that he'll have an heir," Dr. Toogood said. He reached for his bag. "Now, Jonathan, it's your turn to marry. Can't spend the rest of your life roaming."

Jonathan looked at the elderly doctor who had been with his family forever, then smiled. "There is much to be said for roaming."

"One must give up his freedom some day." Dr. Toogood chuckled as he placed his instruments back in the bag. "Funny, I always thought that you and Lady Elizabeth would marry. So did your father."

Elizabeth felt her cheeks heating, and she

couldn't think of anything to say. Evidently, Jonathan didn't have the same problem.

"I've heard other people say the same thing," Jonathan said nonchalantly. "However, we're not suited. But Elizabeth will be marrying very shortly," he said.

Had Jonathan lost his mind? Maybe the carriage had struck him, too. Elizabeth couldn't believe what he'd just said. "I will not," she protested.

"Yes, my dear, you will. You see, Adam has bestowed upon me the task of finding you a husband. Posthaste."

"He wouldn't dare!"

"He would. And he did."

"But who?"

"Someone I deem suitable," Jonathan stated firmly, his eyes smiling into hers. "We will start the parties just as soon as you are on your feet."

"I can see I'm not needed here anymore," Dr. Toogood said. He chuckled. "You take care of yourself, young lady."

"Thank you, Dr. Toogood. Maybe you should look in on my father before you leave," Jonathan said as he walked the doctor to the door.

Elizabeth waited for the doctor to leave and Jonathan to return. Her brother had some nerve, trying to control her life when he was clear across the ocean. And to ask Jonathan to do his dirty work was absurd. She clenched her hands, and would have jumped out of bed if she'd been able. "I don't like this one bit."

Jonathan leaned over and looked at her. "I don't really care what you like," he said coldly, but his gaze was hot enough to burn.

"Jonathan Hird, if you go through with this, I promise you that you'll regret it."

Jonathan took Elizabeth's chin in his hand and tipped her face upward. He gave her a mocking smile. "My dear, I already do."

Chapter Twelve

Elizabeth rolled back and forth on the bed, trying to find a comfortable position, but to no avail. She was hot. She tossed half the covers off, bunched a pillow under her head, then picked up a book she'd been trying to read. She managed three pages before she tossed it aside.

She hadn't seen Jonathan for a week.

She supposed that was for the best. If she had seen him, they would have just argued. Then again, he could at least have checked in on her. She knew she wasn't going to die, but she had been flat on her back for a week, and she was tired of being a patient. And she was bored.

But she didn't want to talk to him about marriage, although she'd thought about it enough. Her heart skipped a beat at the mere mention of the word, because all she could see was a vision of herself fleeing the chapel in New Orleans dressed in her beautiful wedding grown. She could imagine Jonathan's hurt, and she'd seen the ruthless determination in his eyes. He was going to do exactly what her brother had asked him, come hell or high water, and nothing she said or did would change his mind.

She was doomed.

Finally, about midmorning, her head eased a little, so Elizabeth decided to get out of the bed before she went absolutely mad. She'd counted the patterns on the wallpaper more times than she wanted to remember. She had to see her baby! And, most importantly, she had to keep Jonathan from seeing him. Meeting Dawson would only provoke a series of questions she wasn't prepared to answer.

Gathering her courage, she pushed herself up, then stopped. The room spun around, and blackness threatened to close in on her. She took several steadying breaths, then closed her eyes until the room stopped spinning. After a few moments, she felt steadier and opened her eyes again. Thank God, the room was standing still, and her head didn't hurt like it had for the last week.

Slowly, she slid from the bed and waited until she was sure her feet would support her. She looked down at her white cotton nightgown and wondered who had dressed her. Surely it hadn't been Jonathan?

On second thought, she knew it couldn't have been Jonathan because when she last saw him, he looked like he'd be sick if he had to touch her. The thought hurt her more than she cared to admit.

Elizabeth dressed and ran her fingers through her hair to remove the tangles. When she bent down to retrieve her shoes, her head felt heavy and the floor seemed to pull her down. She almost fell on her face and had to grab the bedpost for support. Again the blackness threatened to pull her under. She waited another five minutes before she carefully slipped on her shoes, trying very hard not to lower her head again. After several deep breaths, she composed herself and took a tentative step. With one more breath for courage, she moved gingerly toward the door.

Checking the hallway, she found it empty, breathed a sigh of relief, then started for the staircase. Carefully, she lowered her foot to the first step, then tried it again. She had almost made it to the bottom of the stairs when her luck ran out.

"And where do you think you're going?" Jonathan asked, looking up at her from the bottom of the stairs.

"Home."

He gave her an unfriendly stare. "You're not well enough to go home!"

Elizabeth glared at him. "Since you have not seen me in several days, how would you know how I feel?" She could have bitten her tongue. It was better to let him think she didn't care a fig if she saw him or not.

Jonathan's brow arched. "I've been asking about your progress."

"Well you don't have to bother anymore," she blazed. "I'm going home."

"I do hope you mean the town house across the street."

"No. I mean Briercliff."

"Perhaps you don't recall our last conversation," he said in an ominously calm tone. "So I shall remind you. I'm charged with finding you a husband. The first ball of the Season is next week. Therefore, I will not allow you to go home."

"Allow?" Elizabeth questioned. "I beg your pardon." She shot him an incredulous look. "Allow?" she repeated. "Maybe you haven't noticed but I am a grown woman capable of making my own decisions."

Elizabeth attempted to move around him, but he stopped her. Looking down at the strong hand that held her, she said, "You are not my keeper, Jonathan Hird!" Her gaze snapped back up so she could look him in the eye.

"I am now," he countered dryly. "Your brother has put me in this position, and I will do as he has requested." Jonathan tapped his chin as if he were thinking. "Now let me see. Should it be a banker? Perhaps some titled gent?"

Elizabeth stepped around him. "My brother needs to mind his own bloody business."

"Such language for a woman so gently bred. We shall have to work on that." Jonathan took her arm. "I'll escort you across the street. Wouldn't want any harm to come to you."

Elizabeth stiffened. She couldn't take the chance of him coming into her house and seeing Dawson. "You need not bother."

"It's no bother. As a matter of fact, I insist," Jonathan said as he shoved the door open. "You don't appear capable of crossing the street without someone's help." He would not take the chance of her being hurt again. He hadn't gotten over the last time yet, but he wouldn't let her know that.

Elizabeth's arm tensed beneath his fingers as they neared the street. Jonathan tightened his hold. Evidently, she was reliving the accident. He waited for the street to clear before urging her forward. Once they reached her door, he pulled her around to face him.

Weakness seized Elizabeth's limbs as she saw the expression on Jonathan's face. Damn this man, for the way he made her feel. In the sunlight, his hair glistened and her attraction to him was unmistakable. Clad in buff-colored breeches, shiny brown boots, and a white shirt that lay open in front, Jonathan looked every bit the rake.

Suddenly, his hand cupped her cheek. She jerked back nervously. When he tilted her chin up, she couldn't help gazing into his blue eyes—eyes that were cold and hard. She found herself wanting to erase all the hurt that she saw in the depths of his eyes. She wanted Jonathan to envelop her in his arms and hold her, care for her, love her, and most of all, forgive her. Resisting the urge to touch him was the hardest thing she'd ever done.

"Elizabeth," he said softly, "if I have to go to Briercliff to retrieve you, you will regret it."

Elizabeth snapped out of her daze. When would she ever get this love sickness out of her head? It was evident that Jonathan didn't feel the same. He made it plain at every turn that he didn't want her anymore.

"Don't threaten me, Jonathan Hird," she snapped as she jerked her chin away.

"It is a promise . . . not a threat."

She opened her mouth to say something, but couldn't find the words.

"I will call for you tomorrow afternoon, and we'll visit the dressmaker. I need to make sure you are in a pretty package since you're older now than during your first Season."

"Go to hell, Jonathan Hird," Elizabeth snarled. Then she opened the door and stepped inside. With a backward shove, she slammed the door in his face.

Jonathan jerked his head back to save his nose from being mashed. "I have been to hell, Elizabeth Trent. And you're the one who sent me there," he murmured to himself as he turned away from the door to head back to his town house. He waited impatiently for several carriages to pass before he could cross the street. On his way, he kicked a rock out of his path before making his way to the apartment. The simple act did make him feel a touch better.

She wasn't taking the search for a suitable husband well. He smiled, shook his head, and wondered why Elizabeth brought out the worst in him. He didn't care for her anymore. He no longer loved her. She was completely out of his system.

He was also a liar, he realized with an uncomfortable sinking feeling.

Hadn't he spent the last several days holed up in his father's study so he wouldn't wander into Elizabeth's room? What was it about the woman that stirred his blood like no other possibly could? Maybe he should ask Dr. Toogood for a magical remedy, or a gun. . . . Either would do at the moment.

The bloody damned woman had been invading his thoughts more than he cared to admit over the last few days. He was going to have to master control of the situation this time. Miss Elizabeth Trent would dance to his tune, whether she liked it or not.

And this time he'd drag her to the altar for another man. He would make sure she didn't run away from the bloke like she had from him.

Not waiting for Jeffrey, Jonathan opened his front door, turned, and looked back at Trent House. Perhaps when Elizabeth was married, he would have his revenge, and no longer feel the hurt.

But somehow he doubted it.

Elizabeth didn't know what to do.

Dread gnawed her insides and she felt like running away. Her first thought was to flee back to Briercliff, and Jonathan be damned. But she knew he would come after her, so she didn't have any choice but to stay in London. She sat down at her dressing table and brushed her hair while she thought. She had to be careful combing out the tangles since her head was still tender.

Now what was she going to do? To be on the safe side, she'd have Mary take Dawson back home to Briercliff so Annie could take care of him. Then she wouldn't have to worry about Jonathan seeing the boy or asking any questions.

She placed the brush on the dressing table and stared into the mirror. Oh, how she wished the baby had been Jonathan's! Sometimes she believed that Dawson was like Jonathan in some ways, and she realized that deep down, she often pretended the child was his. She stood and went to her window overlooking the small courtyard behind Trent House.

Perhaps Adam was right, she thought as she leaned her forehead against the cool glass and noticed how green everything was turning. Dawson did deserve a father, but she couldn't marry just anyone. It had to be someone she loved. And she'd finally admitted to herself who that person was—that is, when he wasn't making her angry. So just maybe she should keep an open mind and something would work out for them. Miracles did happen every now and then.

Then she had a brilliant idea. She could make Jonathan love her again. It would take a lot of work on her part, but could she do it? She would never be able to undo the hurt she'd caused him, but maybe she could help him forget it.

She'd never been one to pass on a challenge, and Jonathan would be spending a good amount of time with her. . . .

Elizabeth smiled to herself. She loved him. No amount of time or distance could change what her heart had always known.

She pulled away from the window. When Jonathan came tomorrow, he'd find a completely changed woman. One who would cooperate. . . . Well, for the most part she'd cooperate. She smiled again, anticipating the new challenge.

With higher spirits she went to help gather Dawson's toys and have Mary prepare to take him home to Briercliff.

* * *

What a beautiful spring day! Elizabeth thought as she slid from bed. She could smell the flowers from her open window. The back of her head was still tender, and she ached when she first stood, but she knew she would feel better as the day progressed.

She selected an apple green silk dress. The bodice was fitted and the collar was plain. She picked up a bonnet of white *gros de Naples* with snatches of heather and red blossoms around the brim. She tied the bow full under her chin, then picked up her reticule and went downstairs.

Just as he promised, Jonathan was in her hallway at ten o'clock precisely. When she came down the stairs smiling, he took a step backward as if he weren't sure what she intended.

If he only knew, she thought.

"How are you feeling?" Jonathan asked.

"I'm much better, thank you." She took the arm he offered.

As they strolled to the waiting carriage, Jonathan said, "I thought we'd start at Gafton House."

"It's your money," Elizabeth said flippantly.

"Correction," Jonathan said as he took the seat opposite her. "It's your brother's money."

"In that case, I intend to buy quite a few things," Elizabeth informed him. She glanced at Jonathan from beneath her lowered lashes.

As always, his clothes were immaculate and in excellent taste. He wore a royal blue waistcoat and jacket with fawn-colored breeches. His shirt was white, as were his stockings.

She noticed that his attention was focused on the scenery outside the carriage window as if he were trying to look at anything but her. His brows were drawn down in a heavy scowl, and she could tell he wouldn't make good company today.

The carriage stopped in front of Gafton House— a linen-draper's shop—and the place Elizabeth liked best. Before she went to America, she used to visit Gafton House several times a year. She had even invited the proprietor, Mrs. Hepplewhite, out to Briercliff to bring her dresses and fabric.

A tiny bell rang as they entered through dark green double doors. Two long counters stretched the length of the first room where the clerks waited on the patrons; today there wasn't a single space in front of them. The shop was packed with customers.

Brightly colored bolts of cloth were stored behind the counter in bins along with other accessories.

"Evidently, everyone is doing their last-minute shopping for the Season. I would be happy to stay home and avoid this crunch," she said with a smile.

"Nice try," Jonathan shot back, "but it won't work."

At the back of the first room was an archway with two glass windows that stretched from top to bottom. It was from there that Mrs. Hepplewhite emerged as she headed to the front of the store.

"Lady Elizabeth," said Mrs. Hepplewhite, who hurried over and took her hand. "It is so good to see you again, my dear. You have been away much too long." She turned to look at Jonathan with open curiosity. "And is this the reason you've been away? I'll be crushed if you've gotten married and I didn't make your gown."

Elizabeth blushed bright red. She could see the muscle in Jonathan's jaw tighten. "This is Jonathan Hird, Earl of Longdale and a good family friend."

"It is nice to meet you, Lord Longdale," Mrs. Hepplewhite said, nodding. "I hope I'll be making that wedding gown soon."

"Yes, you will be making a wedding gown, but I assure you I'll not be the groom," Jonathan said, his voice cold and hard. He turned to Elizabeth. "Can I trust you to select the appropriate gowns? If so, I shall come to collect you later."

Elizabeth didn't bother to answer.

"I'm going to take Elizabeth to the back room and assist her myself, so she shouldn't be longer than a few hours at most," Mrs. Hepplewhite said, breaking the icy silence.

"Elizabeth?" Jonathan waited, impatience plain on his face.

"I'm a grown woman, Jonathan. I think I can manage to select my own ball gowns," Elizabeth informed him primly.

"Then I shall fetch you in three hours."

Once he was outside, Jonathan breathed a sigh of relief. He wasn't going to survive this task, he thought as he climbed into his carriage and gave his driver instructions to take him to White's. His bloody head was already pounding. Dealing with pirates was easier than dealing with Elizabeth Trent.

His carriage had stopped. Jonathan looked out the window and found several carriages were backed up, waiting to pull up in front of White's.

He tapped on the carriage, then opened the door and stepped out on the sidewalk. He looked up at the coachman. "I'll walk from here. Come back in three hours."

Jonathan strolled down the street. It felt good to stretch his legs as he walked the block and a half. He passed the large bay window that White's had built in the middle of the club. Jonathan looked up as he passed the window and sure enough, Beau Brummell, dressed in his most elegant attire, sat with the Duke of Argyll and Sir Lumley Skeffington, watching the passersby. It was a game to Brummell that they never acknowledged anyone who walked by the window. But this time was different as all three men nodded at Jonathan.

As Jonathan climbed the steps of the gentlemen's club, all he could think of were the endless balls he would be forced to attend, the first being next week. He hated the bloody affairs. Now, he had to contact friends to let them know that he and Elizabeth were in town, so the invitations would start flooding in. Maybe he'd be lucky and find Elizabeth a husband at the first party. Then they wouldn't have to go to any more. However, his conscience told him, not bloody likely.

Inside the club, Jonathan looked around the oak-paneled room to see who he knew. He saw Lords Alvanley and Sefton, who were seated with George Ragget, the club's owner.

Jonathan moved into the next room where the games were played and the betting book was found. He was just getting ready to join in a poker game when someone called his name.

"Is that the Earl of Longdale? Or am I too far into my cups?"

Jonathan stopped and turned around. "You've always drunk too much, old boy," he said to Ian Duffy, the Earl of Radnor.

"Come," Ian waved from his table. "Join me."

When Jonathan reached the table, he clasped Ian's hand and slapped him on the shoulder. Then he sat down at the private table in the corner flanked by two bloodred wingback chairs.

After Jonathan ordered bourbon, he gazed back at his longtime drinking buddy. "You haven't changed a bit."

"Damned if I can say the same of you, old boy. Look at you. You're definitely wider in the shoulders than I can remember and much more muscular. Where the hell have you been?" Ian didn't give Jonathan a chance to answer. "Have you been doing manual labor? You do know you left me in a bit of a lurch. I've had no one around who enjoys the sports like you do. I even went to Foxmore to find you, only to be told that you'd gone."

"So you've missed me then?" Jonathan chuckled.

"Like a pain in the ass." Ian laughed, too.

"I went to the colonies to visit Adam Trent, and then I did something I never thought I'd do. I went to sea for a couple of years."

"Bloody hell. No wonder you look like a pirate."

"You're closer than you think," Jonathan agreed, but he decided not to explain his year at sea. Better not let what he'd done in the colonies get around or he'd never find a husband for Elizabeth.

"How is your father?"

"I'm not sure. He's bedridden. However, he can still raise hell when he chooses. I'm just wondering how bad he really is. I haven't gotten a straight answer from Dr. Toogood."

"I hope you're home to stay," Ian said as he paused to take another drink from the tray the waiter had offered. "By the way, you didn't marry that pretty little Elizabeth when you went to see Adam?"

Ian could have asked just about anything but *that!* Jonathan thought. "Yes, I'm home to stay. As a matter of fact, I'll need to go to Foxmore before long. But first, I have to fulfill a promise to Adam."

Ian noticed that Jonathan hadn't bothered to answer his question about Elizabeth. Maybe his friend's feeling had changed. "The way you're frowning, I'd say you're not too happy about making this promise."

"You could say that." Jonathan looked down into the drink between his hands. "You see, I promised Adam I would find Elizabeth a husband."

Ian slapped his knee and laughed. "Well, that shouldn't be too hard. Promise her to yourself." He punched Jonathan good-naturedly on the arm.

"Elizabeth and I have had a parting of the ways, so to speak," Jonathan said, his tongue heavy with sarcasm. "And I really don't want to go into the details."

Ian stared at his good friend while he took a sip of his bourbon. There was something that Jonathan wasn't telling him. But if Ian pushed now, he could tell he'd get nowhere. And from the sparks in his friend's eyes at the mention of Elizabeth's name, Ian knew Jonathan was denying what he really felt.

Ian smiled to himself. Maybe this Season was going to be a little more fun than the last.

One beautiful girl.

One jealous rake.

Yes, indeed. It could be quite interesting.

Ian cleared his throat to regain Jonathan's attention. "I'll be glad to help you rummage through London's finest and find Lady Elizabeth a proper husband. That's the least a friend can do. Then you'll be able to retire to your estate in peace."

Ian watched the play of emotions on his friend's face before Jonathan finally said, "Thank you. Our first ball is next week."

It was all Ian could do to keep a straight face. If Jonathan clutched that glass much tighter, it would break in two.

"I'll be there," Ian said as he stood. "By the way, there is a horse race next week, and I've got a sure winner."

"I'd like to see what you've picked," Jonathan said as he stood to leave. "We'll talk more tomorrow night."

"Come right this way," Mrs. Hepplewhite said as she escorted Elizabeth to a private room. "I have another patron in there but she is just finishing up." Mrs. Hepplewhite opened the door for Elizabeth.

"Tiffany?" Elizabeth squealed with surprise.

A young woman sitting in one of the two chairs looked up from the patterns she'd been examining. Her blond hair was piled neatly on her head, and her eyes were so blue they were crystal clear.

Elizabeth's childhood friend was as beautiful as she remembered.

"Elizabeth Trent?" Tiffany sprang to her feet and quickly covered the short distance between them, giving Elizabeth a big hug.

"I guess there is no need for introductions." Mrs. Hepplewhite chuckled. "If you'll excuse me, ladies, I'll go and get the material I have in mind for your gowns, Lady Elizabeth."

"Thank you," Elizabeth said with a smile and then looked at her friend. "You are simply beautiful. You haven't changed one bit."

"Oh, haven't I?" Tiffany patted her stomach, and Elizabeth realized that her friend was in the early months of pregnancy.

"Well, maybe a little," Elizabeth admitted as she took a seat. "We have so much catching-up to do. Who did you marry?"

"Marquess Gray DeGray," Tiffany said proudly. "And who did you marry? No wait. I remember. You were going to grow up first and then marry Jonathan Hird."

Elizabeth frowned. "What a good memory."

Mrs. Hepplewhite chose that moment to return, followed by two assistants carrying bolts of brightly colored material. They spread the cloth out in front of Elizabeth.

"I should leave since I've finished," Tiffany said as she stood.

Elizabeth caught Tiffany's arm. "Stay and help me pick out my gowns, if you have the time. Besides, we have so much to talk about."

Tiffany nodded and sat back down. They chatted

happily as Elizabeth chose several fabrics to make the ball gowns.

When they were left alone, Elizabeth confided everything that had happened to her friend. It was as if she had been storing everything up inside her, and it finally poured out. Tiffany didn't condemn or pass judgment. She just listened patiently.

"You poor dear." Tiffany's eyes had grown misty. "I can tell you still love him."

Elizabeth fought hard against the tears she refused to let fall. "Yes, I do."

"Well, we will simply have to undo a wrong. We're going to get you that earl, if it's the last thing we do."

"I don't know." Elizabeth swallowed hard, barely managing a feeble answer. "It may be too late."

Tiffany thought for a moment. "Rubbish. Listen, my husband is going to be gone for the next month or so, and you'll need a female chaperone in public. What if I move into Trent House so we'll be together? Then we can plan our next move."

"Are you sure you don't mind?"

Tiffany reached over and took Elizabeth's hand. "Listen, these rakes are a tough lot. They don't want to give up their freedom although they know they must, so they play the charade. Gray was the worst. I thought I would never convince him he couldn't live without me." She chuckled. "So you see, my dear, I have experience."

Elizabeth grinned. "I'm so glad I bumped into you. You make me feel as if I might have a chance."

Tiffany stood to leave. Evidently, Elizabeth hadn't looked in a mirror lately, Tiffany thought.

Elizabeth was very beautiful. Men would be flocking all around her. "My dear, Jonathan Hird hasn't met his match. . . .

"Two scheming females against one unsuspecting gentleman . . . he doesn't stand a chance."

Chapter Thirteen

Hours later, Elizabeth was absolutely beaming when she met Jonathan at the front of the dress shop. She'd been talking to a group of ladies when he first entered and was actually laughing. That wasn't the mood he'd left her in.

Jonathan eyed her warily. A spark, like flint striking a stone, flickered in the back of her eyes and told him that she was definitely up to something. He arched an eyebrow. "It appears you enjoyed yourself, madam."

"Indeed," Elizabeth said as she breezed by him. "I saw my old friend who is now Tiffany DeGray. We had a lovely visit remembering times gone by."

And plotting something new, Jonathan would wager. He fell into step beside Elizabeth. "I recall her," he said, pausing to open the shop door. "She was a skinny thing the last time I saw her."

"She has changed," Elizabeth said, taking Jonathan's hand as she stepped up into the waiting carriage. She waited while he took the seat across from her. "Her husband is abroad for the next month, so she's agreed to be my chaperone while I am here in the city."

Jonathan gave Elizabeth a queer look. "Chaperone? That's my job."

"But someone needs to protect me from you," Elizabeth told him with a hint of amusement in her voice.

Elizabeth laughed at the sour look on his face and thought, *if only you knew!* "Every proper lady must have a female companion. Granted, I'm a bit older than most, but at least I'll be proper."

Since when did Elizabeth ever worry about propriety, Jonathan couldn't help wondering, but he forced himself to make idle chitchat. "We're invited to the Cheshire's Ball next week. Will your gown be ready by then?"

"Yes. Mrs. Hepplewhite said she would put someone special on my order. So, don't worry, I will not embarrass you."

"Good," Jonathan said, then dismissed her by turning to the window and viewing but not seeing the many town houses they rode past. He remained quiet for the rest of the trip home, wondering what Elizabeth was up to. She was being much too agreeable.

Did he even care what she wore or how she looked? Elizabeth wondered. There was a time when she could read his every expression but not now. Jonathan had a carefully blank expression. She never knew what he was thinking and it was driving her mad. She only hoped Tiffany's plan would work. At the moment, she believed, Jonathan Hird was completely immune to her.

The morning of the Cheshire's Ball dawned bright and sunny. It was a beautiful spring day. Tiffany had some of her things delivered and she settled into the room next to Elizabeth's.

By mid-afternoon, Tiffany and Elizabeth sat down at a small table in the garden behind Trent House to have tea and to discuss the upcoming ball.

"Has your dress arrived?" Tiffany asked.

"No," Elizabeth replied while placing the second lump of sugar in her teacup. "I expect it will be late, but I know the gown will get here. Mrs. Hepplewhite has never let me down."

"Good. We have three parties in a row to attend," Tiffany pointed out as she stirred her tea. "I have been busy the last few days on your behalf. I have a good friend, Beau Brummell, who I've persuaded to help us." She placed her teaspoon on the saucer and looked at Elizabeth. "Do you know Beau?"

"No, but I've heard of him." Elizabeth picked up her cup. "He's all the rage, and a friend of the Prince Regent, I seem to recall."

"He's very much in demand. Everyone wants him at their party, and for good reason. He is so handsome with his dark hair and green eyes. He has set a new standard in men's wardrobe. You remember when men use to dress in those pastel colors?"

Elizabeth nodded. "Sometime they appeared more feminine than the ladies."

"Precisely. Well, Beau dresses in black and white and looks magnificent." Tiffany smiled brightly. "He has also agreed to help us with our plan."

Elizabeth almost dropped her teacup. "How?"

Tiffany laughed at the surprised look on her friend's face. "Beau is going to flirt outrageously with you. And by the third party, Jonathan should be seeing red."

"Do you really think so?"

"If Jonathan loves you, yes."

Elizabeth focused her gaze on her cup. "Sometimes 'if' can be a very large word."

"We'll have none of that. No fretting." Tiffany patted Elizabeth's hand. "Let's start preparing for the party. It doesn't matter if Mrs. Hepplewhite's dress isn't ready. We want to save that special dress for the third party."

"This sounds so devilishly underhanded." Elizabeth laughed wickedly. "I just love it."

Back in her room, Elizabeth began preparing for the ball. Happily, one of the upstairs maids was adept at styling hair. Elizabeth sat patiently while her dark locks were swept up into heavy curls at the crown. White flowers intermixed with pearls were woven into her tresses. After her hair was finished, she chose a black pearl necklace and earrings to match her gown.

She picked up her skirts and fluffed them, enjoying the feel of the material. The dress was a simple one since there hadn't been much time to do more. It was made of white crepe, spotted with white satin. The skirt was finished at the bottom by a garland of flowers and leaves composed of black silk.

Tiffany swept into the room without bothering to knock. "Are you ready? Jonathan is downstairs waiting."

Elizabeth nodded, pinched her cheeks to add color, then stood up from her dressing table. "It's been a while since I've dressed for a ball. How do I look?" She twirled around and held her arms out.

"Splendid. The dress is so simple, but you dress it up yourself. Come. It's time to have fun." Tiffany slid her arm through Elizabeth's and they went downstairs.

Jonathan waited at the foot of the steps, his arm propped upon the newel post. Dressed in dark blue, he looked very dashing, Elizabeth thought as she came to stand in front of him. His hair was combed to the side and slightly longer than he normally wore it, giving him a more rakish look. She smiled up at him.

Jonathan made sure his expression didn't change as Elizabeth and Tiffany approached him. Tiffany had changed from the little girl he remembered to a beautiful woman dressed in green silk. But she wasn't the one who held his interest.

Elizabeth was simply radiant. It should be a sin for any woman to be so beautiful. The black pearls glistened against the creamy softness of her throat. Her white skin begged to be touched.

Damn, why had he agreed to this?

He wasn't looking forward to watching a room

full of men fawning over her. They had better make damned sure they did nothing more than look.

"Jonathan, do you remember Tiffany DeGray?" Elizabeth made the introductions.

"A pleasure to meet you once again, Lord Jonathan." Tiffany extended her hand. "It has been a long time for all of us."

"Pigtails are what I remember the most about you," Jonathan admitted. "Now you are a very lovely woman."

Tiffany blushed. "I outgrew my pigtails."

"So I see." He offered his elbows to both ladies. "Shall we go to the ball?"

Each woman rested a hand on Jonathan's arm and walked with him to the carriage. Once inside, Tiffany started chattering. "I find these parties so tedious. Don't you, Jonathan?"

"Indeed, I do. But this time it's necessary."

"I hope we'll find Elizabeth a husband tonight— then we can start making wedding plans," Tiffany said, giving Jonathan a brilliant smile.

"She'll want a big wedding," Jonathan quipped before he thought. He frowned.

"Then we'll plan for a big wedding." Tiffany turned to Elizabeth. "Is that what you want?"

Elizabeth reacted angrily to Jonathan's snide remark. Of course, he was throwing her comments back at her. She remembered asking him for a big wedding; evidently he remembered it, too. "I'd prefer not to get married at all, thank you. But since my brother is insistent, I guess I have no choice. Perhaps I'll just go to Gretna Green. That's where all hastily arranged marriages take place."

"No!" Jonathan stated so quickly that both

women stared at him. "You'll be married in a church the proper way. And I'll make certain you show up."

Elizabeth could almost hear the words, "This time!" A stinging reply was on her lips. She could say she had a very good reason to run, but it would dredge up a lot of questions she'd have to answer, so she let his remark go and stared out into the darkness. This night was going to be difficult. Thank God, she had Tiffany to bolster her up.

The Cheshire's Ball was attended by many, Jonathan thought, judging from the carriages lining the long drive. When their turn finally came, a doorman dressed in red and white opened the carriage door and offered a hand to the ladies.

Jonathan pressed his lips into a firm, hard line and prepared to do battle. Between the rakes and the sops there had to be one or two decent prospects attending.

They entered a foyer brightly lit with hundreds of candles. The host, George Cheshire, the Earl of Long, and his wife were standing at the head of a long receiving line.

After greeting the earl, they proceeded to the ballroom where Elizabeth was soon surrounded by people she'd not seen in a long time. She and Tiffany talked while Jonathan disappeared into the crowd. It didn't take any time at all before Elizabeth's dance card was full.

The musicians were playing a waltz as Jonathan got his first drink from a table laden with finger foods and huge punch bowls. He turned, and his gaze swept the room filled with debutantes with their mothers or chaperones in tow and the dandies licking their lips as they tried to pick out the perfect mate. He had never liked these things. "A shocking squeeze" was the first thing that came to mind. Had he not made his rash promise to Adam, he would be anywhere but here.

In a corner, he spotted Ian talking to a pretty young lady, so Jonathan made his way over. The woman had gone by the time Jonathan reached Ian.

"Can you believe we are at one of these disgusting things?" Ian remarked.

"I thought maybe you were shopping," Jonathan teased. "How else are you going to find a wife?"

"Probably not here with all these protective mothers hovering about. However, I must say that young woman I was just with wasn't too bad." Ian turned and looked at her across the room. "But I'd prefer someone older who doesn't giggle at everything I have to say. Perhaps I should consider Elizabeth since you don't want her."

Jonathan's jaw tensed. "I'm supposed to find her a *suitable* husband," he said.

"I take offense to that statement, old friend," Ian said, not meaning a word of it, from the twinkle in his eyes. "I'm titled, wealthy, and single. I think I'm an excellent catch."

"And a rake," Jonathan shot back. "I want someone who will take care of Elizabeth."

"I could reform," Ian suggested as he watched Elizabeth on the dance floor. "She really is beautiful," he said in earnest. "Look at all the men watching her."

"I've noticed," Jonathan stated as he, too, watched Elizabeth. She was quite stunning.

Elizabeth danced with one gentleman after another. So many, she couldn't keep their names straight. By the time she was led back to Tiffany, she was feeling a bit dizzy. However, she wasn't given time to catch her breath. Jonathan seemed to appear out of nowhere. Without a word he took her by the arm.

"Shall we?"

Elizabeth just stared at him. "I'm sorry—you're not on my dance card."

"Perhaps you have overlooked my name," Jonathan said as he led her to the dance floor and swept her into a waltz. She couldn't say anything, she was so stunned. He had not paid her one bit of attention, and now she found herself in his arms. How long had it been since he'd held her? Too long, her mind screamed.

"This seems to be the only way I can talk to you," Jonathan finally said. "Are you flirting with every man here, or are you simply choosing a future husband?"

Good. He *was* jealous. It took all Elizabeth's will power not to smile. Maybe he had been paying attention, after all. "You know what they say about variety," she said matter-of-factly. "I want to make sure I find the perfect mate."

"Finding your mate, as you put it, is supposed to be my job," he responded sharply. "I've been checking, and I think Baron Sandys would do nicely. He doesn't care for London and was a good father and husband to his last two wives."

"Who are both dead," Elizabeth pointed out. "And, he is a bit old, wouldn't you say?"

"But stable and rich," Jonathan returned. "Sometimes, you must have tradeoffs."

"Perhaps you do, but I don't." She could feel her temper heating. How dare he put her with any old coot just to get his job over and done with! She looked around and realized they had waltzed into a corner and he was holding her far too close. And, unfortunately for her, it felt wonderful, and was keeping her completely off balance.

She made the mistake of glancing up at him and their gazes met and locked. And for a moment, there was no outside world . . . just the sizzle of the stare. No words . . . only silent communication that made her feel numb all over. She wanted to kiss him so much that it hurt, but if she did it would ruin all her efforts. With great difficulty, she finally dragged her gaze away.

"I think you will have to do a better job of picking my future husband. Think young," Elizabeth informed him. She glanced around. "I believe the music has stopped."

Jonathan waited a few moments before he finally released her and said, "So it has."

Elizabeth turned and made her way on wobbly knees over to where Tiffany was talking to a devilishly handsome gentleman dressed all in black except for a brilliant white cravat.

"Here she is now." Tiffany held a glass of tepid lemonade out to Elizabeth who gratefully took it.

"Thank you," Elizabeth said and took a sip. It would be better if the lemonade was much stronger, she thought. Especially if she had to stay around Jonathan any longer.

Tiffany touched Elizabeth's elbow. "I would like you to meet my good friend, Beau Brummell. Remember, I told you about him."

Elizabeth stared at one of the best-looking men she'd ever seen. He was almost too perfect. Dressed in black, his waistcoat was bloodred and his cravat snow-white.

"Such a beautiful lady," Beau commented as he took Elizabeth's hand and made a production of placing a kiss upon it. He definitely had an aura of smooth sophistication. "Why have I not met you before today?"

Elizabeth actually felt herself blush at his compliment. She felt like one of the giggling debutantes. When she glanced around the room, she could see people were actually staring. Especially Jonathan. *Good. Let the devil stare!*

"I've been away," she finally said, fanning her flushed face.

Tiffany beamed all over. "See?" she whispered behind her fan. "I told you he was charming, and I've informed him of our plans. He's willing to help us."

"Are you sure?" Elizabeth looked at Beau.

"Fair lady, these parties can be much too dull. I look at this little adventure as a diversion from doldrums," he said, then lowered his voice. "Look, here comes our prey now."

Jonathan approached with David Byron at his heels and stopped at their little group. "Brummell," Jonathan said, nodding.

"Longdale, London has been quiet since you've been gone," Beau teased Jonathan.

"I doubt that. I left the city in Ian's and your capable hands. I wager between the two of you that you could keep the city in quite a stir," Jonathan said, his gaze traveling over Beau, taking in his perfectly tailored black jacket. "I see that you are still setting the style, and quite nicely."

"Compliments from my peer. Thank you," Beau said with a bow.

"Elizabeth," Jonathan said, turning to her. "I would like you to meet David Byron."

Elizabeth extended her hand, thinking Jonathan could, at least, find somebody younger. This man wasn't as old as Baron Sandys, but neither was he a spring chicken.

"Would you care to dance?" David asked politely.

"Sorry, my lord, but Elizabeth just promised this one to me," Beau said as he took Elizabeth's elbow and swept her past the little group and onto the dance floor.

Elizabeth giggled. "I cannot believe you did that."

"My dear, where I'm concerned you should believe everything." Beau held her at a proper distance. "As they say, anything for a lark."

He was a marvelous dancer, Elizabeth thought as he whirled her around the ballroom floor. "Well, thank you for helping. I'm certain I'll hear about this all the way home."

"No doubt." Beau grinned, then added, "By Jove! I know how we might really rub salt into the wound. I'll come tomorrow to take you for a ride in Hyde Park."

Elizabeth nodded. "That would be splendid."

Jonathan glared at Elizabeth. What in the hell was she doing with Beau Brummell? He wasn't marriage material, even though many young ladies fancied him. He was certainly not suitable for Elizabeth.

Jonathan was going to choose a husband for her, by God, if it killed them both in the process.

He frowned.

Elizabeth Trent would have to learn to obey.

Chapter Fourteen

Elizabeth woke early the next morning, pleased at how the night before had turned out. She stared at the lavender wallpaper in her room, and stretched before getting out of bed.

Then she remembered that Jonathan had informed her that he was bringing Earl Stanley Derby to call on her, and that she had lied and told him she was looking forward to the meeting. What Jonathan didn't know was that Beau Brummell would also be calling on her at midday to take her for a ride.

This whole charade with Brummell was keeping Elizabeth off balance. She wanted to see Jonathan react, but he never seemed affected by her while she, on the other hand, was very affected by him. She could recall the tenderness of his touch, and she longed to feel it again. She could remember the expression on his face when he had admitted he loved her. More than anything, she wanted to see that expression again.

Every time he was near her, she could feel her knees weaken. And worse, when he wasn't with her, she was miserable and angry with herself for not controlling her emotions better. Men . . . she hated them!

She went to the armoire and picked out a simple day dress in jonquil. Then she instructed her maid to pull her hair back and tie yellow and white ribbons in it. Finally, she went down for breakfast.

Tiffany had just finished filling her plate with fruit and ham and was taking a seat at the long table. "Good morning," Elizabeth said. She picked up a plate from the sideboard and began to fill it with sweet breads and orange slices. "How do you think it went last night?"

"Splendid!" Tiffany smiled, then took a sip of tea. "If you had seen the way Jonathan kept looking at you, you would realize he's besotted." She sighed and nodded. "It won't be much longer before he explodes."

Elizabeth experienced a whirl of perplexing emotions. "Are you sure? I don't see that at all." She spread her linen napkin across her lap. "He barely acknowledges that I'm around, and when he does talk to me, he's complaining about something I've done or telling me what to do."

"That's because he hides his feelings from you," Tiffany explained as she picked up a sweet roll. "Remember, you wounded him. He's merely protecting his heart, or so he thinks."

"I know," Elizabeth replied in a low, tormented

voice. "I don't think I'll ever forgive myself for causing him that hurt."

Tiffany's blue eyes met Elizabeth's gaze. "You had a good reason. I think Dawson was well worth the trouble you went through."

Elizabeth brightened a little. "Yes, he was. I hope Jonathan will understand one day."

"I think he will. But the rough times are not over yet."

Elizabeth frowned. "I know. Tell me a little bit about Beau. I found him very charming last night."

"You and everyone else," Tiffany said, amusement flickering in her eyes. "He is a favorite of the Royals, you know. Everyone loves Beau's attire. You saw how he dresses. He doesn't dress in those floppy pastel clothes and wigs like so many others." She paused to take a sip of tea. "He usually wears dark clothes. I've heard tell that it takes him three hours, on the average, to get dressed, and many more hours spent in counsel with the cutter of his coats or with the custodian of his wardrobe. It's pure perfection."

Tiffany leaned toward Elizabeth as if she were getting ready to tell a dark secret. "There was some talk about his elopement with a young countess from a ball at Lady Jersey's. But I don't believe it," she admitted and sat back in her chair. "It's probably just gossip."

Elizabeth took her last bite of sweet roll. "Beau might be a dandy, but he's a very likable one. I'm glad you introduced him to me, even if it's to use him against Jonathan."

The butler appeared at the door.

"Yes, Linton?" Elizabeth asked.

He nodded then announced, "The Earl of Longdale and the Earl of York are calling."

"Please show them into the main salon," Elizabeth said to Linton. When he'd left, she turned to Tiffany, placing her napkin on the table. "Are you ready to give it another go?"

"Absolutely." Tiffany's laugh was marvelous, contagious. "I haven't had this much fun in ages."

Together they made their way to the main salon. The gentlemen rose from their straight-backed chairs. Elizabeth had to admit that, at least, this one was younger.

After the introductions, Elizabeth and Tiffany sat on a Grecian chaise longue covered in red velvet. Elizabeth did her best to flirt with Lord Stanley. She asked him all kinds of questions and tried to hang on his every word. She noticed that Jonathan remained very quiet; however, his expression was tight with strain. She couldn't tell whether he was jealous or simply bored.

Once again, Linton appeared in the doorway. "Excuse me Lady Elizabeth, but Mr. Beau Brummell is here to see you. I tried to tell him that you already had guests, but he insisted."

"I'm expecting him, Linton," Elizabeth said quickly. "Please show him in."

"What is *he* doing here?" Jonathan asked as his gaze locked with hers.

"I promised to go riding in the park with him," Elizabeth replied sweetly.

"Elizabeth," Jonathan said, his tone threatening as he stood and moved to the far side of the large room.

"Excuse us a moment," Elizabeth said to Tiffany and Stanley. Then she moved to Jonathan. "Yes?"

"Beau Brummell is not the marrying kind," Jonathan stated emphatically.

Her gaze froze on his lips, remembering how good their kisses used to be.

He shook himself mentally. His thoughts didn't need to wander down that path. "Besides, he has no title, and Adam would never approve."

"I happen to like Beau." Elizabeth tried to keep her voice as normal as possible. "He is kind, and the most charming man I've ever met. I can't say the same of you, at the moment."

He looked at her with a sardonic expression that sent her temper soaring. "I must approve your match," he informed her bluntly.

"In that case, you had better start considering Beau because I just might choose him," Elizabeth said in a broken whisper. "Now, if you'll excuse me ..." She turned away from Jonathan and started to leave

Jonathan grabbed her arm and hissed, "Don't push me too far, Elizabeth."

Instead of jerking her arm free as she wanted to, Elizabeth simply pulled it away so they wouldn't draw the attention of the others. "You don't own me, Jonathan Hird." She left him then, but she could still feel his gaze boring into her back.

"Are you ready, Beau?" Elizabeth said as he entered the room.

"Most certainly, beautiful lady." He bowed graciously.

"If you'll excuse us, Lord Stanley." Elizabeth

moved over and took Beau's hand. "But I already have a previous engagement."

"Quite understandable," Stanley said as he rose. "Perhaps I can see you next week."

"That would be lovely. Come along, Tiffany," Elizabeth said, then glanced at Jonathan. "I'll see you tonight for the play."

"You can count on it, madam," Jonathan clipped.

Outside, a bright red-and-white landau waited for them. The footman held open the door, and Elizabeth stepped into the horse-drawn carriage.

"It's such a lovely day for an open carriage ride," Tiffany said as she stepped up and took her seat.

"It's nice to be outside," Elizabeth commented and then added, "It was getting rather warm inside."

"I'll say," Beau said after instructing the driver as to their destination. "Trent barely acknowledged my presence."

"He might not have acknowledged your presence, but he definitely knew you where there," Elizabeth told him. "He was rather testy today."

Two splendid white horses pulled their carriage onto one of the tree-lined paths of Hyde Park. The well-manicured lawns were a beautiful shade of green, and poppies and foxglove dotted the landscape. White narcissus bloomed along the path. Every little sprig and bloom shouted that spring had arrived.

They nodded to acquaintances they passed, but didn't stop until they reached Serpentine Lake. It was a long, curving lake where swans and geese floated along the gleaming surface, peacefully absorbing the sun.

After climbing out of the carriage, they strolled along the lakefront, stopping when they came upon someone they knew.

Later, when they were out of reach of prying eyes, Beau asked, "All right, ladies. What is our next plan of attack?"

Tiffany thought for a moment. "We're going to Covent Garden and using my box," she finally said. "Why don't you go with us?"

"Jonathan will be livid," Elizabeth said.

"Precisely." Tiffany laughed.

Beau's mouth twisted wryly. "We don't want the old man calling me out, ladies." His voice was soft but slightly alarmed.

"No, we don't." Tiffany smiled and patted Beau on the arm for reassurance. "But since it's my box, I'll just say I invited you, and he won't be able to object."

"In that case . . ." Beau breathed a sigh of relief. "I'll call around—no, better yet, I'll meet you at the theater."

"That's a splendid idea. Jonathan wouldn't dare make a scene in public," Elizabeth said, but she thought to herself, at least I hope not.

After taking a long, leisurely walk along the lake, they headed back to the carriage.

Elizabeth leaned over and whispered to Tiffany, "I feel that someone is watching me." Elizabeth twisted her head. She saw many people milling about, but no one she could single out.

"I'm sure they are," Tiffany admitted. "You're

beautiful, and I'm sure word has gotten out that you're very available.''

"I doubt that very seriously, but perhaps you're right. But I actually felt gooseflesh a few moments ago," Elizabeth said as she turned around again to see if she could spot anyone. When she didn't, she shrugged and climbed into the landau.

It wasn't long before they were once again at the front of Trent House. "I shall see you tonight," Beau said when he dropped them off.

When they returned from the park, it was rather late, so Elizabeth had little time to get ready for the evening at the theater. She hurried over to the armoire and chose a white crepe dress trimmed in gold. She had the maid weave gold cords through her hair, to bring out the accent of her gown.

Once she had dressed, she found Tiffany and Jonathan waiting for her downstairs. Jonathan was dressed in a wine-colored coat and waistcoat. His shirt was snow-white, as was his neckcloth. He looked every bit the aristocrat that he was.

Tiffany wore a stunning, violet-colored dress trimmed in cream lace. The crepe dress hung loosely from under the bust and concealed her pregnancy nicely. Her blond hair was swept to the side and she looked lovely.

Once they were in the carriage, Tiffany and Jonathan carried the conversation while Elizabeth stared out the window at the gas lamps, wondering what tonight would bring. She also couldn't shake the odd feeling she'd had this afternoon that someone was watching her. She was just nervous, she supposed.

When they reached Bow Street, the carriages were again backed up to get into Covent Garden. It was the theatrical home of John Philip Kemble and his sister, Sarah Siddons. Elizabeth hadn't seen a performance by either in a long time. She wasn't sure what was planned for the performance tonight.

Elizabeth watched the ladies and gentlemen as they filed out of their vehicles. Most were laughing and carrying on as they made their way into the theater.

Finally, it was their turn. The coachman opened the door. "What are we going to see?" Elizabeth asked, stepping out of the vehicle.

"*The Clandestine Marriage.* It's a most respectable play," Jonathan answered, taking Elizabeth's elbow.

"I've seen the play, and it is one of the better ones," Tiffany commented once they entered the theater.

The interior was done in dark red and trimmed in gold. Huge chandeliers cast a soft glow on the *haute-ton* who leisurely made their way to their boxes.

An orange seller held up a playbill and Jonathan stopped to purchase one for each of them.

They moved across the vestibule and proceeded up the main staircase, heading for Tiffany's box. Jonathan still held Elizabeth's elbow as he guided her along.

"There you are," Beau Brummell said from the top of the stairs, looking grand in black with a blue waistcoat. "I thought perhaps I was late."

"No, just in time." Tiffany smiled brightly at Beau.

Elizabeth felt Jonathan's fingers tighten just before he dropped his hand. He said for Elizabeth's ears only, "Did you invite him?"

"Tiffany did," Elizabeth said ruefully.

"I hope you don't mind the intrusion, old chap, but Tiffany needed an escort," Beau said to Jonathan as he took Tiffany's arm.

"Of course not," Jonathan lied and then swept his hand toward the box. "We should probably find our seats before the performance starts."

They sat on the four red velvet chairs lined up in the box. Elizabeth sat between Jonathan and Beau. As the curtain rose, she sighed. This just might prove to be a very long evening, she thought.

Looking over the edge of the rail at the gallery and pit, she could see everyone scrambling to find a seat. The auditorium was shaped like a horseshoe with three seating areas. The pit, on the ground level, was close to the orchestra. The second level, where they sat, was considered upper class, and high above the boxes was the gallery where the common folk and servants were seated.

Everyone in the pit appeared every bit as excited as the ladies and gentlemen in the boxes. Elizabeth could smell the beer being served below, and she was thankful they were not drinking tonight so she wouldn't have to have that stale smell around her.

While Elizabeth watched the crowd below, she didn't realize that she herself was also being observed. . . .

* * *

Revenge was sweet, but sometimes the best plans didn't always work out as they were laid.

However, Elizabeth and Jonathan might prove useful substitutes and give him the satisfaction that drove him almost to the brink of insanity.

He desperately needed revenge.

And he would have it!

Rubbing his hands together, he looked up at his victim like a vulture planning his attack. His gaze caressed the lovely Elizabeth. He'd forgo the play this evening to put his plan into motion.

Justice would be swift and deadly.

He licked his lips. He loved it when a plan came together.

Elizabeth shivered. She felt that evil stare again, but this time she shook off her silly notions. Why wouldn't others be looking at her as she'd been looking at them? It was merely nerves, she reminded herself. That was all.

Finally, the orchestra sounded and everyone quieted down. Elizabeth slid back in her chair and fanned herself. She could feel Jonathan's leg pressed against hers, and she found it was hard to concentrate on what went on below. However, she had to ignore Jonathan if she was going to make him jealous.

She leaned over and talked to Beau. They laughed and carried on about the performance, and she found it was impossible not to enjoy herself in Beau's presence.

On her other side, she could feel the tension in Jonathan, and she wondered just what he was thinking. Something about her, she hoped.

Jonathan's temper was being held in check by a slim thread. He'd watched Beau whisper and touch Elizabeth all through the play, so when the final curtain went down he stood abruptly and said, "Let's go."

The other three turned and looked at him, but said nothing as they followed him out of the box. As soon as they emerged into the hallway, several people stopped and wanted to talk to Beau.

Jonathan pulled Beau to the side. "Look, you can stay and socialize all you want with Tiffany, but Elizabeth and I are leaving. I'll send the carriage back for you."

"Are you sure you don't want to stay?" Beau asked innocently when he knew what the answer would be. He dared not smile for fear of having blood splattered on his pristine neckcloth. He'd watched Jonathan all night, and if Beau guessed correctly they had finally made the man quite jealous. Poor Elizabeth. Hopefully she could hold her own.

"Positive," Jonathan bit out. He yanked Elizabeth out of the crowd. "We're going."

"What about a chaperone?" Tiffany asked.

"She won't need one," Jonathan quickly told her.

"But—" Elizabeth couldn't finish because Jonathan was pulling her along, and if she stopped him, she could tell there would be a scene. She also couldn't believe that he was rudely leaving their companions behind.

Once inside the carriage, she asked, "What about Beau and Tiffany?"

"I'll have the carriage sent back to get them."

"But why couldn't we stay?"

"I need to talk to you, and the theater isn't the place to do it."

"Oh, really? What do you want to talk about?" Elizabeth stared at him, waiting for an answer. She didn't receive one.

Instead, Jonathan simply stared at her. She waited for him to say something but the silence grew, as did the tension. By the time the carriage dropped them off in front of Jonathan's town house, she was just as irritable as he was.

As soon as the carriage left, she asked, "Are we going over to Trent House?"

"No."

Jeffrey answered the door. "Good evening, my lord. Lady Elizabeth."

"Good evening, Jeffrey," Elizabeth greeted him. She couldn't be rude to him just because his employer was an ass.

"That will be all, Jeffrey," Jonathan said in a clipped voice that forbade any questions. "You can retire for tonight. I will not need you further."

"As you say, sir." The butler shuffled off down the hall.

Jonathan escorted Elizabeth to one of the private parlors and shut the door. After he lit a couple of candles, he strolled over to where Elizabeth stood, her arms folded across her chest.

"I don't approve of your behavior with Brummell tonight!" Jonathan exploded. "It was totally unacceptable."

Her eyes shot daggers at him. "I don't know what you're talking about. We were watching the play and discussing it. What could be wrong with that?" She threw up her hands in disgust.

"Is that what all that laughter was about? I saw the way he kept holding your hand and touching your shoulder. That had absolutely nothing to do with the play."

"In case you'd forgotten, I'm supposed to be looking for a husband and encouraging him."

"Brummell is not acceptable."

"Then who is?" she asked in a low, tormented voice.

Jonathan opened his mouth to say something, then snapped it shut. It was a good qustion. A damned good question. And one he wasn't sure he had the answer for.

He stared at Elizabeth in the dusky glow of the candles. Soft tendrils of hair had slipped from their pins and her eyes sparkled black with rage. He marveled at how magnificent she looked with her chin tilted up as she awaited his answer. In spite of her obvious challenge, her face was both delicate and fragile, and the confusion in her eyes softened the fury within him.

Suddenly, all logic and reason left him, and he did something he'd never intended to do again. He grabbed Elizabeth, pulling her to him in one swift motion and molding her body perfectly against his.

God, she felt good. His mouth seized hers in a ruthless kiss, and he realized, much too late, that he wanted to punish her for the past hurt. He pulled back and looked at her.

Her lips trembled, and a single tear trickled down her cheek and tore at his heart.

"I'm sorry," he said softly.

Elizabeth looked at the face she'd seen every time she'd closed her eyes over the last years. She'd missed him so much that it made her ache inside, and now he was here, touching her, maybe even wanting her again, and her heart melted helplessly at his feet. "I love you," she whispered.

There was a spark in the depths of his eyes as he lowered his head. His mouth gently brushed over her lips as he murmured, "Elizabeth."

With swift tenderness, his mouth found hers again, touching his tongue to her lips; she parted them and he found heaven. She tasted so good. A jolt of pleasure shot through him, and his hand shifted from her back to her breasts. He began massaging her breasts through the fabric, but it wasn't enough. He needed more.

His mouth moved lower, where he nuzzled her neck as his fingers deftly unloosened the back of her gown. His lips moved to her ear. His tongue traced the outside and then the little curves, and she began to tremble. He nibbled on her earlobe. Shivers of delight ran up and down her spine. She moved her hands around his neck and brought his mouth to hers and slowly kissed him, fanning the heat burning deep within her.

She tugged on his shirt and began opening the buttons until she could push his shirt open and feel his warm skin and muscles beneath her fingers.

He slid the gown from her, and it puddled at her feet, followed by her chemise. "My God, you're beautiful," Jonathan said as his eyes feasted on her. And then he realized that they needed to be elsewhere. But he wasn't letting her loose. He picked up her gown and his shirt, then scooped Elizabeth up into his arms and headed straight for his bedroom. Thankfully, they didn't encounter any servants.

He carried her straight to his bed and laid her down, her black hair fanning across the pillow. He couldn't seem to pull his gaze from her milky white breasts that stood out firm and ripe, ready for his mouth. He stepped out of his trousers, and his gaze moved lower, to her slender waist and long, enticing legs. He finished undressing. His body ached with a need that hadn't been filled in a long time.

Jonathan went over to the bed and leaned across her. With his finger, he traced her face. "You cannot imagine what you do to me."

His mouth settled possessively on hers, and before she knew what was happening, he was kissing the breath out of her. A jolt of excitement surged through her body, and she wrapped her arms around him as his tongue slid past her lips into her mouth, probing . . . teasing . . . wanting.

His kisses grew hotter, and she grew wilder, her hands moving up and down his back, trying to get him closer. When his hand moved lower to cup her breast, she gasped as his palm closed around her, and then his fingers began to play with her nipple until it hardened. His mouth left hers, trailing kisses down her throat and across her chest. His ravenous mouth captured one of her nipples, first sucking and then circling it provocatively with his tongue. She moved her hands from his shoulders to his head where she tangled her hands in his hair, pulling him tighter against her.

She was mindless with desire. Her back arched and her loins ached. She felt his hands seductively moving across her stomach and then lower until his fingers reached her thighs and the warm wetness. He began to stroke until she withered beneath him.

"Elizabeth," Jonathan's voice rasped. "Tell me what you want."

Her eyelids fluttered open. "I want you."

He groaned, then parted her legs and lifted her hips, thrusting full-length into her. She gasped, then wrapped her legs around him as he plunged deeper and deeper inside her. She never wanted this moment to end.

Jonathan watched the woman beneath him. Her eyes were misty, her breasts full and tight, and she was driving him crazy with each thrust. Their passions peaked, and he drove himself into her one final time, shuddering at the flood of ecstasy that swept through him.

When his breathing finally calmed down he rolled to his side but still kept Elizabeth in his arms, stroking her back softly. "Elizabeth?"

"Hum," she murmured.

"Do you love me?"

"Yes."

"Then why did you leave me?" He felt her tense beneath his fingertips.

"It wasn't because I didn't love you. I've always loved you. There were other reasons you don't know about."

"What were they?"

"I don't want to talk about it now."

"And may I ask why not?"

"I'm very tired. Can we talk about this in the morning? Let's just enjoy this night. And we'll talk later."

"Perhaps you're right. I'm tired myself," he said, drugged by the emotion of their lovemaking. He pulled the cover over them. "But tomorrow I want answers."

Chapter Fifteen

The sound of rain hitting the windowpanes woke Elizabeth. She glanced at the window. By the dusky hue of the sky, she guessed it must be daybreak.

She yawned, stretched her fingers, and felt something delightfully warm. The heat of the skin beneath her cheek reminded her she wasn't alone. She was in Jonathan's room curled next to him as he slept peacefully beside her.

Cautiously, she raised her head from his chest and watched him sleep. His tanned face had softened, and he looked more like the boy she'd loved instead of the man she'd hurt. Her chest ached with the knowledge of the pain she'd put him through. She'd never wanted to hurt Jonathan, only to protect him.

Last night had been wonderful, Elizabeth thought as she gingerly moved away from him, but she knew it wasn't forever. She couldn't expect it to last.

She loved Jonathan, of that much she was sure, but he hadn't said one word about love to her when she'd told him how she felt. Thinking back on it now, in the light of day, that hurt.

The only thing he'd said was he wanted answers this morning.

She looked at Jonathan carefully, trying to read what was in his mind.

Elizabeth still hadn't decided whether she would tell him the truth about Captain Lee, or lie and tell him she'd been married briefly to someone else. If Jonathan knew that Dawson was Captain Lee's child, would Jonathan hate Dawson? The child looked nothing like Lee, thank goodness, but more like herself. Still, the thought of Jonathan rejecting her child was unbearable.

Her mind whirled with questions. That old familiar panic raced through her like a raging fire. She had to do something before Jonathan woke up. But what? Should she quietly slip away or stay and face him?

Carefully easing herself from the bed, she looked for her clothes. They were all around the room and she blushed as she retrieved them, remembering the passion they had shared last night. She started to dress, then Jonathan gave a deep sigh and stretched.

Elizabeth held her breath.

Please don't let him awaken, she prayed silently. *I'm not ready yet.*

When she could breathe again, she managed to get her dress partially hooked up the back. She turned to face the bed. All right, now that she was dressed, she was ready to answer his questions. She would start by telling Jonathan that she had a child which she'd named after his father.

No, that wouldn't work, she realized. She had to prepare him. Maybe if she eased into the subject slowly . . .

Looking at his square jaw, she remembered how stubborn he could be. Would he be able to accept the fact that she'd had another man's child? Would he be able to forgive her? What she really wanted to do was get down on her knees and beg. *Jonathan, please love me no matter what I've done in the past. I did it for you.*

Her breath came so fast, Elizabeth felt as if she might faint. Then she remembered Jonathan's words: *If any other man touched you, I don't know what I would do. I can't bear to think of you with someone else.*

She couldn't do this.

She couldn't face him.

Not now. Not until she was sure how Jonathan would react. Maybe later.

Turning, she very quietly eased her way to the door. She didn't know what to do, but she couldn't stay and answer questions. At least not now. She was terrified that her confession would destroy the fragile connection they'd made last night. She'd tell him later.

Later, her mind screamed. Always later.

As she eased out the door, it came to her. She would do what she always did when she was frightened and alone.

She would go home to Briercliff and Annie!

Annie would help her sort out her fears. Annie would know what to do. And if Jonathan really loved her, he'd come after her. That was the answer, Elizabeth told herself as she fled from Jonathan's town house. The rain still fell heavily as she stumbled down the steps, but she didn't care. She darted across the street to Trent House.

Sometime later, Jonathan rolled over and smiled contentedly. He couldn't remember the last time he'd slept so peaceful. How long had it been since he'd felt so rested?

The wonderful night of lovemaking with Elizabeth had everything to do with it. He would never get enough of her. He reached for her, but her place by his side was cold and empty.

His eyes sprang open and cold certainty grabbed hold of his stomach. He was in bed alone.

He sat up and scanned the room. Elizabeth was nowhere in sight, and her clothes were gone.

She was gone!

Would this nightmare ever end? Would Elizabeth constantly leave him without an explanation? She had said that she loved him; that much he remembered. If she had meant it, she had a damned strange way of showing it.

He slid from the bed, walked over to a chair, and retrieved his trousers. Had she lied? he wondered as he dressed. Why would she lie? He was puzzled, to say the least. If he could only figure out this game.

Before, he'd blamed Elizabeth's leaving on his damaged arm. Now he couldn't use that excuse.

Was there something else about him that she couldn't abide? No, she wouldn't have stayed with him last night if that were the case. There was something else that Elizabeth wasn't telling him, and he had to know what it was.

Now!

He jerked on the rest of his clothes. He would go to Trent House and demand that Elizabeth give him the answers, even if he had to shake them out of her.

A loud knock sounded at his bedroom door just as he reached for the knob. Jonathan jerked it open. "What is it?"

Jeffrey was as white as a ghost. "Begging your pardon, sir," he stammered awkwardly. He cleared his throat. "But there are men downstairs demanding to see you right away."

"Get rid of them," Jonathan snapped, his voice lashing out at the old servant. "Where is Elizabeth?"

"I have not seen Lady Elizabeth. But these men are the police, and they have come for you," Jeffrey persisted.

"Bloody hell," Jonathan swore and swept past Jeffrey. "Why do they want me?" This morning was going straight to hell!

When Jonathan got to the lower level, he saw the three Petty Constables dressed in blue. He glared at them. "What is the meaning of this?" he said in a menacing tone that cut through the uncomfortable silence.

"You are under arrest for treason against the crown," one of the constables announced.

"Treason?" Jonathan ground the word out

between his teeth. He couldn't have possibly heard the man correctly. "You must be mad. Do you know who I am?"

"Indeed, we do, my lord," the bigger officer replied.

The three men spread out, surrounding Jonathan, as if they expected him to make a break for the door. The action only fueled his anger.

"You are the Earl of Longdale, and your father is the Marquess of Middlesex," the husky officer said.

"Then explain yourself," Jonathan demanded, his expression tight with strain. "How could I be charged with treason? That is utterly ridiculous."

"The only thing we were told, my lord, is that you are charged with treason for fighting with the Americans in New Orleans. There is a witness who has come forth."

Jonathan didn't know what to say. A cold knot formed in his stomach. Impatiently, he pulled his drifting thoughts together. What if someone who knew him had seen him in New Orleans? "This is utterly preposterous. I am outraged. I shall let your superiors know my feelings once we're down at the station." He turned. "Allow me a moment to instruct my staff."

They nodded.

Jonathan took Jeffrey by the arm. "Listen, let my father know what has happened and tell him it is not true, so he doesn't have an attack over the news. Send for the family barrister. Then go over to Trent House and tell Elizabeth what has transpired. Instruct her to send for Adam right away, in case things go wrong." Jonathan peered down at Jeffrey. "Do you have everything?"

Jeffrey stood slumped over with a worried expression, but he managed to nod. Jonathan wanted to assure the elderly butler that everything would be fine but, at the moment, he wasn't too sure of that himself.

"I'm depending on you, my man," Jonathan said and clasped Jeffrey firmly on the shoulder. He didn't add that his life just might depend on this old man getting the information straight.

Jonathan called for his greatcoat, and Jeffrey scurried away. He returned quickly and helped Jonathan into the coat.

"Gentlemen," Jonathan said as he swept past the Petty Constables, his head spinning as he wondered who could have testified against him. Pulling the collar of the coat up, he ducked his head and walked out into the rain.

He rode in the wagon with the three constables surrounding him. Once they arrived at headquarters, Jonathan was ushered into the building where the Chief Constable sat behind an old oak desk. He appeared to be reading papers on his overcrowded desk and didn't bother to look up until Jonathan was standing directly in front of him.

Finally, the Chief Constable leaned back in his chair, folding his hands across his big belly. He wore a blue coat and trousers and a drab waistcoat with the city button. Of course, the gentleman's stomach prevented him from buttoning the bottom two buttons of his jacket.

The Constable gave Jonathan the once-over. "So

this is the one," the constable finally said to the Petty Constables on either side of him.

His eyes were sharp and assessing. After what seemed like an eternity, he introduced himself. "I am Constable James Bridewell."

Jonathan seethed with cold fury. "I suppose you already know who I am," he said tersely.

"Yes, Lord Longdale." Bridewell's expression stilled and grew serious. "You're a man in a lot of trouble."

"So I've been informed," Jonathan replied, then frowned in exasperation. "I believe the ridiculous charge was treason."

"This is correct." Bridewell nodded, his brow drawn together in a frown.

"Do you care to explain?"

"I believe you deserve that much, since treason is a very serious charge. It seems someone has come forth and is laying information against you."

Jonathan gave the Constable a bleak, tight-lipped smile. "Would you like to tell me who and when?"

"I cannot tell you who, but I do know he claims you were with the Americans fighting against your fellow countrymen."

"That is absurd." Jonathan's temper grew hotter by the minute. He slammed his hand down on the desk. "I demand to be released immediately."

"Quite frankly, you don't look like a traitor to me. But we have a witness . . ." Bridewell spread his hands in an expansive gesture. "Therefore, I suggest you retain a good barrister and perhaps he can work a miracle." Bridewell slowly came to his feet. "Until your hearing, I'm sending you to

Newgate." He waved his hand in dismissal. "Take him away."

When the Petty Constable took his arm, Jonathan jerked. "I'm quite capable of moving on my own." He thought about telling the constable exactly what he thought, but he knew it would do no good.

It was still raining as they rode to Newgate Prison, and Jonathan's mood grew as black as the clouds outside.

"Welcome to Newgate," the constable on the left said when the wagon finally stopped.

Jonathan looked out the window in between the raindrops at the grim outline of Newgate's front door. It was the most notorious prison in all of England, a prison that had stood for a thousand years, a place where he never thought he'd find himself. His stomach plummeted to his toes as he disembarked from the wagon.

Swallowing hard, he headed for the gate to hell. He hoped he'd learned enough from his time with the pirates to survive this hellhole. He fervently hoped that Elizabeth could get him some help, and quickly.

He was going to need it.

Hanging wasn't to his liking.

Elizabeth instructed the upstairs maid to pack as quickly as possible, then she went to find Tiffany. She couldn't just up and leave without explaining to her friend.

She knocked on Tiffany's bedroom door, and when she answered, Elizabeth barged into the room.

"Elizabeth!" Tiffany exclaimed and clapped her hands. "Tell me everything and don't leave anything out."

"I can't." Elizabeth couldn't stand still, so she began to pace. "I have to leave right away for Briercliff, but I couldn't leave without first saying goodbye."

Tiffany placed her hands on her hips. "Well, you're not leaving me like this," she told her with a definite firmness. "Not after what I've been though. You owe me a thorough explanation, so I'm going with you."

Elizabeth stopped abruptly. "What about your husband?"

"He won't be back for weeks." Tiffany waved her hand. "I'll be home long before he gets back. Besides, it will give me a chance to see Dawson," she said as she began picking up a few of her things and placing them in a portmanteau. "However, I don't understand why you're leaving."

"I'll explain once we're in the carriage," Elizabeth said. "I'll have Mary pack your things and send them in another vehicle," she explained, tossing her friend a nightgown from a chair. "Hurry— we must go before Jonathan comes over here."

"I don't like the sound of this," Tiffany said as she hurried to finish dressing.

Without stopping for breakfast, they dashed through the rain to the carriage. Half an hour later, Elizabeth was on her way home. The dark clouds above her seemed to part, and her heavy heart felt lighter. Everything would be all right once she was at Briercliff. She'd be able to think clearly once she got home.

* * *

Tiffany waited patiently until the coach had left the city before her patience wore thin. "There is nothing out the window that's interesting, so quit ignoring me, Elizabeth. Turn around and talk to me."

Elizabeth let out a loud sigh and her shoulders slumped. "Oh, Tiffany, I don't know where to start."

Tiffany hated seeing her friend so miserable, and she wanted to give Elizabeth a big hug, but that would only bring on tears, and then she'd never hear the story. Instead, she straightened her skirt and folded her hands in her lap. "You didn't come home last night, so I assume you stayed with Jonathan."

Elizabeth nodded.

"Well? Did you spend the night talking?"

"No, but I wish we had. We started off arguing, then the next thing I knew, we were in each other's arms."

"Then our mission was successful," Tiffany said, smiling triumphantly.

Elizabeth blushed a bright red. "Yes, we made love."

"I can tell it was wonderful by the look on your face. There is nothing that can replace the special glow." Tiffany watched her friend with smug delight. "So what is wrong? Why are we making a mad dash to Briercliff?"

Elizabeth shrugged and said offhandedly, "We are going to Briercliff because I need time to think."

"Think about what?"

Elizabeth could tell Tiffany wasn't about to give up until she heard the whole story. "Jonathan said he wanted answers this morning when we woke up," Elizabeth told her, frowning. "I thought I was ready, but when the morning dawned, I panicked. I sneaked out of his house before he awoke." Elizabeth held her throbbing head with both hands. "I'm so confused."

Tiffany reached over and patted Elizabeth on the knee, then resumed her previous position against the cushions. "That is the smartest thing you've said. You *are* very confused!"

"I know. I know. I'm hopeless," Elizabeth agreed, then cast her eyes downward. "What am I going to do?"

Tiffany studied Elizabeth with curious intensity. "Are you sure you want to hear the answer? You might not like it."

Elizabeth nodded. "If there is one."

"You must stop running away from your problems," Tiffany said firmly. "Do you know what I think?"

"What?"

"That you're afraid to love Jonathan. You're afraid he is going to hurt you." A long moment passed, then she added, "You don't give him the chance to prove himself. You don't trust him."

"Oh! But I—" Elizabeth snapped her mouth shut. It seemed so simple when Tiffany said it. Maybe she *truly* didn't trust Jonathan. "But he didn't say he loved me," she declared.

Tiffany's gentle laughter rippled through the air. "My dear girl, those are the hardest words to get any man to say," she stated firmly. "It's as if the words don't exist in a man's vocabulary. They assume that women should know when they love them." When Elizabeth looked skeptical, Tiffany went on, "I can tell from watching Jonathan Hird that he loves you very much."

Elizabeth glanced out the window and then back to Tiffany. She sighed deeply. "Do you think I'm making a mistake?"

Tiffany nodded. "I'm afraid so, but we're on our way to Briercliff now, so we'll have to continue. The damage is done. Perhaps, once you see Dawson, you'll feel better. Then you're going to have to tell Jonathan the truth."

"Why am I always doing the wrong thing?"

"Because you're human. We all learn from our mistakes. Granted, some of us are slower than others." Tiffany chuckled.

Elizabeth's voice sounded tired even to her own ears. "You made your point. I will tell Jonathan the truth."

The truth shall set me free, Elizabeth hoped. *Or cost me the only person I have ever loved.*

Chapter Sixteen

Jeffrey made his way to the marquess's room and quietly slipped inside. "Excuse me, my lord." He cleared his throat. "There is no good way to tell you," Jeffrey said, then hesitated. "But they have arrested Lord Jonathan for treason," he blurted out.

"They did *what?*" The marquess sat straight up in bed, something he hadn't done in a month. "Get me a wheelchair, and order the carriage. We're going to see my barrister and then we are going to find my son!"

Jeffrey stepped closer to the bed and peered at the marquess. "But your health, my lord."

"Blast and damnation, my health!" The marquess slapped the bed. "Now, do as I say!"

"Lord Jonathan did ask that I send someone to Trent House to inform Lady Elizabeth to send for

His Grace, but when I went across the street I was informed that she had returned to Briercliff."

"Then dispatch someone to Briercliff with a note immediately." Lord Middlesex placed several pillows behind him. "Get me some paper."

Jeffrey shuffled over to the desk and brought back a tablet, pen and quill, and a lapboard.

The marquess dipped the quill into the ink and started to scribble a note. "Send someone reliable." He folded the letter and handed it to Jeffrey. "Send him on horse, so he can travel faster. Now, where is my carriage?"

Jeffrey's head was spinning, and he felt as if he'd been turning in circles ever since he'd entered the bedroom. However, it felt good to have activity in the house again. Things had been much too quiet. It had been a very long while since the marquess had shown any life.

"I'll have the carriage brought around front, sir," Jeffrey said. He hurried as fast as his old bones would allow.

Before long, he had the staff assembled to help bring the marquess downstairs and load him and his chair into the carriage. Jeffrey watched as they brought the marquess down the stairs and assisted him into the brougham.

Watching the carriage roll away, Jeffrey thought it had been a while since he'd seen such fire in the old man's eyes. Perhaps it was a jolly good sign.

The carriage stopped outside a red brick building. The Marquess of Middlesex waited patiently while they unloaded his chair and rolled it over to the vehicle's door. One of the footmen helped him into the chair, then rolled him into the office.

Once inside, the marquess wasn't to be kept waiting.

"Can I help you?" a young man asked.

"Of course you can. Go and get Edward now," Lord Middlesex commanded.

"He might be busy, sir. Who may I say is calling?"

"The Marquess of Middlesex." He glared at the young man, daring him to ask another question. "I have no time for questions. Now, do as I say."

The young man, whose face, by now, had turned very red, left. In just a few moments, the marquess was shown to the back room.

Edward Turner rose and walked around his desk. "Lord Middlesex, it is wonderful to see you up and about." Turner clasped the marquess on the shoulder. "I'd heard you had taken to your bed. Nice to see that isn't true," Turner said, then reached for a brown box on his desk. He opened the lid and held the box down. "Cigar?"

Lord Middlesex took one of the long brown cigars and smelled it. Then he tucked it into his top pocket. "With the news I've just had, I'd have crawled out of my grave if I'd been dead."

"Sounds serious," Turner commented as he returned to his chair behind his desk. "Tell me, what has happened to make you so angry?"

"Jonathan was arrested this morning and taken to Newgate prison. Or so I've been told."

Turner frowned as he leaned back in his chair. "What was the charge?"

"Treason!"

"Ridiculous. How could he be brought up on

such charges?'' Turner stood up. ''Do you want to accompany me to Newgate to see him? Perhaps we can get the matter straightened out before nightfall.''

Lord Middlesex chuckled. ''You'd have a hard time keeping me away, by Jove.''

The journey to the prison was short, and the marquess had to admit he enjoyed being out in the fresh air. So far his energy was holding up, and he hadn't had any fits of coughing. Perhaps that old sawbones hadn't been correct about his health.

He gazed out the window and, soon enough, Newgate Prison came into view. He groaned as he looked at the ominous building. The walls were a drab-colored stone, and two towers stood on each side of the main gate. In the middle, a door that didn't appear much over four feet high appeared to be the only entrance. The marquess chuckled wryly. ''Look, Edward. The door is so small it appears that they don't want anyone coming into the prison.''

''They don't! And getting out in one piece is even harder, I'm afraid,'' Turner said.

The carriage door opened, and Harry, one of the bigger men employed by the marquess, reached in to help Lord Middlesex down and situate him in his wheelchair.

''I hope you can think of a way to get Jonathan out,'' Middlesex said as they moved closer to the entrance.

''I shall surely try,'' Turner said. ''They have made mistakes before.'' He ducked through the low entrance.

Once inside, they waited until the Warden came

into the small, damp room. "Gentlemen," the Warden said, "I'm Robert Williams, at your service." He was a short man, heavyset with bushy eyebrows, and he wheezed when he spoke.

"I'm the Marquess of Middlesex, and this is my barrister, Edward Turner."

"Yes, I'm familiar with Mr. Turner," the Warden said with a nod.

"I understand you are holding my son, the Earl of Longdale," the marquess stated.

"So I've been told," Williams said.

"Can you explain this outrage?"

Williams opened a book on his desk. "I believe the charge is treason."

"Well, it is ridiculous!" Lord Middlesex slammed his hands against the arms of his chair. "I want him released immediately."

Williams stood. "I understand your concern, My Lord. However, the law is binding."

"What evidence do you have?" Turner asked quietly.

"A witness has come forth to lay information against the earl," Williams said as he went to the door leading into the jail. "I cannot release him, but I'll have Lord Longdale brought to you if you'll wait right here."

It seemed like forever before Jonathan appeared in the doorway. His hands were shackled. His hair was ill-kept and there were dark shadows under his eyes.

"Father! You're out of bed," Jonathan said, shocked by the sight.

"Damn right I am! What are you doing in here?"

Jonathan turned to the other man. "Edward, it

is good to see you, as always . . . perhaps not under these circumstances," Jonathan admitted, arching a brow as he sat down on one of the benches beside a long wooden table. Then he looked at his father. "They have charged me with treason."

"How did they get such a ridiculous idea?"

"As you know, I was in America visiting Adam when the British invaded New Orleans. It seems someone has come forth to 'lay information.' "

"That is what Turner just told us. Doesn't sound good," Edward spoke up. "They just hung Brandeth and others for High Treason." He rubbed his jaw in thought. "I hate to ask this, but did you fight against the British?"

Jonathan thought carefully before he answered because he knew his father would never understand. He didn't want to lie, but the truth would kill his father. "I never fired a shot. I ended up on the battlefield by mistake and was shot by the British."

"Are you bloody stupid?" his father said, his brows drawn together. "How did you end up on the battlefield without a rifle?"

"It was foggy. I couldn't see and took a wrong turn," Jonathan said weakly. "It was a British bullet that took me down."

Edward cleared his throat to gain their attention. "We will not know until we go to court who the informant is, but let me point out that the law presumes that a crime has been committed. It's my job to ferret out the evidence that would prove the opposite is true." He rubbed his jaw again.

A nervous habit, Jonathan supposed. It wasn't a

good sign that his barrister was nervous and the trial hadn't yet begun.

"Is there anyone who could testify that you didn't fight?" Edward asked.

"There are many. Unfortunately, they are all in America."

Edward shook his head. "I will have to be truthful with you. This does not look good, especially if the witness is reputable."

Jonathan frowned. "I was afraid you were going to say that, and I don't know who would testify against me. I suppose I won't find out until the trial. Do you know when it will be?"

"We are in luck there. The Assize judge usually makes one appearance a year, and that will be in two weeks. You'll not have to wait a year."

"A year!" Jonathan shouted.

"Some have to wait that long."

"Father, I've heard that for a price there are better accommodations than this filthy rat hole."

"We'll take care of that right now. Get the Warden."

Edward jumped to do his bidding, and brought the Warden back with him.

"I want my son in a private cell with a bed, clean bedding, everything he needs, plus easement of irons. How much will it cost me?"

"It can get costly," the Warden replied blandly, folding his hands together.

"I'm sure it can," Lord Middlesex said impatiently. "Do it. And if I find that you've cheated me, I'll have you in irons! Then you will enjoy the hospitality of your own prison."

"Everything will be arranged," the Warden said simply, then left.

Lord Middlesex reached over and touched Jonathan's hand. "Maybe that will make things a little better until we can get you out of here." He sighed. "I'm getting a bit tired, Son, but I will be back to visit soon."

"Thank you, Father." Jonathan crossed over and bent to embrace him. Turning to the barrister, he said, "I hope you can do something for me, Edward."

"I shall try, but I will not lie to you. This will be an uphill battle," Edward admitted, walking over to push the marquess's chair from the room.

"Father, have you spoken to Elizabeth?" Jonathan asked before he was taken back.

"Jeffrey went to deliver your message, but found she'd left for Briercliff. I've dispatched a messenger to her."

"I see," Jonathan said as he ducked back through the door to hell.

So she ran away again. Would he ever learn?

Elizabeth breathed a sigh of relief upon finally seeing Briercliff again. The carriage came to a stop, and she and Tiffany waited for a footman to help them down. As she started up the steps of the castle, Elizabeth took a deep breath. Even the air was fresher here than in London.

Giles opened the front door, and Elizabeth actually surprised him with a hug. "It's good to be home," she said happily.

"And happy we are to have you home, Lady

Elizabeth," Giles said, his face a bright red. "I wager you'd like to see Master Dawson."

Elizabeth nodded.

"He is in the garden with Annie."

"Come on, Tiffany. Let me introduce you to my son." Elizabeth couldn't wait to hug Dawson.

As they hurried through the house, Tiffany said, "Briercliff is even bigger and prettier than I remember."

"It is special. I have so many fond memories of growing up here," Elizabeth said as she reached for the French doors which led to the terrace.

"How large is Briercliff?"

"Let me see," Elizabeth said and paused to count to herself. "There are thirty-four rooms, two three-bedroom cottages, and two fish ponds."

"It's definitely not a modest estate. I think 'castle' best describes the place." Tiffany laughed.

"I think so, too. Especially in winter, when it is very cold," Elizabeth said as they descended the slate steps. The back lawn stretched out before them. The lawns were terraced, each level leading to another. She caught a glimpse of Annie's head on the second level, and Elizabeth knew that Annie was working in her favorite flowerbed.

"Annie," Elizabeth called, so she wouldn't startle the woman.

A small, brown-haired boy peeked around Annie. "Mummy," Dawson yelled as he ran toward her, his arms wide open.

Elizabeth scooped her son up in her arms and twirled him around. "I've missed you so much, pumpkin." She hugged him tight, then placed kisses on his cheek.

Dawson leaned back and said, "Look." He handed her a slightly crumpled jonquil, crushed in his chubby hand.

"This is for me?" Elizabeth asked.

Dawson nodded and grinned. "I grew it myself. Annie said it was the bulb I planted last year." Dawson finally noticed Tiffany and frowned as if he were trying to remember if he'd seen her before. "Who's that?" He pointed.

Elizabeth placed Dawson on her right hip so they could face Tiffany. "This is Lady Tiffany. She and I used to play together when we were your age."

"My name is Dawson."

Tiffany smiled. "It's nice to meet you, young man."

"You're pretty," Dawson told her as he squirmed to get down.

"You are home a bit early," Annie said as she laid the trowel down and brushed the dirt off her hands.

"I missed my son," Elizabeth said a little too quickly.

Annie stood and peered at Elizabeth with that knowing look. "Of that, I've no doubt, but I think you're not tellin' me all there is to tell."

"We'll speak of it later," Elizabeth said in a low voice. Then louder, she asked, "You remember Tiffany?"

Tiffany had bent down to talk to Dawson, but she straightened at the mention of her name.

"Aye." Annie hugged Tiffany. "Ye've grown into a lovely young woman, and I see ye are expectin' a wee one of yer own."

"Yes, in about five months." Tiffany smiled.

Dawson pulled on Tiffany's hand. "Come on," he said. Tiffany followed him back to the flower-erbed.

Annie watched Elizabeth with a speculative glare. "Ye've seen Jonathan, haven't ye?"

Elizabeth nodded.

"I dinna think he was comin' home."

Elizabeth shrugged, trying not to meet Annie's knowing eyes. "Neither did I."

"Did ye tell him?"

Elizabeth shook her head, unable to find the words to tell Annie how she felt.

"Ye see how miserable yer feelin'?"

"Miserable would be a good word to describe my emotions," Elizabeth said, understanding the obvious.

"The longer ye wait, the harder it will be."

"I know, Annie." Elizabeth sighed and looked at her. "I've already heard this lecture from Tiffany. And I'm going to tell him. I promise." *I just don't know how,* she didn't say out loud.

Annie nodded her approval. "Good."

Dawson brought Tiffany back, pulling on her hand. He had picked her a flower, too.

"I like her," Dawson said as he looked up at Tiffany and grinned. "She said she'd play with me."

"Good. I hope you are going to be good friends, and when Tiffany has her baby you will have some-one else to play with."

Dawson screwed his face into a frown. "Are you going to have the baby tomorrow?" Dawson asked Tiffany, seriously.

Tiffany laughed. "Good Lord, I hope not. No,

Dawson, it will be a little while. In the meantime, you can play with me."

"Come on, let's go," Dawson said as he ran toward the house and motioned for the rest to follow.

The next morning, Giles came to Elizabeth as she was eating breakfast. "A rider has arrived with a message for you, mum. He's in the foyer."

Elizabeth pushed back her chair and stood. She suspected it was a message from Jonathan ordering her to return to London at once. It would be just like him.

"Do you suppose . . . ?" Tiffany was thinking the same question that Elizabeth had on her mind.

"I don't know, but we'll find out in a few moments," Elizabeth said, then left the room. She went straight to the foyer, her heels clicking on the floor. A young boy stood by the door, shoulders slumped as if he'd been riding all night.

When the messenger saw Elizabeth, he straightened and handed her the note. She immediately opened the letter and scanned the contents. Her heart plummeted to her toes. She had expected a letter from Jonathan demanding that she return to London, but not this.

She looked at the messenger, who couldn't be more than sixteen, and said, "Wait a moment, and I'll send a reply."

He nodded. "Yes, mum."

Elizabeth walked briskly to Adam's study, picked up a quill, and penned a note back to Jonathan's father. Returning to the foyer, she handed the boy her note. "Please make certain Lord Middlesex gets this note."

"Yes, my lady." He nodded.

Elizabeth looked at Giles. "Please have the kitchen prepare something for this lad to eat before his return journey."

She watched them leave, then went back to the breakfast room where she sank into her chair. Her legs had done well to support her for as long as they had.

"What's wrong? You look like you've seen a ghost," Tiffany said as she patted her lips with a linen napkin.

"I've just received terrible news," Elizabeth said, then looked at the empty chair. "Where is Dawson?"

"Annie took him to the nursery. She should—"

Just then the door opened and Annie swept in. "That wee one is full of energy today." She looked at Elizabeth and immediately asked, "What's wrong?"

"I just received a message from Lord Middlesex. They have arrested Jonathan for treason!"

"Oh, my God!" Tiffany said.

"Saints above!" Annie said at the same time.

"I can't believe it, either," Elizabeth said, wringing her hands. "It must have happened shortly after I left. Jonathan wants me to send Derek to get Adam. Can you get him quickly?"

"Aye," Annie nodded. "Derek is in St. Ives. But 'twill take him too long to reach Adam in America."

"I know," Elizabeth said. "But we can't just sit here and do nothing. I know Jonathan will have to appear before the Assize judge, and the judge usually comes in the summer months. That will buy us some time." Elizabeth's thoughts churned. "I'm sure the marquess has hired the best barristers. I don't know what else to do."

Annie shook her head. "I'll go and get Derek right away. In the meantime, lass, ye better be doin' a lot of prayin'. 'Twill take a miracle to get him out of this one."

Chapter Seventeen

Leaning her elbows on the table, Elizabeth rested her chin in her hand. "I don't know what to do," she said smoothly, trying not to frown. She realized she'd been saying the same thing over and over again for the last week, and she was still no closer to the answer.

For a moment, Tiffany studied her intently. "I think you need to go and speak to Jonathan. You'll not be satisfied until you do. Perhaps his father can tell you what has transpired. I'm not sure he can, but at least you might find out something."

"You're right." Elizabeth bit her lip and thought about what Tiffany had suggested. "It's not as if Derek is going to come marching through the door with Adam. He's been gone only a week," Elizabeth reasoned, then looked at her friend. "What about you? Do you want to go with me?"

"If you don't mind, I'd like to stay with Dawson," Tiffany said, pausing to lean back in the chair. She folded her hands across her lap. "I consider it good experience for the future." She patted her stomach. "Remember, I had no brothers and sisters and haven't been around babies all that much. I do know that I want to raise my own children and not leave them with a governess unless it's necessary."

"The way Dawson has taken to you, I think you'll be a wonderful mother." Elizabeth smiled. "I must admit I'll feel better with you staying here with him. Even with Annie here, I feel guilty about leaving him so much. I don't think I can ever repay you for everything you've done for me."

"Rubbish!" Tiffany flipped her hand in a dismissive gesture. "You would do the same for me. I just want to see you and Jonathan happy. I must admit," she added with a sigh, "I never imagined a crisis such as this would arise. But things will work out."

"I hope you're right. I'll go to London and find out what is happening, then return in a few days." Elizabeth rose to leave.

"Take your time," Tiffany said, then as an afterthought added, "Remember, Jonathan might be angry and lash out at you."

"I've thought of that," Elizabeth said as she left the room. At least if he is angry, it is preferable to indifference. His anger shows that I might continue to hold hope for reconciliation, she thought.

* * *

Elizabeth knocked on the front door of Jonathan's town house and waited.

"May I help you?" Jeffrey said, without looking to see the visitor's identity.

"It's Elizabeth." She was glad to see he wore his monocle, but it didn't help when he was looking over her head. "Jeffrey, I'd like to see Lord Middlesex."

"Come in, Lady Elizabeth. I'm so sorry, but things have been in such a turmoil, my mind has been on other things." Jeffrey swept his arm toward the interior, motioning for her to enter. "He'll be so glad to see you. I believe he is still in his study."

"Study?" Elizabeth couldn't believe she'd heard the butler correctly. She'd expected to find him in bed as before. "I thought the marquess couldn't get out of bed."

"So did we all." Jeffrey chuckled. "So did we all. However, upon receiving word of the trouble with Lord Jonathan, the marquess has become a changed man. The energy seems to have knocked ten years off his age."

"They say that some good comes out of every situation," Elizabeth said as Jeffrey left her at the study door.

Elizabeth strolled into the room where the marquess was working. Immediately, he looked up from behind the large English oak desk. Upon seeing her, he smiled, then frowned.

"It is nice to see you out of bed," Elizabeth said.

"Who the hell can stay in bed when my son is in prison?" he barked.

Elizabeth smiled at his gruff manner. She leaned over and gave him a hug before taking her seat in front of the desk. She'd always liked his straightforward personality. "I couldn't believe the news when I heard. What can we do?"

"I wish to hell I knew." The marquess ripped out the words impatiently, shoving a stack of papers aside. "My barrister tells me it's serious. It seems someone has come forth and testified that he saw Jonathan siding with the Americans."

Elizabeth turned the news over in her mind. "We have no idea who this person is?"

The marquess shook his head. His eyes met hers. "None."

Elizabeth masked her inner turmoil with deceptive calmness while she thought for a minute. She was more shaken than she cared to admit. "Jonathan was shot by the British when he rode across the field, so he couldn't possibly have fought with the Americans. I can testify to that, because I saw him in the hospital."

The marquess raised his brow. "But the question will come up as to what he was doing there."

"Checking on his holdings," Elizabeth quickly said. "Just like my brother. We have land in America, the same as we have land here. However, we are still British subjects." She couldn't tell Lord Middlesex the whole truth, because then Adam would be tried for treason as well. Besides, the marquess would never understand anyone fighting against the British.

"I don't know," he said reluctantly. He clenched his mouth tighter and laid the quill down. "Anything is worth a try. But first we must find out the identify of the witness."

Elizabeth nodded in agreement. "I have sent for

Adam. But I don't know how long it will take him to get here."

The marquess looked at her for a long moment, his eyes as blue as Jonathan's, only very tired. "I've heard rumblings that they might hold court soon." He shook his head. "And that is not good. If they find Jonathan guilty, they will hang him, three days hence."

Elizabeth gasped and gripped the chair's arms. "We've got to do something. We can't let this happen!" She didn't know what to do, then a thought crossed her mind and she asked, "May I visit him?"

"Prison isn't any place for a lady, but you can visit him with the proper bribes." The marquess rubbed his chin. "Come to think of it, a visit from you will probably do Jonathan some good. He has asked for you. God only knows how he's holding up, being caged like an animal." Lord Middlesex slapped the desktop. "I can't believe they would not release my son on bail to me. They have some gall!"

Elizabeth stood, straightened her shoulders, and cleared her throat. "I'm going to see him immediately."

"Take Ralph with you. He is the young chap that delivered the message to Briercliff. I'll not have you going about London on your own. Ralph isn't much protection, but he will watch over you."

Elizabeth kissed Lord Middlesex on the cheek. "Thank you," she said. "We'll work something out. All will turn out right in the end."

As she turned to leave, she could only hope that statement was true!

* * *

Newgate Prison looked cold and grim. Elizabeth shivered slightly as she and Ralph crossed the cobblestone street to the entrance. She didn't like the thought of Jonathan being in the place at all, much less one hour longer than he had to be.

"What ye here for?" a turnkey asked as soon as they crossed through the front gate.

Elizabeth looked at the tall, thin man. His coat was wrinkled and his hair wasn't combed. He looked more like a prisoner than a guard. "We are here to see the Earl of Longdale," Elizabeth informed him.

"That won't be possible," he said and turned to walk away.

"Perhaps ten shillings would change your mind?"

He turned back around and grinned. "Well, seeing as yer a nice lady and all." He held out his hand. "Maybe I can arrange something."

He shuffled over to a podium where a large black book was kept. Opening the book, he peered down at the list. "Let me see." He scanned the list with a scrawny finger, and finally heaved a sigh. "I got him. He's in the Press Yard." The man looked at Elizabeth and added, "It's where we keep the condemned prisoners."

"Condemned?" Elizabeth's eyes widened. "Jonathan hasn't been tried yet."

The turnkey closed the book with a solid thud. "Well, Ye Ladyship, 'round here ye have to prove yer innocence. Maybe I should have said it's where we keep the prisoners waitin' for reprieves." He grinned, thinking he'd made a joke and turned.

"My name's Stanley, Yer Ladyship. I'll take ye to him. Follow me."

Elizabeth and Ralph waited for Stanley to get a lantern. He took off the globe and turned up the wick before lighting and replacing the glass. It seemed to take forever. Finally, he gestured for them to follow him. Entering a dark hallway, they could have used two lanterns to better light the way. Somewhere Elizabeth could hear water dripping down the walls. Finally, they turned to a staircase, and she breathed a sigh of relief when they didn't go down to the basement, which she'd heard was the worst place to be held. Instead, they went up to the second floor where there was better lighting.

They passed many cells. The prisoners grasped the bars and called out to Elizabeth to stop and talk to them. She ignored them and kept moving. Ralph edged himself over to her left side to shield her from the riffraff, and it made her feel safer.

"Here's yer fellow." Stanley chuckled and unlocked the door. He stuck his head through the doorway. "Ye got visitors. Get to yer feet."

Elizabeth ducked her head and entered the cell. "Please wait outside," she instructed Ralph and Stanley.

"I don't know, milady," Stanley said hesitantly. "He's been a tough one. He took down two jailers and broke one of their arms."

"I insist," she said firmly. "He will not harm me. I'll be fine."

Stanley shrugged. "Have it yer way. Ye have fifteen minutes," he said and shut the door.

Elizabeth's gaze darted around the gloomy interior of the tiny room. It was perhaps nine feet by six feet at the most. There was a cot under a window that had bars and nothing more ... not even a chair to sit in.

Jonathan sat with his back braced against the wall. One foot was propped up on the cot where his arm rested on his knee. He watched her, waiting. He couldn't believe that Elizabeth had actually come. This was not any place for a lady. He was afraid if he moved she'd prove to be nothing more than a figment of his imagination. His jaw tightened.

Of course, even when she was real, she had a nasty habit of disappearing on him.

"I came as soon as I heard," Elizabeth said. Her voice was raspy because she had to fight to hold back the tears.

"So you're not a figment," Jonathan said in a voice so low she barely heard him.

"I beg your pardon?"

"Never mind. If you hadn't left in such a hurry, you would have been a firsthand witness to my arrest." His voice came out smooth, deep, and very sarcastic. His hand swept the room. "Sorry, I have no chair to offer you."

She flushed. She didn't fail to catch the note of sarcasm in his voice. "I couldn't believe it when I heard of your arrest. The whole thing is absurd," she said with bitterness. "Surely you'll get out of here before long. After all, you did nothing wrong."

Jonathan made no effort to move. "That is yet to be proved. Have you sent for Adam?"

"Yes, but it will take too long for him to get here."

"You're probably right," Jonathan agreed. "I'll

find out next week when the judge will be in London. Then we will know how much time I have to prove my innocence. Of course, we both know the real truth."

Since Jonathan still hadn't bothered to move, Elizabeth took a step forward. He sounded nothing like himself. She felt as though she were talking to a stranger. She wanted so much to touch him . . . to hold him. "What are we going to do?"

"*We* are not going to do anything. This is my problem, not yours. Jonathan ran his hand through his hair and drew in a deep breath. "I wish to God I knew. The only thing I can think of is to dispute this witness." He finally put his foot on the floor and leaned his elbows on his knees. "I wish I knew who spoke against me and then maybe I could prepare better."

"I want to do anything I can for you." She caught her lower lip between her teeth and swallowed hard. "Jonathan, I know this makes no difference now, but I'm sorry I ran out the other morning. I—I was frightened and confused. Please don't shut me out."

Jonathan finally came to his feet. He wanted her so much, but he couldn't trust that his vision was real. He felt like a starving man with a feast standing before him.

Her black hair hung loosely around her shoulders, and her eyes were dark beneath a thick fringe of jet-black lashes. Elizabeth was a tempting morsel to say the least.

Jonathan wanted to say something to hurt her, yet he took another step closer until he clearly saw her soft pink lips and delicate cheekbones blooming with color. He was only an arm's length away from her now.

"Oh really," he finally snapped. "Running seems to be the only thing that you do well, Elizabeth." He grasped her by the arms. "First, you tell me you love me, and then you disappear. I should have learned my lesson the first time, but I was stupid enough to listen again. Is this some sick game you enjoy playing?"

He wanted to hurt her, to let her feel some of the pain he'd felt. However, he didn't wait for her to answer, but took her lips in a hard, punishing kiss. What did he have to do to get her to tell him the truth instead of running away yet again? He pressed hard against her lips until she parted hers slightly. Then he plunged his tongue into her mouth, taking everything he wanted and leaving her with nothing.

From the darkness that engulfed him, he heard her whimper, and he immediately softened his kiss. This time when his tongue met hers, hot excitement exploded, and he held her to him. If felt so right when Elizabeth was in his arms. All his cares seemed so far away. But prison wasn't the place for her to be, so he pulled away, and when he did his anger returned.

He wanted her. No matter where he was, or what she'd done, God help him, he wanted her. He needed Elizabeth.

He'd sworn to stay away from the lady, yet the minute she came near him, he was pulling her into his arms. Was he in love, or just a fool?

Perhaps the bastards that run this place should just

*go ahead and shoot him now and put him out of his
misery!*

Elizabeth shook her head wildly. She wanted so
much to tell Jonathan the truth. "I–I–no. This is
not a game. I do love you," she told him and looked
pleadingly into his cold eyes.

"Well, lady, you have a funny way of showing it.
How can I trust or believe anything you say?" His
hold tightened and Elizabeth willed herself not to
shake his hands away. "What are you not telling
me, Elizabeth?"

The door swung open and the turnkey charged
in. "Get yer hands off the lady!"

Jonathan dropped his hands reluctantly, but did
nothing to hide his contempt for Stanley.

Elizabeth spun around. "Please, give us a little
more time," she pleaded.

"A little more time," the man taunted, "and
ye'd be rolling 'round on that cot."

Jonathan swung his fist and caught Stanley in
the jaw, sending him flying backward. "How dare
you speak to a lady in such a manner!"

Stanley scrambled to his feet and rubbed his jaw.
"Ye'll pay for that, yer lordship," he threatened.
"Get out of here now, milady, or I'll have to slap
His Lordship into irons."

Elizabeth looked longingly at Jonathan one last
time. Impulsively, she leaned in and kissed him
softly on the lips. "For now, you'll have to believe
that I love you. I'll explain everything once we have
you out of here."

"Empty promises? I've heard them before."

With a heavy heart, Elizabeth pulled away.

She didn't remember leaving the prison, nor the

carriage ride back to Briercliff. The only thing she realized was that she'd made a mess of her life, and if she was only given one more chance, she would do everything in her power to make things right.

She glanced out the carriage window, but the scenery was nothing but a blur through her tears. What if Adam didn't arrive in time? He'd know what to do, but she couldn't count on his arrival. How could she keep Jonathan from being found guilty?

Elizabeth prayed that God would send them a miracle. At this moment, that seemed to be the only way to keep Jonathan from the gallows.

If that happened, she didn't know how she would bear life.

Three weeks later, Elizabeth received her miracle.

Elizabeth, Annie, and Tiffany were sitting in the sunroom when Derek came marching through the door.

"Derek!" Elizabeth and Annie shrieked at the same time.

Annie came to her feet and went over to hug her husband.

"You haven't had time to get Adam? What happened?" Elizabeth asked.

Derek turned to Elizabeth, one arm still around his wife. "We had to turn around and come back."

"Why?" Tiffany asked before Elizabeth could.

"I'm a bit embarrassed." Derek looked down, the tips of his ears red. "Somehow, I let a bunch of pirates slip up on us. They fired and crippled one of the masts.''

Elizabeth gasped. "Was anyone hurt?"

"Luckily, no." Derek folded his arms across his chest. "You see, this wasn't any scourge of the sea that attacked us. Unfortunately for me, the pirates didn't notice whom they were attacking until it was too late."

"I prefer to be called a privateer," Jean Lafitte corrected as he strode into the room.

Elizabeth stared at Jean in disbelief. His white shirt, black breeches, and gleaming Hessian boots were immaculate, as usual. And he was here . . . at Briercliff. Why? How?

"What's this?" Jean Lafitte said, holding his arms wide. "Adam's sister doesn't give me a hug after I've traveled so far? He let his arms fall to his side. "I'm truly insulted."

Elizabeth smiled and stepped into Jean's arms. "What are you doing here?"

"I was on my way to see my *protégé*, Jonathan, when I came across Derek's ship. Unfortunately, my men had grown bored without a ship to plunder. When they saw the *Morning Star*, they got excited and fired before I recognized Adam's ship. Merely a small mistake, you see."

"Mistake?" Derek's tongue was heavy with sarcasm. "It was a damn good thing you had a bad aim, or we'd be at the bottom of the ocean."

"Eh." Jean smiled benignly as if dealing with a temperamental child. "He was one of my newer men and needs a bit more training. No one was hurt." He chuckled, then continued, "After the slight mishap, Derek tells me that Jonathan is in prison for treason. Is this true?''

Elizabeth nodded and sat down. She glanced at Tiffany, who was still watching Jean with terrified eyes. Tiffany had probably never seen anyone like Jean. Not only was he devilishly good-looking, but his very presence was somehow overwhelming.

"Mon Dieu, this will not do," Jean swore. "I'll not have my friend in some filthy prison."

Giles entered the room. "I have another message for you, Lady Elizabeth."

"Thank you." She took the note and read it quickly. Her blood ran cold as she read. "Jonathan's trial is tomorrow. It's much earlier than we expected." Elizabeth fell back weakly against her chair.

"Then I will go with you to this trial," Jean insisted. "I will not let Jonathan hang for nothing but an unknown man's lies!"

Elizabeth frowned. Could she handle a wild pirate in a prim and proper English courtroom? "How will you do this, Jean?"

"That depends on the trial. If the court is stupid enough to convict my friend, then we shall simply take matters into our own hands."

"How?" Tiffany couldn't seem to say anything more than one word at a time.

Jean turned to the unknown voice. "Who are you?"

"I'm sorry, Jean," Elizabeth apologized. "This is Lady Tiffany DeGray, a dear friend of mine." She turned to Tiffany. "This is Jean Lafitte."

Jean smiled and sauntered over to Tiffany. He

picked up her hand and kissed the back of it. "Mademoiselle. I believe the question was *how*?"

Tiffany nodded, apparently still unable to speak.

"We'll simply break him out of the calaboose. I've had plenty of experience breaking Pierre, my brother, out of prison."

"But no one has ever escaped Newgate," Elizabeth protested.

Jean's eyes were hooded, like those of a hawk. "That's because the English have no imagination." He turned to Elizabeth. "No offense, *chérie.*" Jean tilted his head to the side. "Let a Frenchman show them how it is done."

Elizabeth took a quick, astonished breath. Had Jean really meant every word he said? "But it could be dangerous."

"Of course it is dangerous." Jean smiled like the devil himself. "I wouldn't want it any other way, *chérie.*

"Dangerously—the only way to live."

Chapter Eighteen

Jean and Derek walked to the stable. "Do you think you can rescue Jonathan?" Derek asked.

"*Oui,* but it will take some planning and a little luck, of course," Jean boasted and then, upon seeing his first mate, he called, "Dominic!"

When Dominic reached him, Jean started issuing orders. "Go to the ship and tell them to be prepared to sail at a moment's notice. . . . Check the sails and don't forget the supplies."

"I'll have it done. What else?" Dominic asked.

"Gather five of our best men and then come back here and get horses. I'll talk to the stableman and make sure the horses are saddled and ready for you."

"Horses, Jean?" Dominic asked with a frown. "Most of the blokes never been on a horse."

"If they give you any trouble, remind them that

they could spend the rest of their days below deck. A horse is a dumb animal. The men will get the knack," Jean said and started toward the horses they'd ridden in on. "I'll ride with Elizabeth to London and you can catch up to us. That way we will not waste any time."

"Remember, Jean, when you said we'd go see Jonathan and have a little fun? We really didn't realize how much fun, eh?" Dominic chuckled.

"You are right, my friend. Now, hurry."

Elizabeth rode with Jean in the carriage. As they traveled, he told her about Jonathan's sailing days. She loved hearing how Jonathan had learned to sail, and she really appreciated Jean telling her the things that Jonathan probably never would.

Six hours into their journey, Dominic and his men caught up with them, and they followed behind the carriage on horseback.

Elizabeth had made this trip so many times lately; it seemed to get shorter each time.

Once they were at Trent House, Jean and his men followed her into the foyer, where they were met by Mrs. Greenow, whose eyes had grown large with fright at the sight of Jean and his entourage.

"I'm sorry I couldn't give you advance notice that we'd be arriving, but it couldn't be helped. These gentlemen," Elizabeth swept her hand toward Jean's men, "will be staying with us while I attend Lord Jonathan's trial."

"A trial? I'm sorry. I had not heard," Mrs. Greenow said. "I hope 'tisn't serious?"

"I'm afraid it is. It's the reason for my haste."

"Where shall I put these gen—men?" Mrs. Greenow couldn't quite get the word "gentlemen" out. And Elizabeth could see why—because of the way they were dressed. She was certain Mrs. Greenow would sleep with a butcher knife under her pillow until the men departed.

Jean bowed and kissed Mrs. Greenow's hand.

The woman gasped.

"My name is Jean Lafitte, beautiful lady. My men might look, how shall I say . . . a little rough around the edges, and the word 'gentlemen' does not quite fit them, but, I guarantee, they are the salt of the earth and would lay their lives down to protect one so beautiful as yourself," Jean said with a wicked smile.

Mrs. Greenow blushed and bowed her head. "I'm sorry if I have offended you, sir. It's just that you're dressed in a peculiar manner that I've not seen before. I—I didn't know who you were."

"Thank you for the compliment. My men are supposed to look frightful, and I can understand that you've never seen privateers before," Jean said, releasing her hand. "Your apology is accepted."

It was apparent that Jean had quickly won Mrs. Greenow over.

"Please put Mr. Lafitte in Adam's room and find suitable accommodations for his crew."

Mrs. Greenow gave all the men a skeptical look, but Elizabeth nodded, showing that she would tolerate no argument. Jean had the woman charmed and, after a moment's hesitation, she asked no more questions.

Elizabeth retired to her room to freshen up.

When she had changed clothes, she went to Adam's chamber and rapped quickly on the door.

"*Chérie,*" Jean greeted with a grin. "You appear troubled. What have we forgotten?"

"Clothes," Elizabeth stated and swept past Jean. "Clothes?"

Elizabeth went to the wardrobe. "You must look English when we go to court."

"I resist that statement." Jean placed his hands on his hips. "I am but a Frenchman."

Elizabeth swung around and frowned. "Then you can look like a Frenchman, but not a pirate. How about this?" she asked as she pulled out one of Adam's jackets.

As she held the jacket out, Jean stared at the garment and rubbed his chin. "The color is nice. And the cut isn't bad."

Elizabeth shoved the jacket toward him. "Why don't you try it on? You're about the same size as Adam."

Jean finally relented and slipped into the royal blue jacket. "Nice fabric," he commented as he rubbed his hand down the sleeve.

"It looks good on you."

"Better than Adam?"

Elizabeth smiled. Jean had some ego. "Much better."

"Then I shall wear this tomorrow," he said. "I will even find some appropriate trousers to complement the jacket."

"I'll see you first thing in the morning." Elizabeth breathed a sigh of relief when she was on the other side of the door. The next hurdle would be persuading Jean to leave his sword at home. She could just picture him losing his temper and drawing his sword in the courtroom.

The morning of the trial, gray clouds obscured the sun. Expecting rain, they went across the street to get Lord Middlesex. Jeffrey peered doubtfully at Jean and Elizabeth felt obliged to introduce him.

After a moment, Jeffrey escorted them in and presented them to the marquess. Elizabeth made the introduction. "Lord Middlesex, I would like you to meet a very good friend of our family and Earl Longdale's. This is Monsieur Jean Lafitte."

"Who?" Jean asked, clearly confused by the name Longdale.

"That is Jonathan's title," Elizabeth said to Jean, but looked at the marquess. "Jean is the man Jonathan sailed with."

"A pleasure," the marquess said with a nod. "My boy is going to need all the help he can get. I'm not looking forward to today." He sighed heavily, his voice filled with anguish as he hobbled toward Jean, his gait slow. "I will follow in my own carriage, since I must take that blasted chair. Let us make haste. We must not be late."

Jean nodded and escorted Elizabeth back to the carriage. They rode down several streets, and in just a few minutes they arrived at the Old Bailey.

Jean helped Elizabeth out of the carriage; they stood to the side to await Jonathan's father and the barrister.

"I rather like old Middlesex," Jean commented. "Direct and to the point. My kind of man."

Elizabeth smiled. "He isn't retiring, if that's what you mean."

Jean laughed. "I see much of Middlesex in Jonathan."

"I do, too," Elizabeth said as the marquess's coach came to a halt behind their carriage. A footman scrambled down to assist the marquess into his chair.

A second coach soon arrived, and another gentleman emerged. He was a respectable-looking man, perhaps middle-aged, with slightly graying hair and excellent black, tailored clothing. He went immediately to the marquess's side.

Seeing that Elizabeth and Jean didn't know the man the marquess made the introductions. "Elizabeth and Monsieur Lafitte, this is Edward Turner, my barrister," Lord Middlesex said. Then he abruptly asked Turner, "Have we found out who is testifying against my son?"

Turner tucked a handful of papers under his arm. "No, my lord, but we shall soon enough. He will have to stand in open court and make his statement." Turner reached in his watchpocket and pulled out a timepiece. "We should go in."

After the barrister and Middlesex had walked ahead, Jean leaned over Elizabeth's shoulder and whispered, "And I shall run him through."

Elizabeth smiled and whispered back, "And then Jonathan will have company in prison," she said through a grim smile. "You must control your temper in the courtroom."

Elizabeth hurried to catch up with Edward Turner before they entered the building. "Excuse me, Mr. Turner. I don't know if it matters, but

Jonathan was wounded in the Battle of New Orleans. He never did fight with the Americans."

Turner's brows arched. "Jonathan has said as much. Do we have any witnesses?"

"*Oui,* we do," Jean spoke up. "I was fighting with the Americans. I saw Jonathan myself when he was shot down, and by his own countrymen, too, I might add."

"I'm not sure what to do with this information." Turner seemed to be thinking out loud. "Would a British court look upon someone who fought against Britain worthy of testifying?"

Jean huffed at the insult. "*Mon Dieu,* you are a pompous lot," Jean muttered, then added, "No offense, my friend."

"None taken."

"Shall we go in and see what transpires?" Turner said, and motioned to the footman to push Lord Middlesex's wheelchair.

"What's wrong with going in there and fighting?" Jean mumbled for Elizabeth's ears only.

"Jean, you're in a different country. You must behave according to the rules here," Elizabeth insisted.

"But, *chérie,* I believe in action."

"I know, but now is not the time. Let's go."

The courtroom was much larger than Elizabeth had expected. There was a high semicircle bench at the back wall. In front, behind a wooden barrier, were the rows of seats with crimson cushions. Over the center of the bench was a wooden canopy, surmounted by a carving of the royal arms. When Elizabeth saw the sword, the first thing she thought was that Jean would now have a weapon to use if the proceedings tested his temper.

As they found seats, the bailiff called them to stand. He introduced the Assize judge, who came in and took a seat in the middle of the semicircle. The judge was flanked on either side by other men. Each man wore a scarlet robe and a white powdered wig. Below them, another group of men dressed exactly the same were also seated.

In front of the judges were several long tables and then a platform where the accused would stand. The jury box was to the right, but was currently empty.

Elizabeth sat with Jean to her right and Lord Middlesex to her left. She was so nervous that she wrung her hands together again and again.

What if they found Jonathan guilty? Would they hang him? Treason was a hanging offense, but they couldn't do anything like that to her Jonathan—they just couldn't!

Jean leaned over to her. "It is hard to trust a man who wears a powdered wig and rouge." He rolled his eyes. *"Mon Dieu,* everything in here is red."

Elizabeth glanced at Jean. "It is the way our courts work. The Assize judge only oversees the worst cases."

"Well, I'll be damned," Lord Middlesex said from his place on her other side.

"What's wrong?"

"Perhaps nothing. The judge is George Surrey," Lord Middlesex said with a smile. "He's an old friend of mine."

"Oui, my friend, things may be looking up," Jean added.

Jonathan couldn't remember when his nerves had been stretched so tight. He couldn't seem to sit still as he paced back and forth in his cell. He felt as if he were standing on the edge of a cliff and one wrong step would send him to his death.

He had no idea what today would bring, but in a way, he was almost glad to have the trial at hand. Each day that he remained caged, he became more like an animal, eager to escape. And one way or the other, he was getting out of Newgate. He just hoped it would be as a free man and not as an executed criminal.

He clenched his fists tightly at his sides. If Stanley dared hit him again with that damned stick, Jonathan swore he would kill the man. Then they could add murder to his other charge of treason. It might be worth the price.

Jonathan glanced at the window. He had been digging at the wall a little each day to remove the dry cement, trying to loosen the bars. If escape was the only way he was going to get out of Newgate, then so be it.

Strange and disquieting thoughts began to race through his mind, and he continued to pace. Damn, he was tired. Sleep had eluded him the past two nights, and he was almost too weary to think. Every time he closed his eyes, he saw Elizabeth. She had told him to trust her. But how? And why did she keep running away? The last time he had seen her, he'd wanted to hold her so badly. Instead, he'd given her a punishing kiss.

The hinges of the door creaked as it opened, and Stanley entered with chains dangling from his hand. "It's time to go, Yer Lordship." He held the irons up. "Have to put these on ye first."

Jonathan hated the notion of being chained, but figured he'd best go peacefully. He extended his arms. "Where do we go from here?"

"I'll take ye to the Old Bailey, where ye'll be held in another cell underneath the courtroom until you're called," Stanley muttered as he snapped the hated iron around Jonathan's wrist. "Let's go." He shoved Jonathan forward.

Jonathan walked in front of Stanley, who seemed to take pleasure in prodding him with his stick. They moved down several hallways until they reached the holding cell. Stanley paused and unlocked the door for Jonathan.

The cell was nearly full with a teeming mass of unwashed bodies. Jonathan turned to Stanley for an explanation.

"They call ye to the courtroom in groups of twelve to hear yer pleas. I'll see ye after the trial," Stanley said and shoved Jonathan forward.

Jonathan stepped inside and found a place to stand and wait. He stood with his back to the wall, observing the other men. Some of them looked as rough as Jean's pirates. A few were scared. Some just stared, but all remained quiet.

It was amazing how subdued this group of men was. The sound of keys jingling down the hall could be heard. Jonathan turned, but the guard kept going. Leaning against the wall with his shoulder, he willed himself to relax as he waited.

Finally, the bailiff came for the next group. Relieved that something was finally going to happen . . . he was also worried. But Jonathan marched out with eleven other men, wanting to get the trial over as soon as possible.

When they entered the courtroom, Jonathan immediately scanned the room. He saw his father, Elizabeth, and Jean. My God, Jean Lafitte in England! What a miracle! That actually brought a smile to Jonathan's lips as he nodded to his friend.

The prisoners approached the bench and waited. The clerk stood and read the names of all present, including the other county officials, sheriff, and mayor.

As Jonathan's gaze wandered to the gallery, he could see the people peering above each other to see his face. A titled gentleman being tried was indeed a spectacle.

"Court is in session," the clerk announced, then looked at the prisoners and said, "When your name is called out, please identify yourself by raising a hand. Then plead guilty or not guilty to the indictment against you."

One by one, the names were called off until they finally came to Jonathan. "Jonathan Hird, the Earl of Longdale. The charge is treason. How do you plead?"

Jonathan raised his hand. "Not guilty."

"And how would you be so tried?" the clerk asked.

"By God and my country," Jonathan said.

"So be it." The clerk nodded to a guard, who

hurried over and removed Jonathan's fetters. He rubbed his wrists and stepped to the side to await his turn.

"Show the jury in," the clerk instructed the guard.

Jonathan watched the jurymen file past him to their seats. He studied them, wondering how his fate lay in their hands. Would they be able to tell that he was innocent or would they believe the informant and find him guilty?

The proceedings began in rapid succession while the other cases were tried, one by one. Jonathan wondered what chance he had.

The jury heard each case and passed judgment before proceeding to the next prisoner. They didn't even retire to discuss the cases. The foreman simply took the consensus of the jury and the decision was reached. Jonathan could glean nothing from the jurors' faces. They might as well have been made of stone. They found the eleven men ahead of him guilty, so Jonathan had a grim feeling about his own case.

Finally, Jonathan's turn came. He was instructed to stand on a platform within a small enclosure directly in front of the Assize Judge.

The clerk again announced, "This is Jonathan Hird, the Earl of Longdale. The charge is treason, Your Honor."

"Who represents this man?" the judge asked.

The barrister stood. "I do, Your Honor. Edward Turner."

"Would the prosecutor please explain the charges against the man?" Judge Surrey asked.

The prosecutor, a thin man with wire-rimmed

glasses perched on the end of his nose, stood. "A witness has come forth and accused Earl Longdale of fighting against the crown at the Battle of New Orleans."

"And where is this witness?" the judge asked.

"In the hallway, sir." The prosecutor motioned toward the doors. "He is waiting for a guard to bring him in."

Elizabeth heard the door open, but that was the only sound as silence fell over the room. Her heart thrummed against her ribs, beating a hundred times faster than it should. She began to feel faint as the witness came down and stood on the platform opposite Jonathan. She could tell the man wore a naval uniform, which would be reasonable since he was at the battle, but she couldn't quite see his face from this distance.

"State your name," the prosecutor said.

"Captain Henry Lee of Her Majesty's navy," Lee said in a raspy voice.

Elizabeth clutched her throat and grabbed the arm of her chair for support. No! This couldn't be possible! Lee was dead! Jewel had told her that he'd drowned. Elizabeth shivered as cold ran through her body.

"The slimy bastard lives," Jean muttered under his breath.

When Lee turned to look at Jonathan, Elizabeth saw the ugly scar. If she had held a gun at this very moment, they wouldn't have to worry about the witness. He would have been dead as he was supposed to be, rather than standing there looking like the picture of health.

"Please state in your own words what you saw," the prosecutor requested.

Lee cleared his throat, looked at Jonathan, then back to the judge. "When the battle took place in New Orleans, Jonathan Hird was on the American side, not his own country's. I saw him myself. He is a traitor and deserves to hang."

Before Elizabeth could stop herself, she jumped to her feet. "That is a lie!" she shouted.

Suddenly, everyone's gaze rested upon her, and scores of questions filled the air. Even the marquess tried to pull her back down. But she'd have none of it. She would not let Lee get away with this slander he spurted forth, especially when he'd been on a ship and not involved with the battle.

That was when he'd held her for ransom. He could not have seen who was on which side of the Battle of New Orleans.

Judge Surrey folded his arms, leaned on his desk, and glared down at Elizabeth. "I don't hold with such outbursts in my courtroom."

"But Captain Lee is lying," Elizabeth persisted. "He was nowhere near the battle. He had deserted the British himself in search of treasure."

The judge looked at the prosecutor and frowned. "This is very irregular, but I would like to hear what the lady has to say. Please remove Lee, and hold him. Young woman, step forward."

Elizabeth wasn't quite sure that she could move. Jean squeezed her hand and urged, "Go ahead, *chérie.*"

She managed to make her way to the stand, assisted by Edward Turner.

"State your name," Judge Surrey said in a loud,

forceful voice that made Elizabeth feel as if she were guilty. She would have to choose her words carefully to keep from revealing her own terrible secret. She would hate Jonathan to hear it this way.

"My name is Elizabeth Trent. My brother is Adam Trent, the Duke of St. Ives."

The judge nodded as he recognized the name. "Tell us what you know."

"My brother has property in New Orleans, which is the reason Jonathan was visiting. New Orleans had not been involved in the war at that time. Jonathan and my brother were discussing shipping business when the war broke out." Elizabeth swallowed hard. She was really stretching the truth, but she'd never let Lee get away with his lies. "My sister-in-law, Jewel, had a treasure map. Lee wanted it, but he couldn't get to Jewel. So, he waited until I rode off our land. Then his men kidnapped me and took me to Lee's ship where I was held until he could exchange me for Jewel."

The prosecutor spoke up. "That doesn't mean Captain Lee deserted."

Elizabeth looked at the judge. "If you'll please let me finish."

The judge nodded.

"Jewel told me the rest of the story. They sailed to a small island to find a treasure chest worth a king's ransom while the battle raged. Jewel could hear the fire from other ships as they sailed by, so she knew a battle was going on, but there is no possible way that Lee could have seen Jonathan. Jonathan was on shore, shot by the British, and unable to fight with anyone."

Silence settled over the courtroom. Elizabeth felt

her legs shaking as she glanced at Jonathan, who was gripping the rails so hard that his knuckles had turned white. What was he thinking?

"She is lying, Your Honor," Lee spoke up. "I have served His Majesty well."

Judge Surrey gazed at the two men on either side of him. Finally, he leaned over and whispered something to one of them, then listened to his reply. "This is highly unusual," the judge said and frowned.

Elizabeth swallowed. She could tell the judge that she had definitely told the truth, because she had a child to prove it. However, she didn't want to bring Dawson into this proceeding if she didn't have to. She waited to see what the judge said.

"In light of these new circumstances, I need to take everything under consideration before we proceed." The judge rose. "We will adjourn this case until tomorrow at ten o'clock and a verdict will be issued at that time. Take the prisoner to his cell and hold Lee in custody until the matter is settled."

Elizabeth watched the guard take Lee by the arm. Before he was led out, Lee turned and glared at her. He was close enough for her to hear him say, "You'll regret this day."

She already did.

Jonathan was escorted past her also, but stopped and smiled his thanks. "Thank you for speaking on my behalf," he whispered. "Bring Jean to see me right away," Jonathan said as the guard urged him on.

He seemed to want to tell her something, but the guard wouldn't let him stay.

Elizabeth's voice had somehow left her, but she

managed to nod. Then she went back to the marquess and Jean.

"That was a brave thing for you to do, young lady," the marquess said, drawing her to him for a big hug.

"Lee was lying, Lord Middlesex. Lee is the scum of the earth," she said, more to herself than to Middlesex. "What do you think they will do?"

"I'm not sure. The evidence is compelling, but no conclusion. They could hang them both or leave them to rot in prison forever. We must pray that Surrey makes the right decision," the marquess said in a low voice. "I'm a bit tired. I'm leaving. Are you coming?"

"I want to see Jonathan first, so we'll stay," Elizabeth admitted.

"And I will go with her," Jean said. "Are you ready to go?"

Elizabeth nodded, and they left the courtroom together.

"*Mon Dieu*, I cannot believe that slimy bastard lives. I wanted to kill him myself when we were on the island, but Jewel said he'd drowned, and I never doubted her. Somehow, he must have escaped his watery grave. But this I guarantee—Lee will not so easily escape the next time," Jean vowed.

Chapter Nineteen

The sun sank lower in the sky. The tall buildings cast shadows across the street as Elizabeth and Jean hurried toward Newgate. They had to see Jonathan before the day ended. They needed time to plan and then set those plans into motion.

Surprisingly, Stanley didn't give them his usual hard time when they arrived. Upon seeing Elizabeth, he merely held out his hand and grinned as she placed a few shillings in his palm.

Elizabeth smiled to herself as Jean checked out their surroundings. His gaze constantly shifted while they walked through the dismal corridors toward Jonathan's cell.

Stanley opened the door to the cell and announced, "Ye've got some company. Ye didn't get as lucky as yer accuser," he said with a chuckle, then added, "Heard tell he's escaped."

Jonathan looked up, startled. "What are you talking about?"

"That Captain Lee escaped 'fore they could get him to a cell. They're already punishing the guard. The way it looks, ye could be in here forever before they get this mess straightened out," Stanley said. "Can't hold the trial without him." Then he looked at Elizabeth and Jean. "Ye got fifteen minutes."

Jonathan rose and greeted Jean with a handshake. "I couldn't believe my eyes when I saw you in the courtroom. Thank God, you've come at the right time. As grateful as I am, I'm still a little surprised. What are you doing here?"

"Ah, my friend. Are you always in trouble?" Jean replied with a chuckle. "Or does trouble just seem to follow you?"

Jonathan gave a sarcastic laugh. "So it would seem." He looked at Elizabeth. He wanted very much to touch her, to hold her hand, and just forget his problems but he didn't dare. "I appreciate what you did for me at the trial. At least it has put some doubts into everyone's minds and has bought me a little time."

"I can't believe that filthy Lee is still alive." Elizabeth shuddered. "Did I hear the guard correctly? Lee has escaped?"

"So," he said, "Lee must be caught and stopped before he strikes again. If I could get my hands on him, he wouldn't be alive long. After what he did to Elizabeth and now me, he deserves no mercy," Jonathan vowed.

Elizabeth swallowed hard. If only Jonathan knew the real damage that Lee had inflicted.

"You would have to wait in line, my friend," Jean said in a nasty voice. His eyes blazed with seething anger. "Remember, Lee shot my beautiful Jewel. He must pay the price.

"When we found her, she told us Lee had drowned, and I had no reason to believe otherwise. With the swift current, it did not seem likely that he survived. The man must be blessed with many lives."

"He's a cat, all right. An alley cat," Jonathan muttered.

Jean went to the window, stepped up on the cot, and glanced out. "I see you have fresh air."

"Aye," Jonathan said with a grin. "And loose bars."

"Ah, I've taught you well." Jean nodded approvingly. "I've come prepared to help you with whatever you decide to do. The decision is yours."

"I'm glad you planned ahead, as usual," Jonathan said, a cold edge of irony in his voice. "There isn't much to decide. My father will have my name cleared. Lee's escape has made his word look doubtful. However, it could take weeks to settle these charges, and I'm not willing to stay behind bars that long. Lee will likely be preparing to sail his ship. As I've said before, I have a score or two to settle with him." Jonathan prowled the cramped confines of the cell.

Jean smiled, a ruthless gleam in his eyes. "Then we shall see you at midnight, my friend."

Elizabeth bit her lower lip. She didn't want to object, but she wasn't sure about the idea of Jonathan escaping. She didn't want him shot. "But the

British will hunt you down. All they will see is an escaped prisoner.''

"I'll take my chances," Jonathan told Elizabeth. He turned to Jean and said, "Midnight it shall be."

The downstairs clock struck twelve as Jean assembled his men at Trent's House. A slight movement in the darkness caught his eye, and he swung around to see Elizabeth coming down the stairs dressed in breeches and a dark shirt. Her hair had been caught up under a cap, and she looked very much like a young boy, not the beautiful woman he'd been with earlier.

"What are you doing?" Jean demanded. He wasn't sure whether to send her back to bed or to be proud of her gumption. She was a lot like her brother.

"I'm going to help you," she announced defiantly. "You will not leave me behind."

"You know this could be dangerous, *chérie,*" Jean warned. "I do not wish to see you hurt."

"Nor do I." Elizabeth took a deep breath. "I'll be fine, she said, heading for the foyer. She would not allow them to leave her behind to worry herself to death. "Besides which, we don't want to waste time coming back to the town house when we can go directly to Briercliff from the prison."

Before Jean could argue further, the front door flew open, and Dominic strode toward them. Elizabeth hadn't realized he wasn't among the other men—she'd been too concerned with convincing Jean she was going with him.

"You were right, Jean," Dominic said when he

stopped directly in front of his captain. "*The Rose* has already set sail."

"*The Rose?*" Elizabeth asked, a little puzzled.

"Captain Lee's ship," Jean explained. "Lee has done just as we expected. He's wasted little time leaving England and removing himself from harm's way. Let us not delay another moment." Jean looked at Elizabeth. "Jonathan will not like you accompanying us. But who am I to argue? Stay close by me."

"I can take care of myself," Elizabeth insisted. Jonathan wasn't her keeper, and he couldn't tell her what to do.

One of Jean's men, Mel, held the horses that had been brought from the stables. When Mel handed the reins to Jean he said, "They'li have the wagon readied by the time we get there."

The group made one stop on the way to purchase a wagon full of hay from the stable where the horses had been boarded. Elizabeth couldn't fathom why they needed the wagon. It would only slow them down. Then it occurred to her that they planned to hide Jonathan beneath the hay as they made their escape.

Soon the dark silhouette of Newgate loomed ahead. They didn't stop at the front gate, but went to the north side of the prison. Jean dismounted and paced the area, taking long strides. He seemed to be counting off his steps. When he reached a certain spot, he stopped and turned toward his men. "Position the wagon here."

The rest of the men and Elizabeth dismounted and tied their horses to the wagon. The horse pulling the wagon whinnied.

"Keep him quiet," Jean snapped.

Elizabeth ran over to the horse, grabbed his halter, and started rubbing his muzzle, but not before the wagon rolled over Mel's foot and he started swearing.

"Why don't we just announce that we are here?" Jean spat.

"Sorry, Jean," Mel managed to say as he rubbed his injured foot.

When everything had quieted down again, Jean stepped back and gazed up at the building. "The window is too high to throw a rope up to Jonathan," Jean said, rubbing his jaw. "That means we're going to have to take the rope to him. Come, Dominic, and grab a coil of rope. Let us make haste, and see what we can do."

"You're going to walk in the front door?" Elizabeth asked.

"That seems to be the only way. The walls are much too steep to climb. Besides, no one would expect a jailbreak through the main entrance. The British are so arrogant; they would never expect a jailbreak at all. It takes a Frenchman to be cunning," Jean said with a smile.

"What can I do?" Elizabeth asked, stepping out of the darkness. "Should I go with you?"

"No, *chérie,* you must stay behind and be ready with the wagon. You've done a good job calming that beast. We don't want him moving at the wrong time. Perhaps you can try to keep the horse quiet, eh?"

Elizabeth nodded, but doubt surfaced. "What if they don't let you inside the prison?"

Jean looked at her as if she were a small child

and sighed deeply. Suddenly, a wicked grin spread across his face. "Then we'll simply use persuasion." He bowed to her and then disappeared into the blackness.

The darkness was aided by a full moon casting weak glimmers of light here and there as Jean and Dominic made their way around the building to the main gate. They found very few guards on watch at this time of night. Jean grinned and looked at Dominic. "Better hide that coil of rope until we are in the building."

Jean picked up the brass knocker and knocked soundly on the thick oak door. When he didn't get an immediate answer, he peered into the small slit in the door. The turnkey, Stanley, stumbled to the door. By the looks of him, he'd been asleep.

Finally, the door opened. "What do ye want? Ye can't see a bloody prisoner this late at night," the man announced sleepily and tried to close the door.

Dominic stepped forward quickly and blocked the way with his leg. "What if we make it worth your while?"

Stanley's eyes grew wide with interest. "Such as?" he asked, opening the door a little further.

"Such as gold?" Jean suggested and held a pouch up by one finger.

"Real gold." A slow, greedy smile crept across Stanley's face, his gaze never leaving the small bag. Then he frowned and gasped as he realized what was going on. "Ye planning a bloody jailbreak!" He turned to call for help, "Guard—"

Dominic had his arm around Stanley's neck so fast that the man didn't know what happened. He could only gasp for air. He struggled, but Dominic pressed the sharp tip of a knife against his back, and then Stanley went very still.

"I see we'll have to do this the hard way." Jean sighed as they stepped through the door, pushing the turnkey ahead of him, and then closing the door quietly behind them. "We tried being civil," Jean reminded Stanley. "Now we will try reason." Jean drew out his knife and ran his thumb over the razor-sharp edge. "Do you see this knife, my friend?"

The man nodded the best he could with Dominic's arm still around this neck.

"If you don't get the keys and take us to Jonathan Hird immediately and very quietly, I guarantee I will cut out your tongue. Then you will never be able to call out again," Jean said, his tone menacing. Jean peered at the guard, his nose mere inches away. "Do you understand?"

Stanley nodded.

"Good." Jean grinned, his teeth white in the darkness. That's what he liked—complete cooperation. "Dominic, you may release him now that we've come to a gentleman's agreement."

Stanley's eyes were large with fear as he reached for the large ring of keys hanging on a big wooden peg. "Follow me," he said, his eyes flickering with fear.

Dominic and Jean flanked Stanley to make certain the fool wasn't stupid enough to try to alert the guard—or worse, to run. Fortunately, since it was late, they didn't run into any other guards on their way. Dominic had placed the coil of rope over his shoulder to make sure his hands were free to handle his dagger.

Stanley's hands shook as he fumbled with the key ring. Finally, he selected the correct brass key and unlocked the cell door. He tried to step aside, but Dominic shoved Stanley through the door.

Jonathan jumped to his feet.

"Ye ain't goin' to kill—" Stanley never finished his sentence. Jean hit him on the head with the butt of his pistol and the man slumped, senseless, to the floor.

"The man talked too much," Jean said, dusting off his hands. "We'll not have to worry about him alerting anyone for a while." Jean stepped over the sprawled body and tucked the gun back into his waistband. "Now let's get out of here."

"I was beginning to think you weren't coming," Jonathan said as he started for the open door.

Jean wagged his finger and shook his head. "Now, let's take a look at those bars." He examined them critically. "Ah, you have done well."

They tugged on one of the steel bars until the mortar finally gave way. Then they chipped away at the other bar while Dominic dragged Stanley over to the side, gagged him, and tied him up to give them a little more time once they had escaped.

Jonathan tossed the rope through the window and looked down. "The rope is too short, and it's a long drop. But it's by far too risky to try walking through the front door. You were lucky enough coming in that way."

"I'm willing to bet we could march out the way we came in. However, knowing you might be cau-

tious, I arranged for another method of escape."
Jean chuckled.

"Maybe you need to think again," Jonathan said,
"Because the rope is too short."

"That's why we have a wagon full of hay below
to break our fall. You'll have to scramble out of
the way quickly because we'll be right behind you,"
Jean said. He slapped Jonathan on the back then
watched as Jonathan climbed up on the ledge and
squeezed through the small opening.

"Here goes," Jonathan said, looking back at
Jean.

"If you break anything, be sure to shout," Jean
told him. "And then Dominic and I will go out
the way we came."

"You're all heart, old boy," Jonathan laughed
before shoving off the ledge. He lowered himself,
climbing down the wall with the rope before letting
go and falling the rest of the way.

Jean heard a soft thud, followed by an oath. He
looked at Dominic. "See? Nothing to it. Let's go."

Jean and Pierre followed, landing safely in the
hay. They scrambled to the horses being held by
one of the men.

"Who's the bloke with the hat? I don't recognize
him," Jonathan asked as he grabbed the reins and
swung up into the saddle.

Jean nudged his horse with his knees and smiled.
"My friend, you've been in prison much too long.
That is Elizabeth."

"Elizabeth?" Jonathan trotted up alongside
Jean. "What the devil is she doing here?"

"She insisted." Jean shrugged. "You know
women."

"Unfortunately, I do," Jonathan said. "I'll deal with her later. Let's find Lee's ship."

"We have already thought of that," Jean said, urging his horse forward. "Lee has already sailed."

Upon seeing Jonathan's frown, Jean added, "Don't worry. With our sloop, we can catch his heavy frigate, but we'll have to hurry. Just think. We'll be chasing the English, and the English will be chasing us." Jean's laughter was a full-hearted sound. "I knew if I found you, you'd contribute to our excitement." He kneed his horse into a full gallop.

Elizabeth and Jonathan didn't speak as they dashed toward Briercliff. She wasn't sure what was running through Jonathan's head, but she had a feeling it was revenge against Lee.

They traveled all night, only stopping to rest the horses. It was late the next day when they finally arrived at their destination.

Elizabeth could barely hold onto her horse, she was so tired, but they needed fresh horses to go on to St. Ives, and she needed to see Dawson. She wasn't going to hide her baby any longer. It was time to tell Jonathan the truth.

Elizabeth dismounted, energized by thoughts of seeing her son. She hurried toward the house. "I can have the cooks prepare some food for the journey," she told Jean and Jonathan.

Jean stayed behind to issue orders to his men while Elizabeth and Jonathan climbed the front steps of Briercliff. As soon as they opened the door and Elizabeth called out, Annie, looking agitated, rushed out into the foyer. Elizabeth wondered while Giles wasn't anywhere in site.

"Thank God ye've returned." Annie grabbed Elizabeth by the arm. " 'Tis awful. Simply awful," Annie cried frantically, tears glistening in her eyes. " 'Tis Master Dawson."

"What's wrong?" Elizabeth tried to push past Annie to see to her son. She'd never seen the woman so distraught. Annie had always been the steady one. She was the one who held everyone else together.

"I—I canna believe it happened," Annie wailed, wringing her hands. "No one was here to stop him. Derek is at St. Ives, and Giles tried but was struck down. He's in bed now."

"What's wrong? Is he hurt?" Then she realized what Annie had said, and a wave of apprehension coursed through her. "Prevent what, Annie?" Elizabeth asked anxiously. "Where are Tiffany and Dawson?"

"Dawson?" Jonathan questioned. "That's the second time I've heard you mention that name. And I don't think you are referring to my father."

Because of Annie's state of distress, Elizabeth brushed Jonathan aside. She had to find out what was upsetting Annie. Elizabeth's heart raced and she began to get an uneasy feeling. It was impossible to steady her erratic pulse. "What is it, Annie? What is it?"

Jonathan grabbed Annie by the arm and turned her to him. "Has anyone hurt you? And who struck Giles? I'll speak with them immediately," Jonathan said.

Annie didn't answer. Tears pooled in her eyes and she blinked to clear them. Finally, she looked away from Elizabeth and reached into her pocket.

Producing a small piece of paper, she handed it to Elizabeth.

In the background, Elizabeth heard the door open, and out of the corner of her eye, she saw Jean coming toward them. But she couldn't leave until she found out what had happened. And where was Dawson?

Elizabeth's hands were shaking as she fumbled to unfold the letter. As she scanned the words, she felt the blood drain rapidly from her head, her knees gave way, and she crumpled to the ground.

"My God," Jonathan exclaimed. He knelt and scooped her up in his arms. She was as white as snow. He shook her head back and forth, but he couldn't bring her to.

"Mon Dieu! What was in that blasted note?" Jean swore and bent down and retrieved the paper.

Annie was crying as she, too, bent down beside Elizabeth. "My poor lass."

"Read it aloud," Jonathan demanded.

"Blast and damnation. It's a note from Lee to Jonathan." Jean cleared his throat and began to read.

> *My life has been hell since I've been involved with your infernal family. I am not a man to take defeat lightly!*
>
> *Revenge is my driving force. You see, I was cheated of my gold by Jewel's trickery. I will not be cheated again!*
>
> *I thought I had my revenge against some of you with the trial. But that bitch, Elizabeth, chose to open her mouth, making me an enemy of my own country. So you see I have nothing more to lose.*

Now you will pay!

I came for Elizabeth, but instead I found a child and Elizabeth's best friend. They will do very nicely as hostages.

If you hope to see them alive again, find Lafitte and deliver to me a chest full of gold to the most northern dock of New Orleans. I will wait five days for you to arrive.

It would be a shame to see what the fish would do to a little boy who can't swim.

Jean crumpled the note. "The bastard will die!"

"Not if I get him first," Jonathan declared.

Jonathan took Elizabeth over to a chair, where he placed her down. Carefully, he pulled her forward until her head was between her legs and she began to struggle. "Wake up, Elizabeth."

She moaned.

"Who is this Tiffany?" Jean demanded.

"She's a friend of Elizabeth's. They grew up together, but she doesn't have a child," Jonathan said, shaking his head. "Tiffany is expecting her first baby," Jonathan explained, then looked at Annie. "Who is this child?"

Annie had finally gotten control of herself, but avoided Jonathan's eyes as she asked Jean, "Can ye find them?"

"Of course," Lafitte declared, "but we must move quickly."

Elizabeth finally opened her eyes. "Wh—what happened?"

"You fainted after reading this note," Jonathan explained, taking her hand.

"My God, I remember," she said. "We must go after them."

Jonathan straightened and looked down at her. "Who is Dawson?"

The moment had finally come to tell Jonathan the truth. "My son." Elizabeth tried to get to her feet, but her legs would not hold her. "Jean, we must save my child!"

"Son?" Jonathan paused as if he didn't understand. "You have a son?"

"We will save him, *chérie*. Let us not linger further. I did not know about your son, but we'll find him and return him to you." Jean put his arm around Elizabeth and walked with her to the door. "Where are the fresh horses?"

"They are being saddled at the stables," Elizabeth said, then twisted away from Jean. "Let me tell Annie goodbye."

She turned and collided with Jonathan's broad chest. He reached out and steadied her. "You cannot go, Elizabeth. It will be much too dangerous."

"I'm not staying behind," Elizabeth insisted. "Tell him, Jean."

Jean held up his hand. "I know better than to get in the middle of this squabble. I will wait outside."

She knew Jonathan wasn't finished, but he didn't realize just how determined she could be. Elizabeth brushed past Jonathan and went to Annie. "We will find Dawson and Tiffany. Don't worry."

Annie hugged Elizabeth and patted her on the back. "I want ye to be very careful and bring that lad back home."

Jonathan waited by the door. "I repeat, this is too dangerous. You should stay behind."

Elizabeth clenched her hands by her side. Maybe she should appreciate Jonathan's concern, but at the moment she didn't. He wasn't a mother, so he'd never understand. And right now he was in her way. "Perhaps it will be dangerous. But I'm going anyway. And I don't have the time to argue with you, so get out of my way."

"You never told me you had a son," Jonathan said.

"I know." She felt her cheeks heat as Jonathan opened the door. "It was . . . what I wanted to talk to you about."

"I should think so," he said as they hurried toward the stable. "One would think it would be a small fact that should have come up in our conversation before now. Like . . . who is the father?"

Elizabeth stopped so suddenly that Jonathan nearly ran into her and had to back up a couple of steps. She glared up at him. "Jonathan, we are losing precious time! Look, there is a little boy out there who is helpless and scared. Does it matter who his father is?"

Jonathan started to say something, but stopped. He frowned as her words tumbled through his brain, making him feel very small indeed. He stared at her for a long moment. "No, I suppose not." He started walking again. When Elizabeth didn't move, he turned and said, "Come, let's go find your son."

Chapter Twenty

Lafitte's ship, the *Ciel Bleu*, rose and fell in long, surging leaps as she bit into one wave after another. A fresh wind filled the billowing white sails overhead, pushing the ship along at a good pace under brilliant blue skies with only a few wispy clouds.

Elizabeth had positioned herself by the wooden rail where she could survey the horizon. The wind blew her hair and her hands gripped the rails dampened by the sea's salt spray.

Jonathan stood at the helm of the *Ciel Bleu* with Jean; Dominic was stationed behind the big wheel of the ship. However, Jonathan's mind wasn't on Dominic—it was on Elizabeth. Feeling completely helpless and not knowing exactly what to do, he watched her. "We must talk," Jonathan finally said to Jean.

They moved a few steps away from Dominic to

keep him from overhearing. "It has been two weeks, and every day she has stood in the same spot," Jean said. "We have made good time. I figure we will catch up with that scoundrel in the next few days. However . . ." Jean paused and sighed. "It breaks my heart to see Elizabeth so sad, even if I understand her worry over her missing child. She reminds me so much of Jewel."

Jonathan gave Jean an incredulous look. "If you think it breaks *your* heart . . ." Jonathan stopped a moment before continuing. "How do you think I feel? She has barely spoken two words to me since we left St. Ives." He leaned back against the rail and folded his arms across his chest. "Perhaps she is blaming me for what happened."

"I doubt that, my friend. She has been quiet around me as well," Jean paused. "Have you tried to speak to her?"

Jonathan shook his head. "No. I thought I should give her time alone."

Jean raised his brows a fraction. "Perhaps you have given her too much time, my friend. I must admit, I was surprised to hear she had a child. Adam has said nothing of this to me."

Jonathan gave a sarcastic laugh. "The lady is full of surprises."

"Has it occurred to you that the child is about three years old, about the same length of time since Elizabeth left New Orleans?"

Jonathan gaped at his friend. "I—I hadn't thought about it."

Jean folded his arms, his feet planted firmly on the deck as he stared at Jonathan sternly. "Did you compromise her?"

"I don't believe that is any of your bloody business!" Enraged, Jonathan turned to leave, then thought better of it since he'd initiated the conversation. "Since you just saved my hide and we are on your ship, I'll answer your question." Jonathan paused before answering. "The answer is yes. But the lady was willing."

"Well?"

"No. It's impossible. Elizabeth would have told me about a child. She would have realized that I'd be very pleased over my own child."

Jean smiled. "Women are fickle, my friend. And very unpredictable. I, most certainly, have never figured them out."

"Yes, they are fickle, as I'm finding out. Elizabeth owes me plenty of explanations, but I'll not press her until this ordeal is over." Jonathan straightened and turned to look out over the water. "You don't think Lee will hurt the boy?"

Jean spit. "He's such slime. Civilization would be better off without him. And I, for one, intend to exterminate him quickly," Jean added abruptly, venting his rage. Then he resumed control. "And, in answer to your question, I wouldn't put anything past the scum."

"Then you had better get to Lee first, because I intend kill him."

Jean chuckled. "May the best man win."

Elizabeth felt the salt spray nip her face as the ship dove into a swell. The cool mist helped her stay focused.

Every night she prayed that she'd come to the

rail and the ship they sought would be within sight. Then her nightmare would be over. But again today, she'd been let down.

Surely, Lee wouldn't hurt his own child. There had to be some paternal sense in him. He'd have to feel some kind of connection to Dawson. And poor Tiffany, Elizabeth thought. Her friend probably wished she'd never run into Elizabeth. Elizabeth hoped no harm would come to her. Since she had sailed during her own pregnancy, she felt that Tiffany's baby would be fine. Elizabeth just hoped that Tiffany wasn't as sick as she'd been.

Elizabeth glanced behind her to see Derek's ship trailing theirs. When they rescued Dawson and Tiffany, Tiffany could sail back to Briercliff and pretend none of this had ever happened. However, Elizabeth and Dawson would probably continue on to Four Oaks. She had a strong need to see her twin brother.

Stretching, she turned back to the rail. It was getting late—another day lost. She sighed as hot tears moistened her eyes. Another day during which her hopes had slipped further away.

Was she a bad mother? She had asked herself that question over and over. She should have been with her child. Maybe then she could have prevented all of this.

Not finding any answers, she turned and headed back to her cabin. She knew she should speak to Jonathan and Jean, but she couldn't. At least, not now. If she tried to talk to them, all she would do is cry, and tears would do nothing to help their situation.

* * *

Mulling over in his mind what he was going to do, Jonathan ate dinner with Jean. By the time the meal was finished, he wasn't any closer to deciding whether he should talk to Elizabeth or not.

Maybe he had his answer because subconsciously he wandered down below and found himself standing in front of Elizabeth's cabin. He knocked lightly and waited.

Several moments passed until the door opened a crack and Elizabeth peeked through. "May I hel—" She stopped suddenly when she saw who stood on the other side. Her eyes were red and puffy from crying.

"May I come in?" he asked softly, still unsure of what he was going to do, but knowing he had to do something.

She said nothing, but stood back and motioned for him to enter.

He could tell her mood was fragile, at best, and he wasn't certain where to start, but she couldn't continue on this destructive path.

She moved slowly back to the bunk and sat down and buried her face in her hands.

Jonathan seated himself in the chair beside the bed. "Staying in your room all the time isn't good, Elizabeth," he told her firmly. "I'd wager that you've not had a thing to eat in several days. I know I haven't seen you at dinner, and I don't see an empty plate in here," he commented as he glanced around the room.

She simply frowned, clenching the white handkerchief in her hand, and said, "I'm not hungry."

Jonathan felt his frustration growing into a knot that kept tightening in his stomach. He needed to put the fire back into Elizabeth, to see that old, familiar spark in her eyes, but he didn't know how. "If you don't keep up your strength, you'll not be of any use when we catch Lee's ship," he said in a challenging manner.

"We're never going to catch Lee," she said, her voice sounding as dejected as she looked. "I thought we would have caught them long before now."

That was more like it! At least he had her talking. "You forget they have a day's head start on us."

Elizabeth wiped her eyes. "I'm such a failure."

"Why?"

"I let you down at the wedding. And if I had been a good mother, I would have been with Dawson and he wouldn't be on Lee's ship."

"I beg to differ," Jonathan told her point-blank, then admitted, "however, I've said the same thing about myself many times."

"You are definitely no failure, Jonathan, and I owe you an explanation. Perhaps several."

"Yes, you do," he agreed. "Every time we've started this conversation, you seemed to disappear. However, that will be hard to do at sea." He chuckled, trying to lighten the mood. "Your explanation can wait until we've rescued your child."

Elizabeth shook her head. "I've waited much too long as it is." She paused and twisted her handkerchief. "I'm just not sure where to start."

"Start from the very beginning—and that unanswered question . . . why did you run away on our wedding day?" He drew in a deep breath and waited for an answer. When none came, he went on. "At the time, I thought it was because of my arm. My arm is well now, and still you ran off the other night, too. Am I to assume that the problem is me?"

"Of course not!" Elizabeth's eyes widened in surprise. "It's more me than you. As someone dear just pointed out to me, I seem to run when I'm frightened. But it was never your arm," Elizabeth assured him.

As Jonathan watched her, that old familiar panic seized Elizabeth. The day of reckoning couldn't be postponed forever. She realized they had reached the point where their relationship had to be resolved. She took several deep breaths and wiped her eyes again.

"When I . . ." she paused, took another deep breath, and started again. "When I was kidnapped by Captain Lee, he didn't just kidnap me. He raped me to get back at Adam," she blurted out.

Jonathan shot to his feet. "By God, the bastard is a dead man!"

"Please. Let me finish," Elizabeth begged. "This is hard enough as it is," she whispered and waited until he sat back down. "I didn't find out I was pregnant until a few days before the wedding. I wanted to marry you, but I couldn't be dishonest and pass off another man's child as yours. So I ran. I—I knew how you felt about Captain Lee, and I didn't want you to hate the child.

"Oh, how I wished the child wasn't within me. Then I realized the child was part mine, and I could never do anything to hurt him. So I felt the simplest thing to do was leave." She got up and stared blankly out of the porthole. "I left with Annie and Derek and went back to Briercliff.

"I—I also couldn't bear the thought of you offering to marry me out of pity," she continued before he could comment.

"I have a beautiful little boy who looks a lot like me. Sometimes I think he looks like you, too." Elizabeth turned back to Jonathan, "You know, Dawson could have just as easily been our child. That's why I named him Dawson. After your father."

"How do you know he isn't my child?" Jonathan asked.

"I can't honestly answer that question," Elizabeth said. "Accepting the shame of being raped has not been easy. It was my fault that I wandered too far from Four Oaks. It was my fault that I was so weak that Lee overpowered me. I have no way of ever proving that Dawson is yours. I have protected him from everyone because I didn't want the word 'bastard' associated with his name. So mainly I've stayed at Briercliff. And if someone asks, I'd tell them I was married for a brief time and my husband died." She admitted the truth graciously and hopefully. "I am truly sorry, Jonathan," she said with light bitterness.

Jonathan said nothing as he watched her. He drew in several deep breaths to regain control. He felt as if someone had just delivered several heavy blows to his abdomen.

"Elizabeth, I couldn't possibly hate your child, but I can't honestly say what I would have done if you had told me," he admitted. "I don't think any man can predict what he'll do until he is faced with the situation. However, you did not give me the chance to find out," he said, turning her to face him. "I don't like the fact that another man has touched you. No! Hurt you."

"I know I'm unworthy of your love, Jonathan," Elizabeth said in a dull and troubled voice. "But it doesn't change the way I feel about you." Her voice choked, and she had to wait a moment before going on. She looked down at her hands. "I have loved you forever. I've just made some stupid mistakes and now I'm paying for them."

"Elizabeth!" Jonathan cut her off. He hated to see what she was doing to herself. He waited for her to look at him. "Over the last several years, I've tried my best to forget you. Didn't care if I lived or died in the process," he said, his gaze never leaving her face. "But no matter how far away I went, it never seemed to be far enough. You were there in my thoughts and my dreams no matter how much I wished you away." He smiled, realizing he couldn't deny the evidence any longer. "God knows, I've made my own share of mistakes." He raised his hands in a helpless gesture. "Who am I to condemn you? There is one thing I have found out, and I guess I learned it the hard way like you did."

Elizabeth's eyes brimmed with tears. "What is that?"

"That you cannot run away from love. Love finds you, no matter where you are or what you are doing. It's the most powerful emotion a person can experience. And, Elizabeth, I do love you."

Tears slipped freely down Elizabeth's cheeks.

"Jonathan, you don't have to be kind. I don't want you pitying me."

Jonathan drew her to the bed and gestured for her to sit. He sat on the bed beside her, putting his arm around her. "I love you, Elizabeth. No matter how stubborn and difficult you can be. And I'm through trying to ignore these feelings." He tilted her chin up so he could look at her beautiful face. With his thumb he wiped the tears from beneath her eyes.

"Please make me forget," Elizabeth pleaded. "Just for a little while, Jonathan. Please make me forget."

Jonathan didn't hesitate. With his heart hammering foolishly in his chest, he grabbed for the chance to make Elizabeth his, and, he hoped, to erase all the old wounds.

His mouth felt like a warm, silken heat against her as his lips began to work their magic, promising fulfillment, something she desperately needed. Elizabeth's pulse leapt with excitement as a delightful shiver of desire ran through her.

As her hand roamed across his back, she felt his hard muscles beneath her probing fingers, but it wasn't enough. She wanted to feel the warmth of his skin next to hers.

With trembling hands, she began to undo the buttons on his shirt until she could push it open. She pulled away from his mouth and began to trail warm kisses across his chest.

"Jesus," Jonathan whispered, and held her away from him. "You know the way to drive me mad," he said with a smile. "Turn around so I can unhook your gown. I need to feel your soft skin as well."

The smoldering flame in his eyes made Elizabeth tingle, and she obeyed. With expert fingers Jonathan unlatched each hook. When he finished the last, he let her bodice fall to her waist, but instead of turning her around he pulled her back next to his chest. His hands came around to cup her breasts as he nuzzled her neck. His breath was warm on her neck.

"You feel so good, sweetheart," he whispered, his breath hot against her ear as he fondled her breasts through the thin fabric of her chemise. Needing to feel her flesh, soft and warm, he tore open her chemise, his hands reclaiming her soft mounds. He looked down over her shoulder at the tempting nipples that had hardened to tight little peaks. She was blessed with the body of a goddess, and he was blessed to possess it. Rubbing her tight nipples between his fingers, he heard her soft moans of pleasure. Her breasts surged at the intimacy of his touch.

Elizabeth gasped as the delightful sensations ran rampant through her body. The mere caress of his hand sent warm shudders through her. She looked down and watched Jonathan's fingers playing with her nipples, producing a heat that spread over her with such swiftness that she felt dizzy.

Suddenly, he spun her around to face him. He lowered his head and began to tease her breasts with his lips and tongue, circling each nipple over and over as his hand slid lower until it settled between her legs. He began to rub with just the right pressure.

Her breathing became shallow as his tongue caressed her nipples. He kissed her again and again, as he drove her crazy with his fingers. The gentle massage sent currents of desire through her. She finally tore her mouth away. "W–will you stay with me tonight?"

"I'll stay," Jonathan said. He released her and removed the rest of his clothing, and watched as Elizabeth removed what was left of her chemise and her stockings, revealing her long legs.

When she'd finishing undressing, she came back to him. She wrapped her arms around his waist. Her warm skin melted into his. The junction of her legs caressed and teased his manhood. His hand moved gently down the length of her back.

"I'll stay with you forever," he whispered, his tongue tracing the outside of her ear. He felt her shiver as he plunged his tongue into her ear. The minute he did, she collapsed against him in total abandonment. He swept her up in his arms and carried her over to the small bunk and lay beside her in the tiny, cramped space.

When his body covered hers, Elizabeth felt the throbbing heat of his swollen manhood, and she looked up into his eyes. Something was very different, she realized. Finally, all the barriers between them had come down, and she actually could see love in Jonathan's eyes . . . mixed with lust, but it was there . . . strong and sure.

"I love you," she whispered with all the love she felt in her heart.

His mouth took hers with a fierce tenderness. There was a dream-like intimacy to their kisses now. Wrapping her arms around his neck, she matched his ardor.

Placing his hands on her hips, Jonathan positioned himself between her parted thighs. Instead of entering her as she expected, he just rubbed his member against her soft, wet petals, producing a raging heat within her. With a moan of excitement, she arched against him as he continued to tease her. He finally believed he'd shattered the shell she'd built around herself. His whole being was filled with desire for this one woman.

"Does it feel good, love?"

"Yes," she gasped in a throaty whisper.

He positioned his manhood and eased into her with such deliberate slowness that it drove her crazy. She'd never felt like this before and she needed to feel him deep within her. Now!

Jonathan felt the beads of moisture as they seemed to pop out, one by one, all over his body. Wanting to give Elizabeth as much pleasure as he could, he held onto his slender thread of control. He realized now that she'd suffered as much as he had over the last years, if not more. He had to make her forget all that had happened. He had to make her his!

The friction was so exquisite as he moved within her that his blood felt as if it were boiling. When he could wait no longer, he drove deep within her, feeling her wet warmth around him.

She wrapped her arms tightly around him and wrapped her legs around his waist, arching her hips upward.

He moved slowly at first, building his rhythm until they were moving as one. His strokes were powerful. He heard Elizabeth gasp with pleasure; then he followed her with a groan as he found his release, sending them both into sweet oblivion.

When he finally rolled to the side, he wrapped his arms around her, cradling her against him. "Elizabeth," he whispered as his mouth rested against the top of her head.

"Mm."

"If I go to sleep, will you be here in the morning?"

He felt her smile against his chest. "Where would I go?" Then, after another moment, she said, "I'll be here."

Chapter Twenty-one

Something was wrong.

Elizabeth couldn't say what had awakened her, but as she slowly opened her eyes she realized it should be daylight outside instead of dark and gray. And the ship seemed to be rocking violently. One glance through the porthole confirmed her worst fears. They were in the middle of a violent storm.

She lifted her head from Jonathan's chest and shook him. "Jonathan, wake up."

He slowly opened his eyes, then smiled at her. "You're actually here. I thought I'd dreamed I was making love with you."

This wasn't the time for sweet words, Elizabeth thought. "Of course I'm here, but look outside. Something is very wrong."

With the haze finally receding from his mind, Jonathan sat up in bed and looked to where Elizabeth had pointed. The moment he did, he noticed the ship's rocking, and wondered why he hadn't felt it before. He threw back the covers and sprang from the bunk. He couldn't believe that he'd slept so soundly. Normally, the least sound woke him.

He snatched up his breeches and dressed quickly. "I think we have sailed directly into a storm. I'm going topside to lend a hand," he told her as he finished buttoning his shirt.

"Wait for me," Elizabeth called as she scrambled from the bed, wrapping a sheet around her unclothed body.

He stopped at the door. "No. You could be washed overboard."

"But you just said they need everyone. I want to help."

"No," he said again, shaking his head. "Storms can be very unpredictable, and you are not a trained seaman. You will be in the way. I can't do my job and keep an eye on you, too."

Elizabeth bristled like an angry kitten. She did look quite adorable wrapped in a sheet, Jonathan couldn't help thinking. "I'll have you know I'm very capable of taking care of myself."

"But not on a rolling ship." Jonathan could see she was going to be stubborn. But then, what else was new? He didn't have time to stand here and argue, and he certainly didn't want to put her in any danger, either. "Let me see what's going on up top. If there is something you can do, I will come back and let you know." When he saw the doubtful look on her face, he paused. "I promise." Going back over to her, he gave her a brief kiss. "Goodbye," he said, and reached for the door handle. Again, he turned back. "You should put some clothes on if you plan to be of any help."

Elizabeth frowned but said nothing further as she watched the door close behind Jonathan. She felt utterly helpless and absolutely no closer to finding her son.

Not knowing what else to do, she knelt down and prayed that Lee wouldn't hurt Dawson. She was thankful that at least Dawson had Tiffany with him. Perhaps he wouldn't be so frightened. But everytime Elizabeth thought of her child crying out for her, and she wasn't there, her heart broke.

She dashed the tears from her eyes, then dressed in a plain gown; she didn't need a lot of frills on a ship.

Suddenly, the ship swayed and Elizabeth stumbled and found herself on the floor. She gasped at the unexpected noise and movement as books tumbled from the shelf, barely missing her head. She'd thought she'd developed sea legs. Evidently, that didn't apply to storms. Carefully, she pushed herself up, using the bunk, and looked around the room. At least she could make herself useful by securing all the loose articles that were bound to hit the floor in these rough seas.

When Jonathan reached the deck, he could tell that the storm was in the early stages because the deck appeared unharmed. There was no loose equipment scattered about, nor did the shrouds seem torn. The brisk winds would grow stronger as the storm's wrath bored down upon them, but for now the winds were mild compared to what would come.

Jonathan had been in two such storms when he'd sailed with Jean, and he remembered thinking that those were quite terrible, but somehow this one seemed yet rougher.

Men hurried all around him, climbing the riggings to retrim the sails. Others were stowing things away and battening down the hatches. Jonathan glanced up and saw Abe, one of the crew, trying to climb down from the crow's nest. He'd just come over the side when a large wave surged over the ship.

Jonathan wrapped his arms around a pole and clung to it until the ship had righted itself. When he looked back at the crow's nest, Abe wasn't there.

Apparently, Jonathan was the only one who had seen what had happened. He had to do something. He tried to run to the other side, but the wind kept pushing him back. Finally he made it to the starboard side where he caught a glimpse of Abe bobbing like a cork and struggling against the waves as the sea crashed around him. Jonathan knew he didn't have much time. The sea could sweep Abe away with the next large wave.

Grabbing a rope, Jonathan tied himself off, then leaned overboard. "Watch for the rope, Abe," Jonathan shouted as he tossed the coil of rope toward the man. It missed.

"Hurry! I'm drowning, mate," Abe yelled in a strained voice. "I can't keep up against this sea."

Quickly pulling the rope back in, Jonathan twirled it over his head, hoping to get more distance with this throw. With the rope being wet and heavy and the wind whipping it about, it would be very difficult to make his aim good. "Here it comes again," Jonathan yelled over the wailing wind. "Grab the rope and wrap it around yourself." He reared back and slung the rope again. This time, Abe managed to catch the line and hang on for dear life.

Jonathan braced himself against the rail for leverage and tugged with all his might. It seemed like forever before he finally got Abe to the side of the ship. Abe managed to climb back up and Jonathan heaved him up and over the rail.

Abe lay on the deck, gasping for breath. After catching his wind, he looked up at Jonathan and muttered his thanks. "Much obliged, mate. I owe you."

Jonathan offered his arm and hoisted Abe to his feet. "Better keep yourself tied off. Don't want to fish you out again."

Jonathan pitched in, helping the crews to secure anything that would wash overboard when the seas became higher and rougher. The task was difficult; with the ship lurching and bucking, each step had to be made carefully. Ropes were strung across the deck to provide hand holds for those who had to be on deck. The ropes could mean the difference between life and death. Being washed overboard and swallowed by the raging sea was more than a vague possibility. Abe had proven that. And most of the time no one would be there to see it happen and throw a rope. Abe had been lucky.

The winds grew stronger with each passing hour. Before Jonathan knew it, night had fallen again. He made his way to the helm, where he found Jean and Dominic. A flickering lantern by the wheel struggled against the relentless wind, providing the only glow in the darkness. The only other light was the constant flash of lightning. A gust of wind tore at Jonathan and nearly threw him to the deck.

"Will we hold together?" Jonathan shouted above the wind.

Jean glanced up and grinned. "But of course, my friend. The *Ciel Bleu* has withstood storms much worse than this one. Seeing as this is your first *real* storm, I can see why you are concerned. The other storms we experienced will seem like a mere puff of wind compared to this one," Jean shouted above the wind. "We will keep a single sprit sail forward to keep her heels to the wind, and she'll ride the storm as a whore would a man." Jean chuckled.

Just then, a gigantic wave crashed over the bow, soaking the men and sending Jonathan sliding down the deck. He grabbed for anything to stop him and, luckily, latched onto a net, which stopped him from sliding overboard. Scrambling back to his feet, he looked at Jean and Dominic, who still stood, grinning at him. He felt like a fool, which only made Jonathan angry. He shook off some of the water and shoved his hair out of his face.

"One thing, my friend. You must lash some rope around you unless you want to sleep with the fishes," Jean reminded him, then laughed with Dominic.

"And I thought I had taught you much," Dominic said, shaking his head. "There is landlubber in you still."

"I'm glad to be of amusement to you both," Jonathan said sarcastically. He tempered his anger and asked, "How much longer do you think this will go on?"

"If we're lucky it will be over by tomorrow," Jean said, then asked, "How is Elizabeth?"

"Worried."

"Perhaps you should go down and reassure her."

"I will. I did promise to tell her what was happening up top." Jonathan turned and made his way slowly to Elizabeth's cabin door. He knocked, pounding hard to be heard above the wind.

Elizabeth opened the door. "Jonathan, you're soaked," she cried, opening the door wider and drawing him inside. "Let me find you something dry to put on."

"No," he protested, knowing he would only get wet again. He did take the towel she offered and wiped some of the water off his face and arms. "It will have to wait. They need everyone up top. I just wanted to let you know I hadn't forgotten you."

"I'll be fine. Isn't there something I can do?" Elizabeth asked as she took the soaked towel from him. "Are we going to make it?"

"Jean assured me we wouldn't sink. So we must have faith in our captain. However, a little prayer wouldn't hurt," Jonathan added with a smile. "I'd better get back up top. You stay below. That's the best way you can help me."

"But I want to do something. I feel so useless shut up in this tiny cabin." The set of her chin showed she was ready to argue.

"This is not the time to be stubborn. Stay below," Jonathan ordered. "You will be of no use on the deck. I've already had to fish one man out of the ocean." He turned and reached for the door.

"Jonathan."

He sighed impatiently, then turned back.

"Be careful," Elizabeth said and was rewarded with a tight smile. Then he left.

The night wore on; the seas grew angrier and the waves surged higher as the crew worked. The *Ciel Bleu* rode the waves strong and sturdy. Finally, toward morning, the gales began to subside.

The next morning, Elizabeth awoke to find herself on the floor. She'd tumbled from the bunk so many times during the night that she'd finally remained on the floor the last time and gotten a few hours of sleep. When she finally sat up, she realized the ship was steady.

She tossed off the blanket she'd wrapped around herself and hurried topside. The deck was a disaster. Crates were scattered everywhere and seaweed dripped from the riggings. Men lay sprawled on the deck, completely exhausted, except the three who stood at the helm.

She carefully made her way over to them, stepping around the sleeping bodies. "How are we doing?"

Jean laughed. "We are much better than we look. You must have been praying for a miracle, because we're barely off course. Look, I want to show you something." Jean took Elizabeth's arm and steered her toward the railing. "See the horizon?"

She nodded.

"There is a little white spot."

"Where?"

"There." Jean turned her head toward the exact point.

"What is it?"

"Ah, *chérie*, if we are lucky, it is the sails of Lee's ship. We will have him by the end of the day."

Elizabeth grasped the rail. "My son. How are we going to get him?"

Jean looked around at the men on the floor. "I hope my men will have their energy back by then. When they do, we'll devise a plan."

Elizabeth looked around. "What happened to Derek's ship?"

Jonathan came over. "He is probably off course, but he'll find us."

The day dragged by for Elizabeth.

Finally they went to the captain's cabin where Jean and Jonathan began to discuss their options. "I say we overtake them and fire a volley of cannon shots," Jean said.

"No!" Elizabeth screamed. "My son's on that ship."

"Easy." Jonathan squeezed her shoulder. "It will be a warning shot only."

"But Lee wants money. He'll never surrender," Elizabeth argued.

"This will be a warning shot to stop. It will sail over the bow. However, you are correct," Jean admitted. "Lee will not give up without a fight. We must devise a plan that will work and not put the child in danger." He wasn't sure how to handle the situation. He'd never had to consider hostages before.

"Well, my friend, do you have any suggestions?" Jean looked at Jonathan. "Normally, we would blow a hole in the ship or perhaps cripple the main mast. However, I have no guarantee that the child would not be harmed."

Jonathan rubbed the back of his neck. His body ached so much from fatigue that he could barely think. "Do we have the ransom aboard that Lee requested?"

"Oui. I always carry gold," Jean said with a touch of irony in his voice. "Just in case of such emergencies." He thought for a moment. "Well, we can make the exchange . . . but if we do, what guarantee will we have that he'll let the child and Tiffany go?"

Jonathan nodded as he, too, pondered the situation.

"And Lee is not stupid, my friend. Therefore, he's bound to have made an additional plan," Jean surmised, then looked sharply at Jonathan. "But what is it?"

"There is only one way to find out what Lee will do." Jonathan sighed with exasperation. "We'll have to call his hand. Let's send a small boat over under the flag of truce and see what Lee has to say."

Elizabeth had been sitting on the bunk as Jean and Jonathan tried to form a plan. However, they kept lowering their voices so she'd only heard bits and pieces of their conversation and was confused about their intent. So she got up and went to the table to find out exactly what was going on.

"Remember, Lee wanted to make the exchange

in New Orleans," Jean pointed out. "Perhaps we should wait."

Elizabeth frowned. "No. You must get Dawson and Tiffany. Dawson could be ill. I'm sure the storm must have frightened him."

With a nod of their heads they agreed with her.

"I guess the time has come then," Jonathan said and motioned toward the cabin door.

Once they were on deck, Jonathan glanced over the railing to see that the boat had already been lowered. He looked at Elizabeth. "I shall see you shortly."

"Please be careful," Elizabeth said.

Jonathan winked at her before climbing overboard. "No harm will come to your child if I have anything to say about it," he said as he gripped the ladder and started down to the small boat.

Carrying a white flag, Jonathan and his small band of men rowed over to *The Rose*, where a rope ladder was lowered for them.

Jonathan looked up top as he placed his foot on the first step. There were many pistols aimed at them, but why should he be surprised at that?

"Come, Dominic, we have a group above who look real happy to see us," Jonathan said wryly and grabbed the ladder.

A first lieutenant, surrounded by several men with pistols, met them at the top.

"We are here to see Captain Lee," Jonathan stated firmly.

The tall, thin man smiled mockingly at them. "Lee isn't aboard this vessel. Figuring you'd catch the brig, he sailed on the *Midnight Rose*. However, he did leave a message for you. He said he'd make the exchange at the Bay of Pirates instead of New Orleans. He judged that would be safer than a busy harbor. And if you try any tricks, the boy will die."

Jonathan tightened his jaw and took a threatening step toward the lieutenant, but Dominic grabbed his arms as several pistols cocked. "If Lee dares to harm that child or the woman, none of you will live to see another day," Jonathan warned. Then he turned abruptly and descended the rope ladder, no longer concerned that these men would harm him.

He and Dominic rowed back to the *Ciel Bleu*, and Jonathan could see Elizabeth standing anxiously by the rail. He dreaded having to tell her that Dawson wasn't on the ship.

"Where is my son?" Elizabeth demanded the moment they were up top.

"He's not on the ship."

Elizabeth sagged and grabbed the front of Jonathan's shirt. "Where is he? He hasn't been harmed?"

Jonathan gently took Elizabeth's hands. "I know you're upset, but as far as I know the boy is safe. Let's go to Jean's cabin and talk."

Reluctantly, Elizabeth let Jonathan guide her back to the cabin as Jean led the way.

Once inside, Jean said, "So it's as we thought. Lee is playing games."

Elizabeth whirled on Jonathan. "Where is my son?"

"I don't know, Elizabeth," Jonathan said, trying to be gentle. "I know it's difficult, but we must remain calm and think clearly. I'm sure Dawson is safe because he's Lee's ticket to the ransom."

Jonathan glanced at Jean. "It seems Lee sailed on a much faster ship, and he awaits us at the Bay of Pirates. I presume you know of this place?"

A slow smile swept across Jean's face. "This is good," he replied wryly, nodding. "Of course I know of this place."

"Why is this good?" Elizabeth asked.

"It is my island, so to speak. After all, I know the place like the back of my own hand. Therefore, it will be easier to form a plan. Why Lee has chosen the island, I can only speculate. More than likely it's because it is isolated so no one can see what he does. Remember, he is not a pirate and cares what others think of him. If he'd docked at New Orleans and your friend had started screaming, the authorities would have swarmed his vessel. Also, the British are after him and they would look at the New Orleans port first.

"However, his stupid move is good for us." Jean rubbed his chin as he thought. "I think once we give Lee the treasure chest, he'll not let Dawson go. He will try to escape, but if he is not able to do so, he will make another deal to assure we let him sail away."

Elizabeth bit her bottom lip as she listened. "So what do we do now?"

"We'll sail to the back side of the island. Lee will never see us approach. There, we will let off a group of men who can go over land and secretly board Lee's ship. In the meantime, we'll sail around to the front side and confront Lee.

"While we are going through the motions of bringing the chest to Lee's ship, my men will have slipped aboard and have Dawson and your friend secure."

"Sounds like a good plan," Jonathan said. "I don't see any other way. And we don't want Lee to escape just to reappear again."

Jean turned to Elizabeth. "What do you think, Elizabeth?"

"It does sound like the only way," Elizabeth agreed reluctantly. "Lee is so evil he might even kill Dawson if he doesn't think we are doing his bidding." She said the words tentatively, then went on. "We mustn't take any chances that he might harm Dawson or Tiffany." She drew a deep breath. "We must try it your way. Let's do it."

Chapter Twenty-two

When Elizabeth caught her first glimpse of the Bay of Pirates, she couldn't believe how beautiful the island appeared—a lush green forest floating in a turquoise blue sea.

Jean had told her a little about the island. Instead of sand, millions of tiny shells coated the beach that stretched for ten miles around the island. The first rays of the sun made the tiny shells sparkle.

Surrounded by coral reefs, the coast was flat with an elevated interior and steep cliffs covered by tropical green foliage. Elizabeth could hear the birds chattering in the trees, a sound she hadn't heard in several weeks. A warm, gentle breeze blew her hair and caressed her face. As she gazed at the island, she thought it could only be described as paradise, but the circumstances that had brought them here made it just another barrier between her and her son. She wondered how many more hurdles she'd have to face.

They sailed around the back side of the island, just as Jean had planned, then dropped anchor. Elizabeth watched as a crew prepared a small boat for a raiding party to go ashore. They were busy so no one noticed when she turned away. She needed to hurry. She'd seen all she needed to see. It was time for action.

By the time Jonathan, Dominic, and three other men were ready to cast off from the *Ciel Bleu,* it was mid-morning. They would row to shore, then scale the cliffs. When night came, they would sneak aboard Lee's ship.

What Jonathan didn't realize was that one of the men in his party was really a woman. Elizabeth had done a good job of disguising herself, thanks to Dominic's help. Dressed in black breeches, a big white shirt, and a red sash around her waist, she could pass for one of Jean's men.

Since Elizabeth was tall, her height didn't give her away. She had tucked her long hair up under a cap and pulled the brim down so it hid most of her face. Carefully, she remained to the rear of the crew and away from Jonathan. The last thing she wanted was for him to send her back. She was going to get her son one way or the other. She couldn't just sit on a ship and worry.

Derek's ship had arrived shortly after Jean's and had already laid anchor. Derek would remain where he was, and when Jean felt that Jonathan had had enough time to reach Lee's ship, Jean would sail around and confront Lee. Jean had said they would probably wait until the next morning before coming around the island.

Elizabeth observed the two ships as she sat in the longboat headed toward shore. Jean's plan would work! It had to.

The longboat bumped the shore, and Elizabeth scrambled out of the tiny vessel along with the other men, helping as they pulled the boat further up onto the beach. She could hear the pop and crunch of the tiny shells as they walked toward the interior of the island.

Dominic pointed to an overgrown path, which went straight up the cliff and would make their climb a little easier. He led the way, since he knew the island better than anyone except Jean. Jonathan and the other men followed. Elizabeth brought up the rear, the further away from Jonathan the better.

At first the climb was easy, but as they approached the top, they had to go around huge rocks and scramble over narrow ledges. After several hours of climbing, Elizabeth paused and wondered how much further they had to go. She rubbed her fingers—sore from grasping the rocks and trees—on her breeches. She only had one more ledge to climb over, and she'd be at the top.

With her next step, the rocks below her feet gave away. She squealed and flailed her arms, desperately grabbing at anything to keep from falling. She grabbed a tree root that stopped her from going over the edge. She dangled precariously from the root.

"What the hell?" Jonathan turned at the sound.

Something wasn't right. One of his men had slipped. How had this happened? He had to go back down for him.

There was no time for questions. He had to do something fast. Jonathan looped a rope around himself and anchored it to a tree. When he was secure, he leaned down to grab the lad's arm. "Grasp my hand with your free hand," he shouted. The boy grabbed his hand. At least the lad was small. When Jonathan had a firm hold on the lad's arm, he hauled him up until he was secure in his arms.

"Obliged," Elizabeth mumbled, trying to disguise her voice.

"Wait a minute." The lad was much too soft, and he seemed to have curves where he shouldn't. Jonathan jerked off the boy's cap. "I can't believe I didn't notice," he ground out. "What in the bloody hell are you doing here? We are going to have our hands full enough without you slowing us down." He handed her cap back to her. "Don't you ever obey?"

Elizabeth's nerves were stretched to the limit. "I don't take orders well. You should know that by now," she retorted. "I will not wait alone while my son's life is in the balance."

Jonathan untied the rope from around the tree and started to coil it back up. "You bloody well will! Now turn around and climb back down!"

"I will not," she said, defiantly, shoving the cap back on. "I'm going with you whether you like it or not." She grabbed his arm. "You can't spare a man to accompany me, and I promise I will not go back on my own. So you have no choice but to let me come."

Jonathan swung around, clearly angry. "Give me one good reason why I should."

"Because my son is involved, and he doesn't know any of you. What if you go to rescue him, and he runs the other way because he's just as frightened of you as he is of Lee."

Jonathan remained quiet.

"I thought she made a good point," Dominic pointed out from behind Jonathan. "That is why I helped her."

Jonathan glared at Dominic, then turned back to Elizabeth. "Come on. We're wasting time."

Elizabeth wanted to smile, but she didn't allow herself the luxury as she followed the men up the incline. The hill was flat on top and blessed with a freshwater lake. They stopped and rested and drank from the cool, clear water.

But any delay, no matter how short, was too long for Elizabeth. She couldn't sit still. She got up from the pool and went to the far side of the clearing to look over the edge. Thank goodness they were not going in this direction, she thought. The cliff was sheer and about halfway down a beautiful waterfall spurted into a pool below. Several gorgeous birds flew around the trees, adding to the beauty.

"Let's go," Dominic called, bringing her back to the mission at hand.

They started down the other side as the sun was lowering in the sky. Soon it would be dark and they couldn't climb down the mountain without light.

Going down was a little easier than going up, but they had to climb through undergrowth that tore at their skin. By the time they reached the bottom, not only was it dusk, but they all looked as if they had fought with a very large cat.

"We'll rest until midnight," Jonathan said, looking around for Elizabeth. He went to her. "Promise me that you'll listen once we are onboard Lee's ship, and that you will obey me. This isn't a game. Our lives could depend on acting very quickly."

"Sometimes you treat me like a child, Jonathan. I already know everything you just told me. I want to get Dawson off that ship, and make sure he doesn't run into the line of fire." She shivered at the thought.

"I don't treat you like a child, although sometimes you act like one. I'm trying to protect you, as you're trying to protect your child," he said as he rose.

Elizabeth looked up at him as he offered his hand to pull her to her feet. "Thank you," she said and kissed him on the cheek.

Jonathan smiled. "I hope you will do better than that when this whole thing is over."

For once in her life, Elizabeth couldn't think of anything to say. At the moment, she couldn't imagine a normal life.

It was just after midnight when Jonathan issued the command to go. They swam to Lee's ship, which was docked in the bay. The water was warm but the salt stung their cuts and scratches.

If everything worked out, Jean should be sailing around the island and be in the harbor by daybreak.

Dominic climbed up the anchor rope and made his way to the rope ladder, which he tossed overboard. Elizabeth heard a muffled scuffling sound and she held her breath until Dominic leaned over the side and motioned for them to come aboard.

Obviously, Lee wasn't expecting trouble. Only one guard had been posted and Dominic had taken care of him in short order.

The crew spread out and quietly began to search.

Elizabeth didn't bother to open the first door, knowing it would be the captain's cabin. She hoped that Jonathan wouldn't, either, because the sight of Lee would probably send him into a rage. She wanted to get Dawson and Tiffany off the ship with as little trouble as possible.

She eased the second door open and very carefully looked inside. There, lying on the bunk, were Tiffany and Dawson. Dawson was curled up next to Tiffany. Elizabeth's heart swelled with love and gratitude as she moved further into the room.

Tiffany gasped when Elizabeth touched her arm, and Elizabeth placed a finger to her lips. Too late, Dawson opened his eyes and said, "Mummy!" He rubbed his eyes, and when he realized it wasn't a dream he scrambled from under the covers and threw his arms around her neck.

"Shh," Elizabeth warned, hugging her child so tight he squealed. "We must be very quiet so we can get you off this ship," she whispered into his tousled hair.

Tiffany sat up. "Thank God you're here," she whispered. "I was beginning to feel we'd never get off the boat . . . or home again."

Elizabeth propped Dawson on her hip and

looked at Tiffany, trying to take in her appearance. "They didn't hurt you, did they?"

"No, but they have kept us locked up most of the time. They only unlocked the door when we dropped anchor here. Wherever here is."

Jonathan stepped quietly into the room. "We must hurry. The sun is just touching the horizon. Everyone will be waking up shortly. Come, Tiffany." Jonathan held out his hand.

"Who's that?" Dawson said, pointing at Jonathan.

"Shh. It's a friend. I'll introduce you later," Elizabeth whispered. "We must be quiet so we can get away and go home."

Dominic and the other men were preparing to lower a boat when Elizabeth and her group joined them at the rail. There were three dead men on the deck that Elizabeth tried not to notice; she covered Dawson's eyes so he couldn't see them.

Tiffany bit her lip to keep from crying out.

"Tiffany, you go first," Jonathan said, his tone brooking no argument.

"Help me get over the rail," Tiffany said, and Jonathan did that. When she had her footing, he let her go.

Two of Jean's men were already in the boat. They kept the craft steady as Tiffany slowly climbed down the ladder and settled herself.

Jonathan took Dawson from Elizabeth. "Are you a big boy?" Jonathan asked.

Dawson nodded.

"Good." Jonathan positioned Dawson in front of him. "I want you to wrap your arms around my neck and your feet around my waist and hang on very tight as I climb down the ladder. "Can you do that?"

Dawson nodded.

"Go ahead, Elizabeth," Jonathan told her urgently.

"No, I'll wait for you to go with Dawson first, and then I'll follow."

Jonathan knew he didn't have time to argue so he went over the rail and got into the boat safely.

"We have company," Dominic told Elizabeth.

She swung around to see Lee and his men advancing.

"Quick, Elizabeth!" Dominic held out a hand to her.

"No! Get Dawson to safety," Elizabeth said and ran to the bow as Dominic dove overboard.

"Get out of here!" Dominic called, pushing the small boat away from the ship.

"Not without Elizabeth," Jonathan said. He handed Dawson to Tiffany and dove into the water. "Get them to safety," he ordered Dominic. "I'll try to help Elizabeth." Jonathan scrambled out of the boat as shots rang out. Jonathan turned to see that Lee's men had discovered them. He shoved the boat and dove under the water, hoping they would make it safely to shore.

"No!" Elizabeth ran toward them, taking several of the men to the deck with her. She felt herself being pulled back up by her hair. Pain shot through her scalp and tears stung her eyes as Lee twisted his hand in her long hair.

"So we meet again, my pretty," he snarled. He leaned over her ear and whispered, his breath hot, "Maybe we can have a little fun, like before. You do remember before, don't you?"

Elizabeth's blood ran cold, but she realized that Lee had hurt her all he could. She managed to glance out at the small boat and saw that it had made it safely to the beach. Her son was safe, and so was Jonathan. She didn't care what Lee did.

"You're a pig!" she cried and spat. Lee rewarded her with a slap to the side of her face. Her head reeled, and she had to blink several times before she could see straight. Her cheek felt numb from the blow.

"Tie the bitch," Lee snarled, shoving her toward one of his men.

The whine of a cannonball pierced the air as it sailed over the bow of the ship. Everyone dropped to the deck. At the last moment, someone pulled Elizabeth down.

"Lafitte," Lee muttered under his breath. "We have company, men. Prepare to return their fire," Lee commanded.

Elizabeth was jerked to her feet, and the first mate tied her hands. She felt strangely calm, in spite of the apparent danger. She saw Jean's ship flying the *Jolly Roger* and knew that Dawson would be safe. Jean probably believed that everyone was off Lee's ship, and he was prepared to finish the enemy off. And as long as Dawson and Jonathan were safe, Elizabeth didn't care what happened to her.

Elizabeth could see the *Ciel Bleu* had turned broadside as Lee's men tied her to the main mast by a long rope. The rope was coarse against her skin—they had tied her so tight her hands felt numb. Before the first mate was finished, shots were fired from the *Ciel Bleu*. One cannonball struck with full force, shaking the whole ship and knocking Elizabeth to the deck. She gasped for air, having had the wind knocked out of her. When she could finally gulp a breath of air, she managed to get to her feet. She saw that many men had been killed or badly wounded. Blood poured freely over the littered wooden deck.

She looked to see Jean's ship drawing closer. There would be no more cannons because the pirates would board the vessel and resort to hand-to-hand combat. She prayed the pirates were successful. It was her only hope.

"Evidently, Lafitte doesn't care if you live or die," Lee muttered from behind her.

Elizabeth whirled around to see him, livid with rage.

"So why should I?" he snarled, and raised his cutlass.

Elizabeth realized that her luck had finally run out.

Everytime Jonathan neared the top of the ladder, Lafitte would fire another volley and send him back into the water. He wanted to curse his friend, but he realized why Jean was firing. Obviously, he had seen Dominic and Tiffany and thought all was well.

If Jonathan lived to see Jean again, he'd damn well punch him in the nose for this, Jonathan swore to himself as he started up the ladder once again.

His hands were sore and raw from handling the wet rope, but it didn't stop him from inching his way up the ladder. Elizabeth's life depended on him getting to her before Lee did.

Finally, he made it to the top and his heart froze.

Lee had reared back, broadsword in hand, preparing to strike Elizabeth.

Jonathan tumbled to the deck and shouted, "Stop!"

Lee spun around to see who had dared to stop him. Then he smiled. "Good. I can kill you both before that blasted pirate gets here."

Lee advanced on Jonathan, who scrambled to his feet and grabbed a cutlass that lay near a lifeless body, prepared to do battle. Lee swung and Jonathan was quick on his feet, eluding the heavy blade. The rest of Lee's men were preparing to fight with the pirates.

Jonathan lunged, piercing Lee in the side before quickly drawing back his weapon.

Lee looked down, an expression of disgust on his face, but the wound didn't seem to slow him down as he fought with more vengeance, swinging his broadsword with powerful blows. Finally, the broadsword caught Jonathan's cutlass and snapped it like a twig.

Elizabeth looked frantically around for a way to help. She saw a pistol lying near one of the dead sailors. The pistol had been cocked but not fired. She stretched, reaching toward it, but missed grabbing it the first time. She tried again and this time she managed to grasp the barrel of the gun.

Lee's arms swung over his head, ready to split Jonathan's skull with his broadsword as Elizabeth fired the pistol. The bullet tore into Lee's leg.

"Bloody hell," Lee swore and grabbed at his limb, but still didn't stop attacking Jonathan. Again, he picked up his sword, but in the meanwhile Jonathan had managed to get away and find another sword.

One of Lee's men came up behind Jonathan. "Watch out," Elizabeth screamed. Lee's first mate, roused now from the shock of the cannon blow, struck her across the mouth, splitting her lip. She winced at the pain and felt her lip swelling.

When Lafitte's men couldn't get much closer to Lee's ship, they went overboard and swam to the other ship where they poured over the rails, boarding the vessel. Lee's men fired at the pirates but they kept coming.

As the smoke of the battle swirled around the struggling men, Lee tired of swordplay and drew his pistol. Jonathan rolled and grabbed a pistol from a dead sailor and fired at the same time as Lee did.

Lee's shot missed Jonathan, but blood spurted from another wound in Lee's shoulder. Nothing seemed to stop the man. Lee turned just as a pirate approached him from behind. Lee slashed the pirate across his midsection, sending him to the deck.

Jonathan scrambled to find another sword. Once again, the sound of metal made Elizabeth's blood run cold. The fighting was all around her now. Blood was everywhere.

Suddenly, Jean was in front of her. "You are supposed to be on the beach, *chérie*," Jean said. "Hold your hands out."

She did and, in a blink of an eye, Jean had cut away her ropes. "Watch out," she cried as a sailor lunged at Jean.

Jean swung around to catch the Englishman with

a knife to the gut. Drawing his knife back, he threw the sailor aside and looked around for the man he really wanted . . . Lee!

Jonathan had him. They were fighting with swords. As Jean watched he realized that he was a much better swordsman than Jonathan was. Besides, he was fighting with a heavy broadsword. That was not a Frenchman's weapon. But he would give his friend a chance to kill Lee first.

"Stay here, Elizabeth. I have a score to settle," Jean said.

Jean drew his sword and fought his way to where Jonathan and Lee battled. "My friend, you have had your chance to finish the deed. Now he's mine," Lafitte said.

Jonathan would have laughed if his arms were not killing him from swinging the heavy broadsword. The clanging continued, with Jonathan cutting Lee several more times, but Lee never gave in.

Lee lunged, knocking the sword from Jonathan's hand. Jonathan stepped aside and called out, "It's your turn, Jean. I've got him worn down for you."

"En garde," Jean shouted to get Lee's attention.

Lee advanced. "So, we finally meet. You don't look so grand to me." He saluted Jean with his sword.

Jean returned Lee's salute. "Our meeting has been much too long in coming," Jean said with a smile and then put his rapier to action. "I do not appreciate you wounding my niece. Or trying to steal my treasure."

Jean fought with a lighter sword, and he was much faster. He had cut three stripes in Lee's shirt, drawing more blood. "Never said I was grand. Just merely good. And you, my friend, have caused many that I love to suffer. So shall you suffer before I end your miserable life," Jean declared just as he inflicted another wound.

Lee roared, his breathing heavy as he swung his sword with all his might.

All eyes were on Lee and Jean. The Englishmen had either surrendered or were dead, and Lee was the only one remaining. Jean's men stood watching the final stage of the battle.

Jean was so quick on his feet that soon Lee's shirt was soaked with blood from the many slashes that Jean had inflicted.

With a final effort, Lee swung his sword and caught the railing of the ship; the sword bounced from his hand, clattering across the deck. Grabbing a pistol, Lee turned to fire, but not on Jean. . . .

Lee aimed at Elizabeth and pulled the trigger.

Jean plunged his dagger into the miserable excuse of a man, then turned to find Elizabeth lying on the deck.

Chapter Twenty-three

Jonathan couldn't believe his eyes.

One minute he was watching Jean finish Lee, and the next minute, Lee had pulled a gun. Instead of aiming at Jean, Lee aimed and fired at Elizabeth.

"No!" Jonathan shouted. He jumped forward, trying to get between Elizabeth and the gun. But it was too late.

Elizabeth was covered with red, sticky blood.

He knelt down, cradled her in his arms, and glanced at the wound. It was in her shoulder and, hopefully, high enough to have missed her heart. He caressed her cheek. "Say something," he whispered, his heart in his throat.

"Mon Dieu," Jean muttered as he knelt down beside Jonathan. "I thought Lee was aiming at me," Jean said, an edge to his voice. Then Jean withdrew his knife and cut open Elizabeth's dress

over the wound. "It's nasty, but not fatal. The bullet needs to come out, though." Jean let out a long, audible breath. "My ship's doctor could look at her wound."

Jonathan remembered Henry, the ship's doctor, all too well. His intentions were good, though his methods were not. "How long will it take to get her to Four Oaks?"

"A day and a half at most."

"Then let's take her home, where she can get proper care. I don't want to take any chances," Jonathan said. He rose with Elizabeth in his arms. "Dominic and Dawson?"

Jean got up, too, and wiped the blood from his knife with a rag he found on the deck. "Dominic will have taken everyone to the *Ciel Bleu* to await us there, my friend."

Jonathan found himself inexplicably dissatisfied. He glanced over at Lee. "It's a shame that Lee can only die once."

"Aye," Jean agreed, his tongue heavy with sarcasm. "But rest assured, this time he is dead." Jean turned to a few of his men. "Dump the bodies and take a skeleton crew to sail this ship home to Barataria Bay. I'll send Dominic over."

Once on board the *Ciel Bleu,* Jonathan took Elizabeth to her room and placed her gently on the bed. He heard a soft moan, the first sound she'd made since she'd been wounded.

"Elizabeth?" Jonathan said softly as he made her comfortable.

Her eyes fluttered open. After a moment or two

she finally focused on Jonathan and said, "He shot me." She sounded as though she could not believe it.

"I know." Jonathan clenched his jaw. He sat beside her, taking her hand. "But you don't have to worry about Lee. He's dead. He can't hurt you anymore. We're taking you home to Four Oaks so we can have the bullet removed."

She hesitated, blinking with bafflement. "Dawson?" she asked, her voice dry and cracked.

"I'm getting ready to check on him as soon as I get you settled in."

"I'll be all right," Elizabeth assured him. "But I want to see Dawson and Tiffany."

"Your slightest wish is my command." Jonathan bowed and Elizabeth gave him a weak smile.

"You haven't always been so agreeable," she reminded him.

"I've just hidden my agreeable side from you," he said, reaching for the door. "Rest. We'll be home soon."

Elizabeth's eyelids drifted downward, but she forced them up. "Go," she whispered. "See to Tiffany and Dawson. I'll be fine."

Jonathan found Jean giving Dominic orders. "After you have taken Tiffany to Derek's ship, sail Lee's ship back home," Jean commanded. "I've already given the orders. The men are preparing the ship as we speak."

"Jonathan," a feminine voice called from behind him.

Jonathan spun around. He had walked past Tiffany and Dawson without even noticing them. His mind had been on Jean, and he hadn't seen them standing to the side.

"How are you, Tiffany?" Jonathan asked, more pleased to see them than he could have imagined. They looked at each other and smiled in earnest. "Did Lee hurt you?"

"I'm doing well under the circumstances, and much better since you've gotten us away from Lee," she told him. "I'll be going home soon, but I want to tell Elizabeth goodbye. Where is she? I haven't seen her."

Jonathan started to say something, but was stopped when Dawson tugged on his hand.

"What's your name?" Dawson asked as he looked up at Jonathan. His head tilted to the side in a familiar gesture.

For the first time, Jonathan really had a chance to look at the boy. He stooped down so he'd be at eye level with him. Dawson had long black hair that curled under his ears. His eyes were dark like Elizabeth's and Adam's. The child favored Elizabeth, he could see that plainly. But, Lord help him if he had his mother's stubborn streak! Lord help them all.

Elizabeth hadn't introduced him to Dawson when they were onboard Lee's ship, so Jonathan introduced himself, "My name is Jonathan," he said and straightened back up. "You look very much like your mother."

"My name is Dawson, and I'm two years old," he said in his childish voice, holding up two fingers. Then he gave Jonathan a brilliant smile. He noticed the child's dimples. Where had he seen them before? Dawson held up his arms, so Jonathan picked him up.

"You're tall," Dawson said.

"And you are very small," Jonathan replied for lack of anything else to say. He wasn't used to talking to children, but he was finding Dawson hard to resist.

"One day you'll be just as big as Jonathan," Tiffany told the child. She looked at Jonathan. "Do you know where Elizabeth is? Why isn't she up here looking for Dawson?"

"Elizabeth is down below in her cabin," Jonathan said, not wanting to frighten Tiffany with the news that her friend had been wounded. "Follow me."

Once they were in the cabin, Tiffany hurried over to Elizabeth's bed. "You're hurt!" Tiffany looked at Jonathan for an explanation.

Elizabeth reached and took Tiffany's hand, demanding her attention. "I'm so sorry I got you into this situation. Can you ever forgive me?"

Tiffany gave her an incredulous look. "Forget about me, Elizabeth. You're bleeding."

"Mummy." Dawson squirmed to get down out of Jonathan's firm grasp. He placed Dawson on the floor, and the boy ran to his mother, climbing up on the bed and lying down beside Elizabeth on the side that wasn't hurt. He hugged her with gentle, chubby hands.

She smiled at her son, then looked back at her friend. "I'll be fine, Tiffany. We are going to Four Oaks, and a doctor will care for my shoulder. Are you returning home?" she asked weakly.

Tiffany nodded.

Elizabeth had to fight the pain in her shoulder, but she knew if she let Tiffany know of her pain, her friend would stay and never get home. "I want to thank you for all you've done for Dawson." Elizabeth swallowed hard and bit back the tears. She would miss her friend when Tiffany left. "And when I return to London, I will visit you and your baby, I promise."

Tiffany's eyes filled with tears. "I don't want to leave you like this."

"Go. You have your own child to think about."

Tiffany brushed away her tears. "What about Dawson?"

"I'll take care of Dawson," Jonathan said. "He will be well cared for."

Elizabeth looked at him and smiled. She was too startled by his suggestion to offer any objections. She'd never seen Jonathan around children before, and she'd wondered how he would manage.

Jonathan realized how much Elizabeth looked like a mother with Dawson curled up next to her. It seemed so natural. Dawson didn't even realize that his mother was hurt, and that was probably for the best. It would be quite a long time before she'd be able to take care of her son.

"All right," Tiffany finally agreed. "I can see that you're in capable hands." She squeezed Elizabeth's hand and then gave Dawson a hug. "You be a good boy for your mother."

Once Tiffany had gone, Jonathan moved closer to the bed. "I'll have the ship's doctor cleanse your wound, and I will take Dawson up top with me. You must rest. Don't let the doctor do anything more. He isn't the best physician, but he's all we have. I think he was the cook before he was a doctor." Jonathan smiled.

"I'm very tired," Elizabeth said with heavy eyelids. "I appreciate your taking care of Dawson for me."

Jonathan hated leaving Elizabeth, but he knew it would be better for her, knowing that Dawson was being taken care of. He kept Dawson with him the rest of the day, and no matter what he was doing, Dawson seemed content to play at his feet.

"We've had a fair wind and made good time. If the breeze holds, we'll be in the harbor of New Orleans tomorrow morning," Jean said and glanced down at Dawson. "I believe the boy likes you."

Jonathan smiled. "He's been a good lad," he admitted, then looked down at him. "Dawson," Jonathan said.

The child looked up at with his big brown eyes so much like his mother's that Jonathan could see the trust in Dawson's gaze.

Jonathan leaned over and asked, "Would you like to steer the ship?"

Dawson nodded, his eyes wide with wonder. Jonathan took the child's hand and led him behind the big wooden wheel. He upended a bucket so Dawson could stand on his own. The boy giggled.

Together they steered the ship, and something deep inside Jonathan stirred as he placed his big hands over Dawson's small ones.

Dawson tilted his head back to see Jonathan and grinned. "This is fun."

Jonathan's heart melted.

"Looks like father and son to me," Jean commented as he walked by them.

Jonathan started to say something, but stopped. He liked the notion of having a son like Dawson. If circumstances had been different, Dawson might have been his.

When the sun finally set, they went below to check on Elizabeth. Henry, the so-called doctor, sat beside the bed. When they came in, he got up. "Ya sure ya don't want me to take this 'ere bullet out?"

"No. We'll be in New Orleans tomorrow, and then she can be in a proper hospital." Jonathan frowned at the man. "You may go."

"I think she's developed a fever," Henry said as he started for the door. "I'd keep an eye on her if I were you."

Jonathan put Dawson down, and, placing his hand on Elizabeth's forehead, looked down at her. Sure enough, she was burning with fever. He pulled back the covers and examined her wound. It was angry and red, and he'd never felt more helpless in his life. He muttered a curse.

Dawson tugged on his hand. "Shh," he whispered. "Mummy is sleeping."

Momentarily distracted from his problem, Jonathan smiled. "Speaking of sleep, I think it's time for you to go to bed, lad." He pulled open a drawer and retrieved a hammock, which he strung across the room. He eyed Dawson. "Have you ever slept in one of these?"

Dawson shook his head, his eyes huge with wonder.

Jonathan placed a pillow and blanket in the hammock. "You're going to like this," he said as he scooped the child up and placed him in the hammock "See, it's like a swinging bed."

Dawson giggled. "Will you tell me a story?"

Jonathan pulled a chair over beside Elizabeth, and then turned back to Dawson. He didn't want to alarm the child, but he needed to see her, to know she was breathing. "Shut your eyes," Jonathan told Dawson softly. Then he dug way back to his childhood to find an entertaining story for Dawson.

In less than ten minutes, Dawson was fast asleep, and Jonathan could once again focus his attention on Elizabeth. He called for the cook to bring him water, made cool compresses, and bathed her down. To be on the safe side, he poured some whiskey into Elizabeth's wound to prevent infection.

She jerked and cried out when the alcohol hit the raw wound. Jonathan swallowed past the lump in his throat, and whispered soothing words to her until she settled down, then slipped back into her fever-induced sleep.

"Don't leave me, Elizabeth." Jonathan heard his ragged voice as if it came from far away. "I won't let you leave me again."

All night, Jonathan bathed Elizabeth with cool compresses until sometime early in the morning when he fell into an exhausted sleep.

Dawson woke up screaming. "Mummy, Mummy, I don't like this man."

Jonathan came to his feet in one swift motion. He shook Dawson awake. "You're having a bad dream," he said, trying to soothe him.

Dawson opened his eyes and huge tears rolled down his cheeks. When he saw Jonathan, he held his arms up to him, and Jonathan took the boy and sat back down beside Elizabeth with Dawson in his arms. He withdrew a handkerchief from his pocket and wiped Dawson's face off.

"I don't like that man," Dawson whispered.

"What man?"

"The one on the other ship."

"Shh." Jonathan wrapped his arms a little tighter around the child. "You don't have to worry about him anymore. He won't ever bother you again."

Dawson squirmed and looked up at Jonathan. "Will you keep us safe?"

"You mean protect you?"

Dawson nodded.

Jonathan leaned down and kissed Dawson's forehead. "Yes, I'll protect both you and your mother."

Jonathan spent the rest of the night with one arm around Dawson and the other hand resting on Elizabeth. Something told him that all would be well.

Once the ship docked at New Orleans, Jonathan wasted little time getting Elizabeth to the hospital. The doctor started working on her right away.

A messenger was sent to Four Oaks for Adam and Jewel.

When Adam arrived, he found Jonathan and a child who looked a lot like Jonathan sleeping in a chair. Adam nudged Jewel, who smiled at what she saw.

Adam shook Jonathan. "You look like you've had a long night," he said as Jonathan jerked awake.

Jonathan's jump woke Dawson. "Adam. Jewel," Jonathan said, a little startled. "I'm glad you both are here." He looked at Jewel and smiled. "I see you have changed since the last time I saw you."

"Yes, I am a little smaller." Jewel laughed and then asked, "Why are we at a hospital?"

Adam looked around. "And where is my sister?"

"The messenger didn't tell you?"

"Only that both of you were at the hospital."

Jonathan's eyes burned from lack of sleep. The few moments in this hard chair were hardly enough. "Elizabeth was shot. The doctor is removing the bullet."

"What happened?" Confused, Adam paced restlessly around the room. "I told you to find her a husband, not shoot her!"

Jonathan gave him a sarcastic look. His back ached between his shoulder blades, and his temper was short. "She was shot by Captain Lee."

"Lee?" Jewel gasped. "He's dead. He couldn't have shot her."

"Lee is dead now, because Jean killed him. Believe it or not, Lee survived the treasure hunt, then appeared in England and accused me of treason. It's been a bloody mess."

Dawson rubbed his eyes and yawned. Then he glanced curiously at the two strangers. His gaze followed Adam as he moved around the room.

"Look." Jewel nudged her husband. "I bet Dawson sees Elizabeth in you since you're twins."

Adam's attention turned to the child. "Hello,

lad. I'm your Uncle Adam, and this is your Aunt Jewel."

Dawson didn't say anything, but his expressive face became somber as he absorbed what he'd been told.

Jewel held out her arms. "Do you want me to hold you for a little while?"

Dawson seemed to think about the offer. Finally, he went to Jewel. Jonathan rose and stretched, trying to rid himself of aches from too many nights with too little sleep. It would be a miracle if he ever got all the kinks out.

The doctor swept through the door. "That bullet was deep, but I got it," he told the group. "She'll be all right with a little rest."

"Can we see her?" Jonathan asked.

"Yes, but don't stay long."

The doctor showed Jonathan and Adam to Elizabeth's bedside, while Jewel stayed in the waiting room with Dawson.

"Elizabeth," Jonathan said gently. "I have someone here to see you."

Elizabeth opened groggy eyes and blinked. Finally, her vision seemed to clear. "Adam?"

"Yes, sweetheart." Adam bent down and hugged her, and she started crying. "Don't cry. I'm here. I won't let anyone hurt you."

"It's not that—it's just that I've missed you so much. Have you seen my son?"

"Yes. He's a fine boy," Adam told her. "Jewel has him at the moment. Dawson will enjoy meeting his cousin when we go back to Four Oaks." Adam had no more finished his sentence than Elizabeth had drifted off to sleep. "We'll take her home tomorrow," he said to Jonathan.

"The last two months have been hell, old boy," Jonathan said as he raked his hand through his hair.

Adam folded his arms and asked, "Did you find my sister a husband?"

Jonathan gritted his teeth. "I tried."

"Tried isn't good enough."

A suggestion of annoyance hovered in his eyes. "Don't push it, old boy," Jonathan warned. "Especially when you knew damned well what you were doing."

Adam chuckled. "And just when did my plan occur to you?"

"Not until after your sister gave me a lot of grief," Jonathan retorted, a critical tone to his voice. "She doesn't listen worth a damn."

Adam nodded. "I agree. Never has. You know, she's a lot like you."

With a mischievous smile, Jonathan said, "When she is well again, I intend to marry her."

An arched eyebrow indicated Adam's humorous surprise. "Is the lady willing?"

"She says she is. But will she show up at the church? That's the big question."

Three weeks later, under a cobalt blue sky, Elizabeth and Jewel sat on the lawn at Four Oaks watching their children play. Dawson scampered on the lawn while Jewel's baby, Nelson, kicked and gurgled on a blanket as he watched his cousin running around.

"How are you feeling?" Jewel asked.

"Much better," Elizabeth admitted, shifting in her chair. "I'm growing stronger every day. The nightmares have finally stopped."

"That's a good sign."

"I think so," Elizabeth agreed with a delighted smile. "I can't believe that both our children are here playing in front of us. Of course, Nelson is still too young to play, but it won't be long before he'll be tagging along behind Dawson."

"It does seem strange, doesn't it?" Jewel said with a sigh. "If someone had told me that I'd be a mother in a couple of years, I would have laughed in disbelief. Now I can't imagine life without Adam or Nelson. I know you were scared to death when Lee kidnapped Dawson," Jewel said and looked at her sister-in-law.

"It was a nightmare that I don't ever want to relive," Elizabeth admitted.

Jewel reached for the pitcher that had been set up for them and poured two glasses of lemonade. "I also can't believe what you went through in London with Jonathan's trial and everything with Lee. As for that matter, I can't believe that Lee survived. I would have fainted dead away if I'd seen him."

"I almost did," Elizabeth admitted. "It was our worst nightmare in the flesh. Thank God we don't have to worry about him anymore." She sighed. "I hope Jonathan's father got everything straightened out so Jonathan will be able to return home."

A ball rolled over and bumped Jewel's foot. She picked it up and tossed it to Dawson. "And will you go home with Jonathan? You haven't said much about him since you've been back."

Despite all she'd been through, thoughts of Jonathan took up much of Elizabeth's day. "I feel Jonathan has been waiting for me to regain my strength before we talk," she said and looked pensively at Dawson. "I must admit that he and Dawson get along very well."

Jewel's faint smile held a touch of sadness. "I think Dawson favors Jonathan. Are you sure he's not the father?"

"I would love to know that he is, but I have no way of proving it." She cast her eyes downward. "I'm just grateful that Jonathan seems to accept Dawson even if he is Lee's child."

"Then we should be planning another wedding."

"I sure hope so." Joy bubbled in Elizabeth's laugh and shone in her eyes. "Maybe I can start by setting everything straight."

Jewel laughed. "There is one thing I've learned about life," she said. "It is never a smooth road. There is always a bump or two in the road."

Elizabeth's gentle laughter rippled through the air. "Well, lately, I've been hitting all the bumps."

That night after dinner, Jonathan invited Elizabeth out onto the verandah. The warm breeze and star-filled sky made everything feel peaceful. Crickets chirped nearby and the scent of honeysuckle was all around them.

Jonathan leaned against a post and looked at her and smiled. "Elizabeth, the bruise on your cheek is gone, your lip is healed, and your shoulder is recovering. So, tell me, how do you feel?"

Her laughter was like a bird singing and it made his heart feel light and carefree. "I'm well. But I have missed your kisses."

His gaze dropped from her eyes to her shoulders to her breast. "Let me remedy that right away," he said with a chuckle. Gathering her into his arms, he held her snugly. "It's been much too long, my love."

"Yes, it has," Elizabeth whispered as her fingers slid into his hair. She loved its silky feel.

He traced her lower lip and the motion sent shivers through her. His lips produced a tantalizing blush that covered her body as they moved to her earlobes, where his warm breath made her melt.

As his grip tightened, he pressed tender kisses along her throat, then finally moved back to her mouth, where he claimed her as his. He thrust his tongue deeply inside, and she responded ever so gently until he gave a husky growl.

Fire raged in Jonathan. Blood pounded in his brain. It seemed this was the only woman who could cause such a blaze. He wanted her to be his forever.

He tore his mouth from hers, and as his lips grazed her earlobe, he whispered, "Marry me, Elizabeth."

Joy filled her, but she had to be sure. She pressed a kiss on his chin. "Will you accept Dawson?"

Jonathan took her by the upper arms and held her from him. "How could you even consider that I wouldn't want your son?" Jonathan said. "He's part of you, so why shouldn't I love him?"

Elizabeth gave him a brilliant smile. "I want a big wedding."

Jonathan chuckled. "Then you shall have it. I believe you already have the dress, though I've never actually seen it."

"*Touché,*" Elizabeth quipped. "I'll marry you in two weeks."

"I do have your word that you'll show up?"

Elizabeth's knees weakened as Jonathan's mouth descended. "I'll be there, Jonathan Hird. You can count on that."

Chapter Twenty-four

It was early, Elizabeth noticed as she slid out of bed and went to her bedroom window. She wondered what Jonathan was doing. Was he awake? Was he thinking of her? She hoped he was looking forward to today, but she suspected he could be a little nervous after their last try.

She stood by the window, leaning against the wall as she waited for the morning sunrise to spread its glow silently across the horizon.

Finally, the orange ball peeked up over the trees, bathing the new morning with warmth. She opened the window. The air smelled of fresh pine and warm earth. It would be a beautiful day.

It was her wedding day. The day Elizabeth had waited for.

Then the queasiness struck.

She ran for the chamber pot. What was it about

getting married that made her nauseated? Unfortunately, she knew the answer to her question. The harder she tried to ignore the truth, the more it persisted. She was wiping her face when she heard Sally behind her, clucking her tongue.

"You done done it again, didn't you?" Sally asked.

Elizabeth chuckled. Her heart swelled with a special tenderness for Sally. "Yes, Sally. It seems I'm pregnant again, but this time I'm sure I'm marrying the right man, and I know he will be happy when I tell him. Do you know, Sally, that Jonathan's crazy about Dawson?" An easy smile played at the corners of Elizabeth's mouth.

"He's the spittin' image of his ma. How could anyone not love him? Now, let's get you dressed before you go gettin' sick on me again or gettin' cold feet and runnin' off like you did before. I ain't never gonna forgive you for that. That fellow was torn up when I saw him."

Elizabeth hugged the big black woman. "I love you, Sally. And I'm not going to run off. Just think, soon you'll have two babies to tend."

"I'll be lookin' forward to a new baby. But probably goin' to have to convince all those people that attended your weddin' last time."

Sally helped Elizabeth dress in her lovely gown. The bodice had an off-the-shoulders top made with delicate Brussels lace. The long satin skirt fell to the floor. The prettiest part was around the hemline. The seamstresses had embroidered pink roses connected by snowy pearls. She would wear a simple wreath of roses around her head to hold her veil, and carry a single pink rose in honor of her mother.

Elizabeth had forgotten how lovely the gown actually was. As she gave herself a final look in the mirror, Dawson rushed in, dressed as a miniature Jonathan.

"You're pretty," Dawson told her. "Look at me."

"You are very handsome." She bent down and gave him a kiss. "You be a good boy in church. And do everything that Jonathan and Uncle Adam tell you."

"Yes, ma'am," Dawson said. He kissed her again and ran out of the room.

Elizabeth sighed as she stood. "He's growing up too fast."

"They all grow up too fast, Miz Elizabeth."

"It's such a pretty day, Sally. I'm going to walk to the chapel."

"Well, ifen you goin' to walk, I'm comin' too so you don't go messin' up that pretty gown."

They waited a half hour until they were sure everyone was at the church, then Sally and Elizabeth headed toward the chapel with Sally holding the back of Elizabeth's gown so it wouldn't get dirty. "Hear the birds singing, Sally."

"Birds are always singin', Miz Elizabeth."

"But today is special. The birds are singing, the flowers are blooming, the air smells wonderful." Elizabeth sighed. "I think I'm in love."

Sally chuckled. "In love or just plum crazy."

They climbed the steps of the beautiful gray stone chapel that sat in a grove of pecan tress. Wildflowers surrounded the church on all sides and provided a colorful array.

She went into the small room to wait. The room brought back many memories, some not so good. Had she made a mistake the first time? She would never know.

This was it. Now or never, she thought. She said a small prayer that her legs would support her during the walk down the aisle. The closer the time drew near, the more nervous she became. So much so that the thought of running crossed her mind.

Jonathan knew it was his imagination, but it seemed that everyone's gaze was on him.

They were probably wondering—would she or wouldn't she? And the closer the time got, the more apprehensive he became. Surely Elizabeth wouldn't run out on him again. She couldn't possibly make him look like a fool twice. He glanced to the back of the church. Wasn't it time for her to appear?

Adam leaned over to Jonathan. "She will show this time."

"How can you be so sure?" Jonathan asked.

"Because we have some insurance this time." Adam looked down at Dawson. "We have Dawson."

Dawson glanced up at Jonathan and smiled. He was tugging on the neck of his shirt. Jonathan bent down and loosened the collar for the child.

Jonathan let out a slow breath, feeling much better. Elizabeth Trent would never run out on her child.

The music began. The doorway was empty.

The congregation turned in their seats and looked to the back of the church. Suddenly, Elizabeth was in the doorway and walking toward him.

She was beautiful. A vision in white. And she was here. She hadn't run. She was actually coming down the aisle. Was that a sigh of relief he heard from the priest? Jonathan smiled.

And then, as if in a dream, Elizabeth was beside him, holding his hand.

The simple service lasted only twenty minutes. Then the priest announced that Jonathan could kiss the bride.

Looking down at the woman whose hand he held, he realized that Elizabeth was finally his. He smiled like a lovesick young lad. She had taken him on a wild chase, but that was behind them. His lips pressed against hers, then gently covered her mouth. He was shocked at her eager response to the touch of his lips, and he pressed closer until Adam and the priest finally cleared their throats to indicate that it was time to stop. Reluctantly, they pulled away from each other.

As they walked down the aisle, Elizabeth winked at Jean and Pierre; then she smiled at all her friends who had come and given her a second chance.

Outside the church, they shook hands with everyone as their guests left the church. Dawson kept pulling on Elizabeth's dress. Finally, when the guests had left, she bent down to her son. "What's wrong?"

"Foot hurts." Dawson pointed at his shoe.

Elizabeth sat him down and took off his right shoe and sock. There was a tiny stone that had somehow slipped into the shoe. She shook out his sock and was preparing to put the shoe back on when Jonathan stopped her.

"Wait a minute," Jonathan said. He bent down and examined Dawson's ankle. "Look at this."

Elizabeth stared at the brown spot on the child's ankle. "It's his birthmark. It looks like the shape of a heart to me. He's always had it."

Jonathan immediately sat down next to Dawson.

"What are you doing?" Elizabeth glanced around and found Jean, Adam, and Jewel watching them.

"You'll see," Jonathan said as he removed his right shoe and sock, putting his foot next to Dawson's. He pulled up the leg of his breeches. And there, on Jonathan's ankle, was the identical birthmark. "It's the Hird birthmark. My father has one, too."

"Dawson is yours!" Elizabeth cried as she knelt down beside both of them. "I always wondered, but never had any proof. Oh, Jonathan, I'm so happy. No, wait. I feel bad." She frowned. "I'm sorry I put you through so much when there was really no need. If only I had known. . . ."

"I love Dawson whether he is mine or not," Jonathan said as he hugged the child. "Now, it's even more special between us."

"This is wonderful," Jewel said.

"I have some news that is just as good," Elizabeth said, looking at her new husband.

"I can't think of any better news," Jonathan admitted. "I have you. I have a son. What else could there be?"

"How about another son or perhaps a daughter?"

Jonathan's mouth fell open. "You don't mean—"

Elizabeth nodded.

"Does this mean that you once again have compromised my sister?" Adam said from behind Jonathan.

"So it would seem." Jonathan laughed. "Where your sister is concerned, I just can't seem to help myself."

Adam chuckled and Jean said, "I do recall Jonathan saying that he never wanted to see a woman again."

"I remember that," Adam joined in the fun.

"I didn't want to see *just any woman*," Jonathan said as he reached out for Elizabeth. "When you love only once there is only one woman." He crushed Elizabeth to him and finally found the happiness he'd thought he'd lost.

AUTHOR'S NOTE

I want to thank all of my fans who wrote to me about THE DUKE'S LADY and asked for this story about Jonathan and Elizabeth. I enjoyed receiving your letters and I hope you like LOVE ONLY ONCE as much as you did THE DUKE'S LADY. I would love to hear your comments. You can write or e-mail me at the address below. As always, the writer of that first fan letter I receive will get a special gift from me, and the first five will receive an autographed cover. So keep those letters coming. . . .

Brenda K. Jernigan
80 Pine Street W.
Lillington, NC 27546
bkj1608@juno.com